PRETTY
drunk

Lacey Black

Pretty Drunk

Pine Village Series, book 3

USA Today Bestselling Author
Lacey Black

Lacey Black

Pretty Drunk
Pine Village Series, book 3

Lacey Black

CHAPTER
one

Hallie

I stare down at my phone and sigh. Ignoring the third text message in as many days, I toss the device onto the bed, determined to put Curtis and his long-winded apologies and promises out of my head. It's too late for them. It's been almost two years since we broke up, and like clockwork, he sends me his monthly text messages. Usually, they start on the same day every month and go on for days. It's probably on his very busy calendar. *Text Hallie.* It's bullshit, to be an item on someone's to-do list. And of all the times for him to try to plead his case, this is the day I'm not having it.

Today, my friend is getting married.

It's a bit of a shotgun wedding, but not for the reason you may think. No, she's not pregnant—though I believe that'll happen pretty soon. Ellie and TD, friends of mine from high school, wanted to get married quickly before her son, Brody, starts college. She manages the diner in town and he's a police officer. A May engagement resulted in a July wedding ceremony, but that's okay. I work best under pressure. Plus, I have summers off from teaching preschool in town, which left me plenty of time to help her plan a wedding to the man of her dreams.

That's my focus. Ensuring every detail is executed perfectly to her vision, which really was pretty simple, since Ellie Daniels is a simple woman. As long as TD is standing at the end of the aisle waiting for her and at the end of the day they're pronounced husband and wife, that's all she cares about. Everything else is just fluff.

Well, fortunately for her, I specialize in fluff.

A knock has me spinning toward the sound and opening the door. I'm prepared to see Blair, who was getting ready at her house before joining us at Ellie and TD's, but that's not who stands before me. It's Logan, TD's best man and professional thorn in my side.

He flashes me a grin, which seems to drop from his lips just as quickly as it appears. His eyes slowly take in the dress I picked to wear for today's celebration. It's light blue and hugs my curves to perfection. When I first saw the dress, I knew it was the one I wanted to wear. Ellie gave Blair and I free rein to choose our own dresses for the wedding, and I fell in love with this one. Timeless, simple, yet sexy.

"Jesus, Cupcake. You look stunning."

A blush creeps up my neck and burns my cheeks at the rare compliment. I take in his navy-blue slacks and ivory button-down with the top button open. He's sans necktie, and even though his arms are covered, I can picture his intricate ink hidden beneath the material. "You clean up nicely yourself, Johnson."

For years, I've despised the man. Honestly, I'm not even sure how it started anymore, but the bickering has sort of been our thing. I'm sure it has a lot to do with his cocky I know everything attitude, but all I know is he's always been cocky and completely full of himself. Of course, he's also one of the most attractive men I've ever had the privilege of seeing in a pair of swim trunks.

Not that I'd admit that out loud.

He glances down, running a hand over his abs. "I know," he states with a smirk and a wink.

Sighing, I shake all thoughts of Logan and how yummy he looks out of my head. "Can I help you?"

"TD wanted me to give you this," he states, holding out his fist.

Hesitantly, I lift my palm below his fist. His fingers brush against my skin as he slowly opens his hand and drops the basic silver band. I glance down at the ring, my heart skipping a beat for a moment at the sight. It wasn't that long ago I thought I'd be wearing one of these. Of course, Curtis ruined that dream by deeming his career more important than me. Since then, I've found little desire to actually try dating again. It just seems so pointless at this stage of the game. All the good ones are taken, at least in our small town, and I can't seem to find the time or willpower to look outside my hometown.

"Don't you have something for me, Hallie?"

There's something in the tone of his voice that goes straight to the apex of my legs. The deep timbre of his voice is like an electrical charge to my clit. I've always had that reaction to him and spend a considerable amount of effort to keep that little nugget hidden. No way can he know how attracted I am to him. If he were to find out he'd use it against me, no doubt.

I spin around and walk toward the small velvet bag sitting on the guest bed beside my phone. Just as I lift the pouch, which contains Ellie's wedding band, the device lights up again. I instantly spot Curtis's name on the screen once more. I try to stop the groan, but it slips past my lips quickly and must catch Logan's attention.

I feel his broad chest brush against my back as he reaches for the phone. "Curtis? As in the douchebag with the misguided priorities?"

I snort. "That's the one."

His eyes narrow just a bit. "Are you seeing him again?"

"No," I insist rapidly. "He just texts every now and then. I haven't had time to block him yet."

His dark eyes bore into me with their intensity and scrutiny. "Want some help with that?" he asks, reminding me how much Logan didn't seem to like Curtis. Don't get me wrong, he was always polite, but I just sensed his displeasure anytime they were in the same place together.

"No thanks, I can handle it," I assure him, handing the small bag over. "Her ring. Don't lose it."

He rolls his eyes dramatically. "I somehow managed to make my way from Brody's room across the hall to this one without losing TD's ring. I think I can manage the return trip."

"See that you do," I sass back, pasting on a sugary sweet smile.

He snatches the velvet bag from my hand and slips it into his pocket. When he turns toward the door, my eyes automatically drop to where his pants hug his rear. Let me tell you, Logan Johnson has one hell of an ass. Of course, he *is* one hell of an ass too, but that's not what I'm focusing on right now. His ass is firm, round, and looks amazing in a pair of jeans.

And I can now confirm that statement holds true for dress slacks as well.

"I can feel your eyes on my ass. Make sure you keep your focus on the bride and groom out there, yeah? I know you'll want to keep checking me out, but we're here to celebrate our friends. Keep your priorities straight, Cupcake."

And with that, he exits the guest room and leaves me in stunned silence.

"Fucker," I mutter, a wave of annoyance washing through me.

I give myself a few minutes to calm down from our exchange before grabbing my phone and duffel bag and exiting the bedroom. I take my personal belongings to my vehicle, and as I'm getting ready to go back inside, I see Blair and my brother, Gabe, pull into the driveway, so I hang back and wait for them.

"Is this not the *best* day for a wedding?" Blair asks, sliding out of the passenger seat of Gabe's truck.

"It is, and my goodness, you are smokin' in that dress, Blair," I state, fanning my face as she heads my way.

Blair pauses and does a little spin, showing off her light blue dress, a similar color as mine but in a halter top style. Where mine sits just above my knees, her hits just below hers. When we went shopping together early last month, we were able to secure Ellie's wedding dress and our bridesmaid dresses at the same place, which was a huge relief to get that crossed off the to-do list.

"Stay back. This beauty is all mine," Gabe announces, wrapping his arms around Blair's waist and pulling her into his chest. They make out like the cute, completely in love couple they are.

"Eww, gross. Stop, please. I just ate and the last thing I want to do is have my lunch return because my brother is making out with his girlfriend in front of me," I mutter, sticking my tongue out and closing my eyes.

"Fiancée."

"What?" I ask, eyes flying open as I look at the two people in front of me. "Seriously?"

Blair holds up her hand and flashes a large solitaire diamond, and my heart sings with happiness. Blair was my best friend growing up, and even though she moved away right before our senior year of high school, we remained close and in contact. Three winters ago, she came to Pine Village for a visit and ended up hooking up with my big brother. It was for one night, but when she returned to town that next summer to help her dad at his medical practice, that one night turned into love. Now, she's going to be my sister, and I couldn't be happier.

"We're not telling anyone though. Today is Ellie and TD's day," she insists, a smile on her lips as she gazes down at her ring.

"I'm so proud of you, big brother. You finally got off your ass," I josh. I knew this day was coming, I just didn't know when. "When's the big day?"

"I'd marry her tomorrow if she'd let me," Gabe states, peering down at his fiancée with so much love it makes my heart skip a beat to witness.

"Soon," Blair says. "We've been talking about starting a family."

"Yay!" I bellow, throwing my arms around them both and squeezing. "I'm going to be the best aunt ever."

"You will," Gabe agrees.

"I was going to take off the ring for today," Blair says, a look of concern in her eyes. And I get it. She doesn't want to take away from Ellie by announcing her engagement on their wedding day.

"You better not!"

We all look over at the window at the far left of the house. The very window Ellie is standing in front of, without a care of who might see her.

"Seriously! Get in here so I can see that ring," Ellie hollers through the open window.

"Come on. Let's not keep the bride waiting," I say, reaching for my best friend's hand. Even though she places hers inside mine, she pauses and turns to kiss Gabe. "Eww, stop," I mumble. "We don't have time to suck face."

"There's always time to suck face, Hal," my disgusting brother proclaims before locking lips with my bestie once more.

With a groan, I turn and enter the house. Before I can close the door, my brother is there, escorting Blair inside. She slips her arm in mine and as my brother heads toward the opposite end of the house where the two smaller bedrooms are located, Blair and I go in search of the bride in the master suite.

The door opens as soon as we approach. "Get in here," Ellie proclaims, reaching for Blair's hand and zeroing in on the ring on her finger. "Oh my gosh, I can't believe you're engaged. Finally!"

Blair rolls her eyes playfully. "We weren't in a hurry. Between my dad's health, moving into Gabe's house, and then finishing the remodel, we've had our hands full."

"How is your dad?" Ellie asks, still ogling the ring on Blair's finger.

"Much better. He's spending all his free time with Aggie and Patience," she says, referring to her eight-year-old sister, Agnes, and her stepmom, who just so happens to be about seven years older than our thirty-six years.

"Aggie is going to be so excited to help plan a wedding," I say. Blair spends a lot of time with her young half sister, as well as rebuilding her relationship with her father, Frank, and stepmom. It hasn't been easy, considering Blair was seventeen when her father's affair with his nurse, Patience, came to light, breaking up their home. But over time, she's forgiven them both and has relocated back to Pine Village with my brother and joined him in taking over Frank's medical practice.

"For sure," Blair replies with a chuckle. "Enough about that though. Today is your day, El."

"It's my wedding day, but I'm sharing it with everyone, and that includes celebrating your engagement," Ellie insists.

Blair looks down at the simple ivory satin dress Ellie chose to wear today. "My God, TD is going to lose his mind when he sees you."

Ellie giggles and glances down. "He will, won't he?"

"He'll be throwing you over his shoulder and carrying you back in here before dinner is even served. Dresses will be ripped off. Babies will be made," I tell them, looking toward Blair. "Probably two babies. You both will be knocked up before the end of the night, and I'll be eating extra wedding cake and drinking all the champagne my body can handle. I'll definitely be hungover tomorrow. Alone."

As if he sensed I was about to embark on a private pity party, my phone vibrates with a text message. I already know who it's from, and I refuse to acknowledge it in any way.

Unfortunately for me, Blair notices. "Your phone is buzzing," she says, pointing to the device in my hand.

"Yeah, I know. I'm ignoring it."

They exchange a look before returning gazes my way. "Who is it?" Ellie asks hesitantly.

Sighing, I shake my head and toss the phone onto the master bed. "Curtis."

"Curtis?" they both ask simultaneously.

"Yep," I reply, popping the P.

"Why?" Blair inquires, taking a seat on the bed.

I shrug. "He wants to talk."

Ellie carefully has a seat on the bed beside Blair. "Again, why? It's been, what? Two years?"

I nod. "Exactly. What could he possibly say now, after all this time? Nothing new. It's the exact same messages every month when he tries to tell me he's sorry and wants to get back together."

"It's definitely fishy, if you ask me," Blair chimes in. "Text messages?"

"You could answer him," Ellie suggests, but that feels like a terrible idea. When we broke up, I did everything in my power to make a clean break. Yet, he's continued to try to plead his case and get back together. He knew my biggest issue was the fact I always came second to his job. If he really wanted to make it work, he would have tried harder—before now—and would show me he's really trying to change. Not just sending me monthly messages, stating the same garbage.

"It doesn't matter," I state, giving my two friends a big smile. "It's your wedding day, and it's almost time to head outside."

At the topic change in conversation, Ellie grins widely. "I'm so ready."

As if on cue, there's a knock at the door. "I'll get it," I offer, since I'm standing.

I carefully open the door and find Ellie's eighteen-year-old son, Brody, on the opposite side. "Look at you, Brode. So handsome," I say, stepping back so he can enter the room.

"Ladies, you look beautiful," he replies as he enters the room. Suddenly, he spots his mom sitting on the bed, and the biggest smile spreads across his lips. "Wow, Mom, you look..."

Brody doesn't shy away from the tears swimming in his eyes as he takes his first look at his mom. She stands up and goes to him, and I quickly grab my phone to catch their first embrace. I'm not big on crying, but I find my own eyes getting a little misty as I snap a few pictures of them together before setting my phone on the bed.

"You are the most beautiful woman in the world," Brody says to Ellie as he steps back and takes her in once more. "TD is going to freak when he sees you. In a good way."

Ellie chuckles and looks at her simple, yet incredibly elegant dress. "You think?"

"Definitely," he replies, leaning forward and kissing her forehead. "Are you ready? I'm here to escort the bride outside."

"I'm ready," Ellie announces with a renewed sense of excitement. "Let me grab our bouquets." She chose a small grouping of classic white roses and daisies to carry, which fits her personality. Classic and dainty. "All right, let's get this show on the road."

Blair and I follow them through the house to the back door leading to the backyard, where their wedding and reception will take place. It's a small affair, with his family and their closest friends in attendance.

Just as Blair and I take our spots at the front of the line to walk the makeshift aisle, Ellie stops and turns her attention to her son. "Brody, I want you to know you'll always be my number one."

He grins and kisses her forehead once more. "I know, Mom. But if it's all the same to you, I'd rather share that spot." He nods toward the door. "He's a good man. I've looked up to him my whole life and giving you away to marry him—" He clears his throat and shakes his head. "I'm honored, because I love you both so much. Now, come on. We're making the poor man sweat out there."

And cue the waterworks.

Gabe steps up and offers his arm to Blair. Once she's secured at his side, they make their way toward the trellis Logan made for today's ceremony. Movement at my side causes me to pause, as does the intoxicating cologne I catch a whiff of hanging in the air. Logan extends his elbow, and I try to ignore the hum of desire sliding down my spine as I casually link my arm with his.

"Ready, Cupcake?"

I turn my attention toward the audience and paint a smile on my lips. "As I'll ever be, considering I'm stuck with you for the next few seconds."

His chuckle vibrates through my veins, landing squarely at the apex of my legs. "Hallie, Hallie, Hallie. When are you going to admit you really do like me?"

"Never."

He tsks as we step forward and slowly make our way toward the front where TD waits. "One day. One of these days, I'll get you to admit how you really feel about me."

"Don't hold your breath," I mutter without so much as the slightest slip of my grin from my lips.

He pulls me closer as he leads me to the spot where we'll stand with our friends. I try to ignore the fact my body seems to buzz with anticipation and lust with every step I take, especially considering his arm is resting against the side of my boob. Thank God I wore a padded bra. I'll be damned if I let him see just how much he truly affects me.

It'll be a cold day in hell when I let Logan Johnson see how badly I want him.

CHAPTER *Two*

LOGAN

"So, you're next, huh?" I hold up my beer bottle for Gabe to tap before we both take a drink.

Once he swallows the cold brew, he grins from ear to ear. "Yep, I'm next. Hopefully before the end of the year."

"Yeah?"

He shrugs, turning his attention toward the dance floor where Blair, Ellie, Hallie, and a few others dance. "We're ready to have kids. None of us are getting any younger, you know?" he states, his eyes never leaving his fiancée.

I shift in my seat at his comment.

Honestly, I thought I'd be a dad by now. Even when I was young, I saw myself with a wife and kids. Of course, that was after my dream of playing professional football was over, and thanks to an extensive knee injury in college, that dream crashed and burned before I was able to enter the draft.

That still left the whole marriage and kids thing. Unfortunately, I came back to my hometown and went looking in the wrong places. Oh, it was easy to find, don't get me wrong. Everyone seemed interested in dating the former hometown quarterback, who took his team to state and almost went pro. Too bad I jumped at the first woman to throw herself at me, which was my first mistake. Thinking she was in it for love and marrying her was my second.

I always knew I'd come back to Pine Village, though I assumed it would be later in life and not when I was twenty-two. I started working for my dad at our family-owned hardware store and lumberyard, something I always loved to do while I was growing up in this small town. So it was the logical fit to transition back to the business I was raised in. I even invited my wife to join us, which was my third fatal mistake.

Now, even after the marriage is dissolved, I can't get her to leave.

"Earth to Logan." Gabe snaps his fingers in front of my face, pulling me out of my thoughts.

"Sorry." I draw a long pull from my beer. "Spaced out for a minute."

"I'd probably zone out too if my ex-wife showed up at my best friend's wedding."

It takes a moment for his words to register, but when they finally do, my wide eyes move from the dance floor to him. He uses his beer bottle to point toward the bar area, where my ex-wife, Shay, is getting a drink. She's laughing and trying to flirt with Marcus, who looks like he'd rather be anywhere but trapped by the beer cooler and talking to Shay.

"Christ," I mutter. "Doesn't she know it's a private event?"

Gage shrugs his shoulders. "When has that ever stopped Shay?"

He's right. Shay does what Shay wants to do. She wouldn't know how to put anyone before herself, and I just wish it wouldn't have taken me the time it did before I saw what everyone had always known about her. I was just too dumb and blinded by the magic of pussy to see it myself.

Lesson learned the hard way.

"Is it just me or are we a guest heavy all of a sudden?" TD asks, dropping into the empty chair beside me.

"Nothing gets past you," I grumble, teasing my best friend and making Gabe snort.

"You mean you didn't invite her?" Gabe asks between drinks of his beer.

"My best man's ex-wife?" TD jokes, eyebrows pulling to the sky.

"Just making sure," Gabe states before returning his gaze to the dance floor. And really, there's no floor. Ellie decided she'd dance with her husband and friends in the middle of the grass, beneath strands of twinkle lights we hung from the trees earlier in the week.

"What are you doing over here, anyway? Shouldn't you be out dancing with your new wife?" I ask, finishing off my second and final beer of the night. I promised the groom I'd make sure everyone leaves safely and everything is shut down and secure.

The newlyweds are using my cabin for their wedding night. I guess someone should be getting some action there. Lord knows I'm not. Not that I've been trying. Between running a business and cleaning up my ex-wife's messes, I stay pretty busy. So while they're away, I'll be here, making sure everything is taken care of the way a good best man should. Brody will be staying here, and I'm going to assume his girlfriend, Morgan, so my plan is to get the big things taken care of tonight and come back in the morning to finish cleaning up.

"I've danced with my lovely wife twice," TD states. "I'd much rather sit back and watch her."

My eyes scan the dance floor, where a handful of women are all moving to an upbeat song, and eventually land on Hallie. She's a natural out there, her hips doing things that make my libido stand up and take notice.

"Shit, she's spotted you, Logan. She's coming over here," TD mutters quietly.

I don't need to ask who *she* is. I already know he's referring to Shay.

"We should go dance," Gabe states just as the song changes to a slow number.

TD stands up, a grin spreading across his lips. "You won't get a complaint out of me. Anything to get my hands on my wife."

I'm left with a choice. I can hang back, sitting alone at the table and giving my ex-wife an opportunity to come wreak havoc on my night, or I can offer to dance with Hallie, potentially risking injury to my face or balls when her claws come out in protest.

"Logan!" I hear Shay call over my shoulder.

I'm up and moving before I can think twice.

Gabe already has Blair in his arms, as does TD with Ellie. Brody and Morgan are gently swaying to the music too, so as Hallie starts to exit the dancing area, I reach out and lightly grab her wrist. "Come on, Cupcake. Let's show everyone how it's done."

A shock lights up my arm and races through my veins. Her gasp is loud, her eyes wide with surprise. I'm not sure if it's from the zap of our contact or the fact I'm asking her to dance, when she's made it clear she'd rather streak naked through downtown than be anywhere near me.

What's equally surprising is she doesn't say a word as I guide her back onto the dance floor and pull her into my arms. Her eyes hold a hint of defiance despite being glassy, a result of the several glasses of wine she's had tonight, and her cheeks rosy. She's definitely buzzed, and perhaps I can use that to my advantage. At least she's not hissing and scratching at me like a caged animal trying to make a break for it.

With her chest pressed to mine, we gently sway to the beat of a classic Shania Twain ballad. She opens her mouth, but quickly closes it, and even though I want to ask what she was about to say, it's probably best not to poke the bear. We're getting along and not bickering. Perhaps she thought it best to just let it go for the moment.

Then again...

"Is this a trick? Are you about to dip me and let me fall to the ground? Tramp my foot and break my toes?" she finally asks, skepticism written all over her gorgeous face.

"Would I do that?"

Her eyes narrow, and I try to ignore how much I like the fire dancing in those little slits. I also try to ignore the way she feels in my arms. Soft in all the right places, and it's difficult not to flex my fingers into the curve of her hip. "Would you do that? Is that another trick?"

I huff out a deep breath. "Can't a man just dance with a friend?"

"When that man is you?"

A chuckle slides from my lips. This is what's the most comfortable with Hallie. Sparring.

Her left hand rests in the middle of my back, while her right one wraps around my shoulder, and I try to keep my brain from dwelling on how much I enjoy the simple contact.

Or my body from reacting to it.

Just as I'm about to comment on how it's been a solid two minutes without either of us threatening to kill each other, I feel her tense. Her entire body goes rigid, and a soft gasp slips from her mouth. I catch the moment her eyes narrow on something behind me.

Or someone.

"What is she doing here?" Hallie seethes, confirming my suspicions about who she saw. There's only one woman who can piss Hallie off with just her appearance, and that's Shay.

"I don't know," I tell her honestly.

"Really? You have no idea? Did you bring her?"

And there it goes...Our civil little bubble popped.

"Seriously? You've seen me almost the entire day, Hallie. Where did I stash her? In my pocket?"

The annoyance radiates off her body like a furnace. "Anything is possible," she mumbles, but with a little less venom behind it.

Apparently, she realizes I didn't invite my ex-wife to my best friend's wedding.

With a sigh, I spin her around so she's no longer facing the woman she despises. Shay was the mean girl in school and knew exactly how to push everyone's buttons. Well, she knew how to piss off the girls. She had a way of wrapping the boys around her pinky finger, which is a big reason why she was so unpopular amongst the females in our school. Shay was gorgeous and knew it. She used her looks to get whatever she wanted.

Or *whoever* she wanted.

And even though I saw the vulnerable side a few times throughout the course of our marriage, she's still the same stuck-up, petty, incredibly catty woman she was in high school.

"She's coming over here, isn't she?" she grumbles.

"Oh yeah." I take the opportunity to pull her even closer, our chests pressed firmly together. "We should kiss."

Hallie sputters, choking on air. "What?"

"It'll detour her from coming over here and talking to us. You better make it quick. She's almost right behind you," I challenge, holding her ice-blue gaze.

Before I'm able to prepare for the assault, she goes up on her tiptoes and slams her mouth to mine. Any hesitation I feel at kissing Hallie flies out the proverbial window the moment her hands move to my neck, her fingers dancing at the nape and driving me wild. I coax open her mouth and catch the wine on her tongue, practically getting drunk myself on her taste.

The kiss doesn't last nearly as long as my body begs for, and when she pulls her lips from mine, shock is registered on her face. "Umm," she says, clearing her throat. "Is she still back there?"

"No, we're clear," I reply automatically.

Hallie's gorgeous blue eyes narrow. "You didn't even look." Before I can open my mouth, she spins around and looks, confirming the fact my ex-wife was never really behind her. Shay is over by the bar, giggling and flirting with one of the assistant coaches on the high school football team, who was unfortunate enough to be at the wrong place at the wrong time. "Really? Was she even heading this way?"

I shrug and paste on my best innocent smile.

"You're unbelievable," she grumbles, dropping her arms. "It wasn't even a good kiss," she adds, lifting her chin and shoulders in defiance.

Leaning in, I whisper, "Liar." And with a wink, I turn and walk away, leaving her standing in the middle of the dance floor. I can feel her daggers, as well as the eyes of practically everyone else at the reception, on me as I go, but I refuse to look anywhere else but straight ahead until I reach my table and take a seat.

It's not the first time we've kissed. A couple years ago, with Shay bothering us at Shiner's, she laid one on me and scrambled my brain. Much like she has tonight.

"Why were you kissing my sister?" Gabe asks when he's finished his dance with Blair and rejoins me at the table.

"She kissed me," I reply, fighting the smile threatening to take over. Of course, I might have strongly suggested it, but I'm not telling him that. Instead, I watch as she walks over to where she left her wineglass and chugs the contents.

"You two have the weirdest relationship."

"There's no relationship. She'd rather castrate me with a dull butter knife," I quip, even though my statement holds a lot of truth.

Gabe pulls a traumatized face. "True."

"All right, friends, I'm taking my wife away to the cabin," TD announces as he approaches the table. "You've got this, right?"

I nod, knowing what he's referring to. I promised them I'd help get a few things cleaned up after the last guest leaves, and then finish with the big stuff tomorrow. Since my house is behind theirs and just down the block, it's no hardship for me to hang around and clean up the yard a bit. Plus, I'm the best man, so this goes with the territory. "Of course."

TD nods and glances over to where Ellie is hugging Brody and Morgan. "They're both still planning on staying here, so you don't have to worry about anything inside the house. Just make sure no food is left outside and all the lights are off."

"Got it."

A squeal erupts from across the yard, grabbing our attention. Hallie pulls Ellie into a huge hug, doing this odd dancing/swaying thing as she squeezes. "Perhaps make sure Hallie doesn't drive? It appears she's had plenty to drink," he states with a grin.

"I've got Hal," Gabe mutters, shaking his head at his sister's antics.

"Okay, well, I think that's all. I'm going to say goodbye to Brode and head out."

"Enjoy your night," Gabe proclaims with a grin.

TD slaps him on the shoulder, a wolfish grin on his lips. "Oh, I plan on it."

We watch as he heads over to his stepson and holds out his hand. Brody pushes it away and throws his arms around TD's shoulders, pulling him into a hug. Morgan is there and gives TD a polite hug as well before the man walks to where his new wife stands. In one fluid motion, he lifts her into his arms—as if he were carrying her over the threshold—and to a chorus of cheers, walks through the backyard toward the driveway where his truck is waiting.

Gabe snorts. "I'll be confirming her pregnancy in about a month."

Nodding, I can't help but agree. TD has loved Ellie for as long as I can remember, even if he was too stubborn to admit it for a long time. As Gabe mentioned earlier, we're not getting any younger, and I know my friend would kill to have the opportunity to have a child or two with Ellie.

"Logan."

With a deep sigh, I glance to my right. "What are you doing here, Shay?"

She seems surprised I'd even ask, her hand coming up to her chest. "I was invited!" she insists loudly before flipping her long blond hair over her shoulder.

My eyebrows crawl up toward my hairline as I gaze back at her skeptically.

"Whatever, they're my friends too," she counters, pulling out the chair beside mine and taking a seat.

"Please. Sit." Those two words have a touch of bite to them.

"Thanks, I will," she counters with a big grin, clearly missing my animosity. "Hello, Dr. Rhodes," she coos, batting her eyelashes.

"Shay," he replies politely with a nod, but quickly returns his eyes to watching Blair.

"I was doing some thinking," she starts, and I know I'm not going to like where this is going. "Do you know Taylor Swift?"

"Personally?" I quip, wishing I had a shot of something hard like Jack Daniels.

"Oh my God, wouldn't that be, like, amazing?" she gushes, leaning in closer and trying to invade my personal space.

Ignoring her question, I glance to my right and find Hallie standing there, sending a glaring look this way. Funny thing is, I'm not sure if her eye daggers are meant for me or Shay. Even when she's trying to kill me with her baby blue peepers, I can't help but get a little turned on. I narrow my eyes back at her, holding her gaze as she downs another glass of champagne. Yep, Cupcake is gonna be hurtin' tomorrow.

"...and so I went ahead and ordered all new signage."

"I'm sorry, what?" I ask, returning my attention to the woman sitting in front of me.

Gabe barks out a laugh, clearing enjoying the moment as Shay just rolls her eyes. "New signage for the aisles and departments. All in a Taylor Swift theme, based on her songs."

Am I being punked right now?

"You've got to me shittin' me," I mutter, rubbing my thumb over my temple where a headache is quickly forming.

"Don't you worry about a thing. I've taken care of it all," she boasts before standing up and stepping beside me. "We make such a great team, don't we?" she asks, leaning forward and getting right in my face. Her ample tits are practically spilling out of her cleavage and her expensive perfume tickles my nose, making my stomach turn. "See you Monday, partner." Then, she leans in and kisses my cheek before I can move away. Call it shock or whatever. I can't believe she just did that, right here in the middle of TD and Ellie's reception.

Wait.

Yes, I can.

Shay loves to put on a show.

"Can't wait to see your new Taylor Swift signage," Gabe states before bursting into a fit of laughter.

"Fuck off." I run my hand down my face. "Can you believe her?"

"Actually, yes, I can. The funny thing is you still seem shocked by her behavior."

"What does that make me?" I ask, more to myself than anyone else.

"I don't know, man, but by the end of next week, you'll be a business owner with fun new Taylor Swift signs," he quips.

Again, I run my hand down my face in frustration. None of this would be happening if my dad hadn't left my then-wife half the family business. I understand he thought he was doing a great thing for us as newlyweds, but that simple gesture in leaving our family business to both of us has done nothing but cause me headaches and heartburn. No matter how much I offer to buy her out, Shay won't sell me her fifty percent, and because my father was of sound mind when he finalized his will—oddly, not long before he died of a massive heart attack—there was no way of getting around it.

We are business partners; despite our divorce and the fact she knows nothing about the industry.

This is my life.

I've got two women who drive me absolutely fucking insane, and the wild part is I'm not sleeping with either.

Can't make this shit up.

CHAPTER Three

"I'm not feeling well."

I spin around, which was a bad idea. The earth moves, causing Blair to tilt funny and blur. "What?"

"I'm not..." She pauses and holds her hand to her mouth. "I think I need to sit a minute."

By the time I'm at her side, she's already dropping into the nearest chair. Her face looks pale, and despite the amount of alcohol I've consumed tonight, I can tell she's on the verge of throwing up. Her eyes are glassy and her skin splotchy.

I look over her shoulder, my eyes connecting with my brother. He must register the panic on my face and is up and heading our way moments later.

"What's wrong?" Gabe asks, dropping to his knees in front of Blair.

"I got a little dizzy and feel like I'm going to throw up," Blair mumbles, her head dropped down as she tries to breathe slowly. "No big deal."

"No big deal? Honey, you're ghost-white. What was the last thing you ate?" Gabe asks, slipping into physician mode.

"Cake about an hour ago. And I haven't drunk enough alcohol to feel this queasy."

"Oh my God, you're pregnant! I'm going to be an aunt. I'll be the bestest aunt in the history of all aunts," I state proudly, suddenly incredibly happy for my brother and best friend. Of course, it might be the alcohol talking.

"I'm sure it's just the excitement of the day, mixed with a little champagne and sweets," Blair insists, but not before I catch a hint of joy in her eyes.

"All right, let's not get ahead of ourselves here," Gabe replies diplomatically. "Can you stand, Blair?"

She nods and carefully stands. "The wave of nausea has passed."

Gabe gently grips her arm, offering her the support she needs. "Let's get you home."

"I told Hallie I'd help clean up," she says, glancing around at the thinning crowd.

"Just go. I got this," I insist with a dramatic wave of my hand.

"I'm supposed to take you home," Gabe realizes.

"I'm a big girl. I can walk."

"You're not walking," my brother counters. "I can run Blair home, and then come back for—"

"I can make sure Hallie gets home."

My eyes narrow as I slowly turn to face the owner of that voice. "Thanks, but I'll be fine. It's only a few blocks," I contend, swaying just a touch on my tired feet.

"Don't argue. I'll make sure she gets home," Logan maintains, wrapping his hand around my waist. The contact, despite being through my dress, sizzles against my already-flushed skin. It makes me wonder if a little contact in *other* places would burn just as fiercely. You know, his fingers...maybe his tongue...

Yep. Time to stop drinking.

"Whatever," I grumble, determined to slip out before Logan has a chance to be a hero and escort me home.

I give my brother and future sister-in-law a hug and send them on their way, secretly hoping she really is pregnant, before turning my attention to the backyard mess. Logan, Brody, and Morgan have already started throwing plates and empty cups and cans in the trash, so I grab a half-empty bottle of sweet white wine and take a big swig straight out of it.

I'm not usually a big drinker. I enjoy the occasional drinks with friends or a glass of wine at the end of a hard day, but I'm not big on getting this intoxicated. I hate throwing up, for one, and two, I despise hangovers. They're the absolute worst. The nausea, the pounding headache, the sensitivity to light and smell, let alone the undeniable urge to lie around all day on the couch, forgoing any and all basic chores like laundry, grocery shopping, or dishes.

You know, things most people spend their Sunday doing.

I carefully make my way over to where the DJ was set up, and even though he's starting to tear down his equipment, the music is still playing softly. With the bottle of wine still in my hand, I let the beat of the song move me, swaying my hips to the rhythm. I know I should be helping clean up, but sometimes you just need to dance. With my eyes closed, I focus on the way the music sweeps through me, the warm breeze rustles my dress, and the cool grass tickles my bare feet. But it's more than that.

I feel...free.

Free to move, to laugh, to cry, to love. Free to do whatever the hell I want to do, and it's the greatest feeling in the world.

I can feel his presence, his warmth, before anything else. Logan's behind me. Spinning around, I move too fast and stumble forward, essentially throwing myself at him. He catches me easily in his strong, muscular arms, and even though I'd never admit this out loud, it's not the first time I've thought about these very arms wrapped around me.

A giggle spills from my lips, and I almost drop the bottle of wine. "Oops."

There's humor dancing in his dark chocolate eyes, and suddenly, the urge to kiss him again is so strong, it's practically a living breathing entity between us. "Are you ready?" he whispers, his warm breath tickling my forehead.

The alcohol makes my brain a little foggy. "Ready?"

"To go home," he replies, the corners of his kissable lips curling upward.

"Home?"

Now, he smiles widely, showing off his perfectly straight pearly whites. "Yes, home, Cupcake. I'll drive you."

"But we have to finish cleaning up," I insist, turning and looking at the empty, clean backyard. Somehow, between my dancing and my...well, dancing, they managed to pick up the entire space, turn off the twinkle lights hanging from the trees, and help the DJ get all his equipment into his truck.

"It's taken care of. We'll come back in the morning and take down all the lights and return the tables and chairs to the church. Brody and Morgan just went inside to go to bed, so all that's left is to take you home."

Take you home.

I really need to ignore the way my body hums with anticipation and my nipples pebble against my strapless bra right now.

He continues to watch me, and when I don't say anything, he adds, "Do you have anything inside you need to get?"

Shaking my head, I confirm, "I don't think so. My purse and bag are in my car already."

"And your phone?" he asks, glancing down at my waist, as if trying to figure out where I've been hiding the device all night.

"Oh, uh...I don't know." Where is my phone? When was the last time I saw it?

"It's okay, Hal. We'll find it," he says, pulling me into his side and escorting me through the yard and toward the driveway.

I don't sway as much, thanks to his hold on me, and it isn't until we reach the sidewalk that it hits me, I'm not wearing shoes. The sooner I get inside my Jeep Cherokee, the better. We move to the passenger side door, but when Logan goes to open it, it doesn't budge.

"Uhh, Cupcake? Where's your keys?"

I glance at the purse sitting on the seat and mutter, "In my purse."

Logan walks around and tries the other doors, just in case, but I know it's useless. I remember hitting the lock button after I dropped my stuff in my vehicle. They'll all be locked. I lean back against the Jeep and close my eyes, the exhaustion of the day and the alcohol starting to lull me to sleep.

"Okay, plan B. I'm guessing you have a spare key, right?"

I nod. "In the basket on my counter. In my locked condo, which I can't get into because that key is in my vehicle too."

"All right," he says, walking back over to where I rest. "No spare house key hidden under a flowerpot?"

"Nope," I announce, popping the P before standing up straight and swaying. "Gabe has that, and he's dealing with Blair and making babies."

"Okay, so short of breaking and entering, we need another option," he states, running his hand down his face. "Come on, Cupcake. You're going to my place for the night."

Before I can open my mouth, he reaches down and picks me up. "What the hell are you doing?" I holler, wiggling in his embrace.

"Stop it or I'll drop you," he states with a grunt when my elbow connects with his chest.

"Where are you taking me?"

Logan pauses and exhales. "I'm taking you to my place. Unless you want me to take you to your brother's, where he's tending to Blair and making babies and stuff."

"Eww, gross," I mumble.

"All right, so we're about out of options. You can crash at my place for the night, and in the morning, when we come back here to help TD and Ellie finish cleaning up, we can have Gabe bring the spare key to your condo. Deal?"

In my drunken state, I struggle to come up with another logical possibility for the evening. One that doesn't involve me sleeping in Logan's guest room, under his roof, in the same space as him. Unfortunately, no other route seems convenient or reasonable. Showing up at my parents' house this late would rate about the same as showing up on my brother's doorstep, and all my friends are either home and sleeping by now or enjoying their wedding night.

And I'm *not* interrupting that.

"What do you say, Hal? Wanna crash at my place?"

I want to argue and find some other option. *Any* other option that doesn't involve sleeping inside on the couch and possibly disturbing Brody and Morgan, but it appears I'm about out of choices. Plus, the alcohol is really starting to work its magic, and the sooner I get to bed, the better I'll be. "Ugh, fine," I grumble, closing my eyes and letting the scent of his cologne and the feel of his strong arms wrap around me like a warm blanket.

We start to move, and I force my eyes open. "I can walk," I insist before the heaviness of my eyelids closes them once more.

"I'm not so sure about that," he wisecracks, the smirk on his lips heard in his reply.

Deciding not to argue—might be a first for me—I snuggle into his body and relax. I mean, if the man wants to carry me to his house, who am I to stop him? "I'm not sleeping with you," I whisper. The act of speaking causes my lips to brush against his neck, and I'll admit, I might leave them there for a few seconds.

Oh, that's definitely the alcohol talking...

Logan tenses but doesn't stop moving. "I'm not taking you back to my house to take advantage of you, Hallie. You're safe with me."

"I know," I whisper, shifting to get closer to his amazing scent, "but I haven't decided if you're safe with me yet." The confession rolls off my lips so easily, there's no chance to stop it.

Logan chuckles, the low, gravelly sound going straight to the undersexed apex of my legs. "Good to know, Cupcake. Good to know."

I wonder how he's able to carry me so easily. I mean, I know Logan's strong, but I'm not one of those tiny little Barbie dolls like his ex-wife. I've got thighs and an ass. Oh, and great boobs. More than a handful, that's for sure. I'm sure it's not easy carrying me from TD and Ellie's place around the block to Logan's. I should definitely walk...

I'm jostled awake a moment later as I'm placed on a soft, warm surface. A groan echoes through the space around me as I try to open my eyes, but for some reason, they're extra heavy. Too heavy to open. "Logan?"

"I'm here, Hal," he murmurs close to my ear. "Get some sleep."

I curl into my side and burrow into the pillow as a cool blanket is pulled up and placed on my body. "Smells like you," I purr, inhaling the scent of his shampoo, bodywash, and laundry detergent.

He doesn't reply, just places his lips on my forehead and slowly backs away.

There are so many things I should do. I should get up and change out of my bridesmaid dress. I should brush my hair and teeth and use the bathroom. I should take some Tylenol and drink some water, because I know I'm going to be feeling like crap in the morning.

But as I lie here, cocooned in Logan's warm, comfortable guest bed that smells way too much like him, all that other stuff just falls away. I need to sleep, and as the seconds tick on, I feel myself being dragged under the abyss of consciousness.

The last thing I remember is how magical this bed feels, and how I secretly hope I get to sleep in it again.

Don't tell Logan.

CHAPTER *four*

LOGAN

I stand in the doorway and watch her way longer than what would be considered appropriate by society's standards. Yet, I don't move. Even when she starts to lightly snore, I don't move. Seeing her hair fan out across my pillow is fucking with my head. It makes me want things I have no business wanting, thinking things that are so far past the line of inappropriate, I can't even see said line anymore.

Plus, my little head is sending dirty images straight to my big head, ensuring they're on the same wavelength.

I should have suggested she change out of her bridesmaid dress. I'm sure she won't be comfortable, but the moment I placed her in my bed, she seemed to settle immediately. Even though she called for me, the second I spoke, she snuggled into my pillow and proceeded to pass out for the night.

Needing to stop staring like a stalker, I head for the bathroom and retrieve two ibuprofen tablets from my cabinet before moving to the kitchen to grab her a glass of water. She probably should have taken it before passing out, but I think I was just so transfixed on seeing her in my bed, it sort of scrambled my brain.

I take the glass and tablets of pain pills she's definitely going to want in the morning and return to my bedroom. Hallie's right where she was a minute ago. Only this time, her mouth is hanging wide open as she snores. Probably going to drool on my pillow too.

Setting the things in my hands down on my nightstand, I slip over to my closet and grab a pair of joggers before quietly exiting my room, leaving the door cracked open as I go. The first thing I do is toss the joggers I'll sleep in onto the bathroom vanity and then stop at the hallway closet to retrieve a sheet and blanket. If I'm going to sleep on the couch, I'd rather have my pillow, but there's no way I'd remove Hallie's head from it just so I could use it.

Also, I kinda like the idea of it smelling like her fruity shampoo.

I'm a masochist like that.

As I tuck the sheet under the couch cushion and grab one of the throw pillows that came with the couch, I realize I probably should have turned the second bedroom into one for a guest. But I've never really had a reason to. All my friends are here and have their own places. My mom lives in town still, and any distant family we have usually stays with her during a visit.

Once my bed for the night is ready, I return to the bathroom to shower. I'm pretty certain Hallie's down for the count, but still, I try to be quiet. This house isn't too old, but it's a tad on the smaller size, sitting at about eleven hundred square feet, so I'm sure sound travels easily. I crank up the hot water and let it run while stripping out of my dress shoes, socks, slacks, and button-down. After tossing them in the hamper to deal with tomorrow, I remove my boxers and undershirt and step into the shower, adjusting the water before moving beneath it.

The heat feels like heaven. It's been a long couple of days prepping and setting up for the wedding. From making the arch they stood beneath to moving tables and chairs and setting them up, it's been quite the task, even for a small affair, but I wouldn't change a thing. I'd do anything and everything they asked, just to see my best friend finally marry the woman he's loved for years.

My cock is hard, reminding me there's a woman lying in my bed. An *untouchable* woman, but one still. When was the last time a female joined me in bed? Way too long ago, if you ask me. I've dated off and on since my divorce, but nothing serious. I even engaged in a one-night stand about two years ago when I was out of town for a convention thing.

But I refuse to be that guy now. I'm not jacking off to images of the woman who'd rather douse me in honey and leave me outside to see what happens. So I ignore my dick and turn the water a little cooler, grabbing the soap and giving myself a quick wash and rinse. I do the same with shampoo and conditioner before rinsing all the suds from my body. When I'm finished, the water is turned off and I'm grabbing my towel.

As soon as I'm dry, I slip on the joggers and exit the steamy bathroom. I usually sleep in less than the sweats, but with having a guest, I don't want to be walking around in my underwear, even just to sleep on the couch. So, although though they're warm and a little constricting, I'll deal with it for one night.

My mind conjures up more images of Hallie. How incredible she felt in my arms, and how natural she appeared sleeping in my bed. Of course, thanks to the half-hard dick in my pants, I'm also thinking about bending her over every flat surface in my house just to watch her amazing ass move. I've always been an ass man, which is another weird fact questioning my decision to marry Shay. She has no ass, or at least, not one as round as Hallie's.

I know her weight has always been a sore subject for her. She's not big by any means, just curvy in all the right places. Shay and her mean girl minions used it to poke fun at her when we were younger, but I've always found her curvy figure to be incredibly attractive. Case in point: my hard-on that won't seem to quit.

When we were married, Shay was always dieting. She counted every calorie she ate, which in turn, meant I was always under the microscope. She refused to eat red meat and didn't want it anywhere near our refrigerator, like it could contaminate her fresh chicken with its unhealthy, artery-clogging abilities.

I, on the other hand, didn't give two shits. Sure, at first, I tried to abide by her strict diet rules she put in place for both of us, but after a while, I craved a juicy cheeseburger, an Italian beef sandwich, or a medium steak with mushrooms and onions sauteed in butter. Eventually, I started cooking what I wanted, adding in dishes she'd eat too. Why? Because she refused to cook. But I was determined to compromise and find even ground between her meal choices and my own. She still bitched and moaned every single night, but I didn't care. I was trying to make it work, even when she'd throw continuous wrenches in my plans at living peacefully.

Hallie doesn't seem to care what she eats. Yes, I've heard her talk about dieting over the years, but if she wants to eat half a pizza or a plate of nachos, she does. Plus, she always seemed to enjoy the hell out of her food. Whatever it was, she wasn't afraid of getting her hands dirty and eating. More than once I wanted to lick barbecue sauce off her lips while she was eating wings from Shiner's, but I figured that would have resulted in a knee to my balls, so I never did.

Just fantasized about it way more than any male ever should.

I bypass my living room and head straight to my kitchen. It's midnight now, and even though I'm exhausted, I'm not tired. My mind is spinning and my libido too amped up to sleep. So I do the next best thing. Grabbing the bottle of tequila from the cabinet, I pour myself a shot and swallow the liquid. Then, I refill the small glass and take a second. It's not like I'm leaving anytime soon, and two shots aren't going to completely impair me; just help me shut off my brain and give me a nice little buzz so I can sleep.

I consider pouring myself a third shot but think better of it. I want to make sure I hear Hallie if she wakes in the night, and knocking myself out with tequila won't help. I place my hands on the counter and exhale deeply. When my eyes close, I see her, which isn't helping things below the belt, but I can't seem to shake her either. I don't know what it is about Hallie. One minute I want to shake the hell out of her for giving me lip and rolling her eyes, and then next I want to kiss her until we're both breathless. It's a vicious cycle, a merry-go-round of emotions I can't seem to shake.

My shoulders are tense as I try to take a few calming breaths and crack my neck from side to side to try to ease the tension. What I really need to do is get laid, but that's definitely not happening tonight. Maybe I need to ask out Jordan Lovejoy, the new boutique owner in town. Every time she's come into the hardware store, she's flirted a bit, letting me know she's interested. She has dark hair, big green eyes, and always dresses like she fell out of a magazine. Perhaps that's why I've barely given her a second glance, because she reminds me a bit too much of my ex-wife. Always put together like a model. But I should be able to put that aside for one night to see if there's any spark.

"Are you pouring shots?"

My entire body goes rigid as her soft, sleepy voice washes over me like spring rain. Slowly, I push off the counter and turn around, but I'm not prepared for what I encounter when I do. Her long, coppery brown hair is messy, the soft curls from earlier flat against her head, and her makeup is smudged beneath her eyes.

But that's not what catches my attention and holds it with a death grip. No, it's my shirt. One of my Johnson Hardware T-shirts hugs her curves and hits mid-thigh.

"Don't you think you've had enough?" I ask, ripping my eyes from her bare legs and bringing the conversation back to the alcohol.

Hallie steps into the kitchen and shrugs. "I haven't had any of those yet."

"What?" I ask, my throat a little dry.

She steps up beside me, her light perfume wrapping around me, going straight to my cock. "Shots."

My eyebrows draw together in confusion. "You want to do shots? At midnight? After drinking your weight in wine?"

The sweetest giggle slips from her lips. "Not quite my weight, but I had plenty. Feeling no pain right now."

I prop my hip against the counter and cross my arms over my bare chest. "What are you doing up, Hal? You should be sleeping."

She shrugs, her arm brushing against mine. "I've never been a particularly heavy sleeper and woke up because it was too quiet."

My eyes narrow just a bit as I try to keep up with her line of thinking. "It was too quiet?"

Nodding, she reaches for the shot glass on the counter and fills it with alcohol. "I'm used to sleeping with a TV or music on, so it was just too quiet. Let's play a game."

"A game?"

"Yeah, kinda like truth or dare. We'll ask questions or make dares, and if the other person doesn't want to do it or say, they have to drink."

"So...truth or dare."

This can't end well.

"Whatever," she replies, opening the first cabinet directly in front of her. "You got any snacks? I get snacky when I drink."

"Maybe you should just go to bed," I suggest, walking toward the dry food cabinet and grabbing a bag of pretzel sticks.

She rips the package out of my hands and grabs a fistful, popping the first one in her mouth. "Got any peanut butter?" she asks while chewing.

With a shake of my head, I return to the cabinet and pull out the jar of peanut butter. "That's multiple questions. Does that count as two?"

"No," she quickly replies, scooping a glob of peanut butter out of the jar with the end of a pretzel and shoving it into her mouth. "My first question is why am I sleeping in your bed?"

My cock kicks at the memory her question conjures up. "Because I only have one bed."

Her eyes narrow a bit in consideration. "But you have a guest room."

I shrug and grab a pretzel stick from the bag. She holds up the jar of peanut butter, but I shake my head. "I do, but it doesn't have a bed. There's an old weight bench in there and a desk I always say I'm going to use as my office at home but have never gotten around to actually using."

"Hmm. So you were going to sleep on the couch?"

After swallowing my snack, I nod. "Yep."

"Interesting. Okay, your turn."

"Why are you wearing my shirt?" I find myself asking.

She glances down. "When I woke up, my dress had ridden up to my waist, and if I was going to fall back asleep, I knew I needed to get comfortable. I usually sleep in old T-shirts, so I scrounged through your drawer and found this one."

The corner of my mouth curls up. "Last time I was near your drawers, I got accused of rooting through your panties."

"You were! You threw them on the ground," she insists, even though that wasn't exactly what happened. The drawer I was pulling out to move fell and discarded her panties all over the place. It took me days to get the image of her red lace thong out of my head.

"Hardly," I counter, grabbing a second pretzel and popping it into my mouth.

"Besides, it's not like guys keep things hidden in their panty drawer like women do," she mutters, sliding the pretzel into the peanut butter once more and taking a bite.

My brain grabs on to her statement and refuses to let go. "Wait, what did you have hidden in your panty drawer that you didn't want me to see?"

The cutest blush creeps up her neck. "Nothing," she insists quickly.

"That's my question, Cupcake. I want to know what you didn't want me to see."

Her blue eyes narrow. "You jumped your turn. It's my question. You have to drink," she states, sliding the shot glass my way.

I hold her gaze and down the liquid before reaching for the bottle and refilling the glass. "You still have to answer," I tell her, sliding the glass in her direction.

She takes the glass and, while maintaining eye contact, tosses it back and hisses as the tequila slides down her throat. "Damn, that's good. Not as much burn as I expected."

"It's the good stuff straight from Mexico," I tell her as she refills the shot glass, wondering why she took the shot at all. It wasn't her turn.

"I didn't have anything in the drawer. I had moved it."

"It? What was it?" I ask with a big grin.

Hallie glances around, as if looking to see if anyone else is listening, and leans in. "A small pink vibrator named Little Richard."

My cock weeps with joy.

A gargled laugh flies from my mouth as I do all I can to ignore the images her reply creates. I even reach over and take the shot of tequila, praying it helps cool my suddenly too-hot body. Of course, it doesn't. It only helps amp it up even more.

"What about you? Got anything hidden in your panty drawer you don't want me to see?"

I snort at her question. "My panty drawer? I don't have panties, Cupcake."

She waves her hand. "Fine, fine. Got anything in your manly underwear drawer you don't want me to see?"

"Like?" I inquire, raising an eyebrow.

She seems to ponder her own question. "Porn? Dirty magazines? Oh! Do you have a giant sexy toy stash somewhere? I've always wondered if you were the secret Dom type. Quiet in public but totally take-charge in the bedroom. Do you have handcuffs or a flogger?"

I choke on the air I'm breathing. "A flogger?"

"Yeah, a flogger," she says. "I'll take this shot right now if you have a flogger in your bedroom."

A gravelly chuckle slides from my mouth as my brain starts to feel a little fuzzy from the booze. "Sorry, Cupcake. No flogger in there."

"Damn," she mutters, taking the shot glass and throwing it back.

I reach for the bottle and glass, moving them away from her at this point. She's had two shots of strong tequila, and she definitely doesn't need any more. "You should head back and try to get some sleep," I suggest, even though my dick doesn't agree.

She leans forward, invading my personal space as she whispers, "But we didn't get to any dares."

I almost groan but bite it back at the last second. This woman has no idea how much of a temptress she is. Seeing her standing in my kitchen, wearing my shirt, after lying in my bed, is putting all sorts of bad ideas in my head. "Maybe next time," I suggest as the warmth of the alcohol starts to roll its way through my blood.

"There's gonna be a next time? Are you asking me to sleep over again, Johnson?"

The corner of my mouth curls up as I gently grip the counter to keep from reaching for her. "Only if you're ever drunk, lose your keys, and need a place to crash."

She tsks, reaching for the shot glass. I watch as she spins it with her fingers, her eyes watching the liquid inside. I can practically see her brain spinning, deep in thought, and the moment she looks up with determination and challenge in her eyes, I know I'm in deep fucking trouble.

"One little dare before we call it a night?" she whispers softly, batting those baby blues my way.

Sighing, I slowly nod. "Fine. One little dare," I repeat her words.

She holds up the glass, a coy little smile on her lips as she faces me head-on and drops her bomb straight into my lap. "I dare you to kiss me."

CHAPTER *five*

Hallie

I have no idea why I dared him to do that, other than the fact I'm pretty drunk, and he's standing in front of me wearing nothing but a pair of gray joggers. He's literally one of those dirty memes women share about guys in gray sweatpants.

I can see the outline of his dick, and as far as I can tell, he's been sporting a chubby since I walked into the kitchen. Not to mention his muscular chest and arms are on full display, complete with sexy tattoos. I've never been one to find them so alluring, but there's just something about Logan's ink that seems to turn me on all of a sudden.

His eyes burn as they gaze down at me. I wish I knew what he was thinking, but I never know on a normal day, let alone one fueled by alcohol and bad decisions. His mouth is so kissable, so perfect, and I secretly—or not so secretly at this point—really hope he lays one on me. Something tells me it would be pretty epic; despite the decade's worth of annoyance and arguments we've endured.

Maybe my friends are right. Maybe all of that has just been foreplay, a dance leading to this very moment. We've been circling each other, going round and round for years, trading jabs like Mike Tyson. Perhaps every comment has been exactly what they've suggested it to be.

Foreplay.

Logan steps forward, his chest almost brushing against mine. My nipples are pebbled against the soft cotton of the borrowed shirt, and a quick glance down confirms he notices. When his eyes return to mine, he reaches for the shot glass and takes it from my hand. Disappointment settles in my gut, but I refuse to let it show. I won't let him know how much he affects me, how much his rejection burns.

Slowly, he lifts the shot to his lips and downs the liquid without so much as a flinch as the tequila hits his throat. Logan sets the glass on the counter, and just as I go to take a step back, he wraps his hand around my waist. His grip doesn't hurt as his fingers flex into the material of the shirt, and for the first time, I catch a hint of desire swirling in his brown eyes.

"You don't really want me to kiss you, Hallie. That's the alcohol talking," he murmurs as his other hand comes up to the back of my neck.

"Maybe, maybe not. Are you telling me you don't think about that kiss we shared a couple years back at Shiner's?" I lift my chin in a challenge and refuse to look away.

"Are you telling me you do?" There's something gravelly about his tone that goes straight to my lady bits.

I lift a single shoulder to shrug. "Not really. It just popped into my head right now," I insist casually, even though it's a total lie. I've thought of that kiss way more than I should.

"Hmm," he hums, lowering his lips to my ear and whispering, "Are you telling me that kiss wasn't memorable enough?"

"I barely recall it." My throat is so dry, the words practically stick to my tongue.

"That's too bad. It was a pretty good kiss."

"Was it?" I lift my chin again in challenge.

His eyes zero in on my mouth, and I can barely breathe. "Maybe I should give you a refresher. You know, see if it jogs your memory at all."

"Might not hurt. It would be more for research purposes, right?" I murmur, my heart trying to leap out of my chest.

"Absolutely. Research."

His fingers slip around to my lower back, dancing along the top of my ass. It takes every ounce of self-control I possess not to just leap into his arms and wrap myself around him like a spider monkey. Warm breath tickles my lips as he inches closer and closer, hovering just above my mouth. I feel like I might die from waiting, which is why I might be the one who moves first. Even in my more than buzzed state, I realize I'm the one who initiates the kiss.

There's a flash moment where we both freeze, our lips fused together like lovers do, but then he moves, opening up and letting his tongue slip out and stroke the seam of my mouth. That one motion ignites embers deep in my soul, causing them to blaze to life for what feels like the first time ever.

The kiss turns ravenous. Our tongues duel as our bodies start to grind against each other, searching for the relief the other offers. My hands dive into his hair, gripping the strands and digging in deep, needing the contact. I crave him in a way I never have before, and even though that should be enough to stop this whole thing, it only drives my desire further.

Logan backs me up, caging me against the cabinets before lifting me off the ground and setting me on the counter. My legs wrap around his waist, and I feel exactly how excited he is in the moment as well. My panties are soaked, useless by most standards, and all I can think about is having them ripped from my body before being ravished.

Preferably by his tongue.

Before I'm ready, Logan rips his mouth from my own. We both pant for air, while our hands continue to explore. "This is a bad idea," he murmurs, his eyes glassy from alcohol, yet dark with desire.

My nipples pebble against the soft cotton T-shirt, and my ankles lock around his back. "Very bad," I reply, grinding my clit against his erection and gasping in ecstasy.

A loud groan fills the room as his hips rock forward, seeking more glorious friction. "Fuck, Hallie. I can't think when you do that."

I shake my head. "No thinking, Logan." I meet his lust-drunk gaze and whisper, "Let's be bad. Just for one night. Let's be bad together."

Sure, it might be the alcohol talking, but deep down, I know that's not the entire reason I'm basically throwing myself at him. I've always wanted him. Since high school, he was my crush, the one I used to dream about writing my first name attached to his last name in my notebook. I never did, though. Never vocalized I liked him or the fact I thought he was the most gorgeous guy in high school.

Logan didn't see me like that. I knew it.

I heard it.

One evening senior year, I was at the high school finishing my civics project while a group of classmates were hanging around the weight room. They were talking about girls, of course, and the ones they'd had sex with or wanted to. I was just about to get as far away from the testosterone-filled hallway as I could when I heard my name, followed by laughter. I was used to the mean girls making fun of me or the boys teasing me about my ass, but this was different. It was the moment I heard Logan Johnson say, "She's cute in the face, but her ass needs its own zip code."

I had never let the words of my classmates get to me. Until that day. That was the moment my crush on Logan turned into something else. I didn't hate him—much like I don't hate him now—but my tongue seemed to hold a touch of venom when we spoke, and in return, he gave as good as he received. It continued over the years until that was all we knew. How to push buttons and poke the bear.

What he said all those years ago, as a stupid high school boy, wasn't exactly untrue. My butt and thighs were always a little thicker than all the other girls we went to school with. I've never been a size two or four, and I've always been okay with that. As I grew more comfortable with my body in adulthood, I realized my J.Lo bootie was one of my best assets. Well, that and my boobs.

Now, here we are, Logan and I, ready to rip every stitch of clothing from our bodies and do things fueled by a mix of alcohol and years of pent-up frustration—both sexual and otherwise. I bend forward and run my tongue up his neck before latching my lips around the sensitive skin beneath his right ear. I suck hard, not caring if my action leaves a mark.

He grunts in response, pulling me hard against his body, slipping his hands beneath the T-shirt, and gripping the globes of my ass. "My God, Cupcake, your ass is fucking amazing," he mutters, squeezing and rocking his erection into my core.

"You should see it in the air when I'm on my hands and knees," I insist, earning the reaction I was going for.

Logan squeezes my ass hard and grinds himself against me once more. Then, we're moving. I'm lifted against his chest as if I weigh nothing, my legs locking at his lower back and my arms anchoring myself to him around his neck. His mouth fuses to my own as he steers us toward his bedroom. This kiss is carnal and raw, teetering on the edge of insanity.

And let me tell you, I am here for it.

When we reach the bedroom, he rips his mouth from mine and somehow tosses me onto the bed. Considering I was climbing him like a tree and grinding against his erection like a stripper to a pole, I'm left a little stunned by the sudden change in position. I land in a bouncing heap of limbs but have no time to dwell on it because Logan is there, monopolizing my thoughts by sliding his joggers down his thick, muscular legs. His cock springs free, making my mouth water at the first sight.

Keeping my eyes zeroed in on his erection, I rip the T-shirt I'm wearing over my head and throw it on the floor before lying back on the rumpled bedding. A strangled noise comes from his throat as he reaches down and strokes his hard cock. His eyes burn pure fire as he stares down at me, almost as if he's afraid to move.

Needing to find release, I spread my thighs and push aside my panties. My fingers eagerly dive between my folds, coating in the wetness already there. I keep my eyes glued on Logan as I gently stroke my clit, gasping as a rush of sensations flood my body.

"Two fingers. I want to see you fuck yourself," he states, his voice raw and gravelly.

I do as instructed, gently pressing into my body. I stretch around my fingers, imagining it's the moment he thrusts his cock inside me. My core clenches, gripping my fingers as I try to move them in and out. With my other hand, I cup my left breast, squeezing the nipple and rolling it between my fingers.

"Enough."

My eyes fly open—I didn't even realize they had closed—and my hands stop moving. Before I can ask what's wrong, he releases the death grip hold on his cock and makes a spinning motion with his finger. "On your hands and knees. Now."

I waste no time flipping over, slipping off my panties as I go. The moment I'm on my hands and knees, I glance over my shoulder and almost orgasm right here and now. Logan crawls onto the bed, slowly approaching me as if he were a wolf stalking his prey.

Suddenly, he smacks my ass. The jolt of pain mixed with pleasure causes me to gasp and groan at the same time. I feel my core clench as a fresh wave of wetness slides down my thigh.

"Hallie," he whispers as he moves into position behind me. His hands grip my thighs as his cock grinds between my ass cheeks.

My nipples pebble hard, and I push back against him, desperate to get closer. Frantic to find that sweet relief his body is promising. He shifts his cock into position, the tip nudging my entrance.

Just as he starts to press forward, he pauses, the head breaching my pussy. "Tell me to stop, Hal. Tell me, and we go no farther. Last chance."

I want to scream in frustration, to chastise him for stopping when we could already be fucking. Instead of opening my mouth, I decide to answer with my body. I rock back, taking his cock all the way inside me. A mixture of his groan dancing around the room tangles with my own. The stretch is intense, but thanks to being incredibly wet, it only lasts a second.

Then he moves.

I barely have time to prepare as he pulls out and pistons back inside. His pace is fast, intense, and exactly what I need. He thrusts hard, his grip firm, as Logan Johnson takes me for the ride of my life. Yes, that's right. I'm having sex with the one man who drives me absolutely insane with frustration, and apparently, insane with desire too.

He shifts his hands, stroking his palms over my ass cheeks and digging his fingernails into my flesh. My back automatically arches, adjusting our positions just a bit and sending him even deeper into me. A curse slips from his lips as his hands massage the globes of my rear, his fingers moving closer and closer to the place no one has ever touched.

"Touch yourself, Hallie," he demands, rocking his hips and making my eyes cross with pleasure.

I do as instructed, slipping one hand between my legs and circling a finger over my clit. I know I'm about to come. The sensations are too much. He's hitting so deep, stroking that elusive G-spot Curtis swore was impossible to reach.

Wrong, Curtis.

So. Fucking. Wrong.

"Logan," I groan, my fingers stroking even faster.

"Jesus, Hallie," he mutters, slamming into me and sending me flying over the edge.

My orgasm rips through my entire body, white light bursting behind my eyelids like fireworks on the Fourth of July. A loud cry fills the space around us, and I don't even care it's coming from me. All I can do is feel, and what I'm feeling is fucking amazing.

Just as I start to float down from my release, I move my hand between my legs and cup his balls. They're tight and hard, and the second I wrap my fingers around them and give them a firm stroke, Logan detonates like a bomb. He slams forward, grinding his groin against my ass, while my internal muscles milk every drop he possesses.

"Holy shit," he mutters, dropping down to cover my back with his chest.

"Mmm." My body is practically singing, my limbs numb and boneless, and all I want to do is let the tequila rock me to sleep.

With his arms wrapped around my waist, he turns us both and lies down on the bed. I want to say something witty about being cradled against his chest, but I'm in some sort of orgasm stupor, unable to properly function. All I do is lie here, my back pressed to his incredibly fit abdomen, and listen to the sound of our rapid breathing. My heart is still hammering in my chest as he shifts one arm under my neck and throws the other over my waist.

I try to ignore the nagging feeling of rightness in the moment. Being in his arms feels...perfect. But I push that thought from my brain as quickly as it enters. The last thing I need is to entertain ideas of having more with him. We're not in a relationship. There's no happily ever after for the two of us. We had sex—epic sex—but casual nonetheless.

After a few minutes, Logan shifts his position, bringing his mouth closer to my ear and whispers, "Feels good."

"What does?" I ask, trying to fight from falling asleep, but knowing it's a losing battle.

"Being bad with you."

A small smile curls my lips as his breathing evens out and he starts to snore lightly. Never in a million years did I think I'd be here, in his bed, wrapped in his arms, but right now, my brain is unable to process everything that's happened. The overthinking will come in the morning. Tonight, I'm just going to enjoy being here, riding the high from too much alcohol and amazing sex.

Everything else will still be there in the light of day.
I'll deal with it then.

CHAPTER
six

LOGAN

My head is pounding and my stomach churning. It takes extra strength to crack open my eyelids, since they seem a little weighted. My mouth is dry and full of cotton, and my limbs feel heavy and numb. And despite all that, my brain is able to conjure up perfect images of Hallie's naked body in every position we used.

And damn, did we do a lot of positioning.

I woke up after only an hour of sleep with my hard cock being swallowed down Hallie's throat. I was still buzzed, desperate for sleep, but when my eyes opened and landed on the gorgeous naked woman between my legs, I was suddenly wide awake. So wide awake, as soon as she sucked me off, I returned the favor and buried my face in her pussy, where I stayed until she was screaming my name and coming on my tongue.

There was another round of epic sex. I was on top, then she was on top in reverse cowgirl. There was bending and lunging and more aerobics than I thought were possible, and at the end, we were both so sated and satisfied, we passed out before our heads hit the pillows for the final time.

I'm going to be dehydrated for a week.

Running my hand over my face, I reach over to find the space beside me empty and cold. I turn in that direction, surprised to find her gone. A quick check of my watch confirms it's late morning, well after the time I was supposed to be at TD and Ellie's to help finish cleaning up from the wedding, but what I can't understand is why Hallie isn't here.

In my bed.

I toss the rumpled sheet off my lower body and slide out of bed. My legs hurt, and my back is stiff, and my head could definitely use some pain meds. Not to mention the fact I smell like sweat and sex. I'm not complaining—those sweet flashbacks parade through my mind again—but a hot shower is just what the doctor ordered.

Forgoing pants, I move through the house naked and verify what I already know. Hallie is gone, having slipped out at some point between four this morning and eleven when I woke. This is equally perplexing, since she didn't have a car or keys, and disappointing, because I wouldn't mind asking her to join me in the shower.

Something tells me I'm going to have a hard time forgetting our night together anytime soon.

I grab a bottle of water from the fridge before making my way to the bathroom. First things first, I pop two tablets from the bottle of pain reliever and toss them in my mouth. Once I chase them with half the bottle of cold liquid, I flip on the shower and grab my toothbrush. The room slowly fills with steam as I start to scrub my teeth with toothpaste, spitting the remnants into the sink and rinsing both the brush and my mouth. Finally, I chug the remainder of the cold water, toss the bottle into the trash, and climb into the shower, adjusting the temperature so it doesn't scald me.

"Fuck," I grumble, placing my hands on the shower wall and dipping my head under the spray. The hot water running down my back is welcome and relaxing as I twist my neck from side to side, trying to stretch out my achy muscles.

Memories parade through my brain once more, reminding me exactly why my body is so sore. Marathon sex will do that to a guy, even one who enjoys running and working out a few times a week. I have to admit, sex with Hallie was definitely the best workout I've ever had.

Grabbing the bar of soap, I wash myself from head to toe before reaching for the shampoo and scrubbing my hair, despite having washed it last night. As much as I'd love to stand here until the water turns cold, I have plenty of stuff to do today. First up, head over to my friend's house and complete the list I promised I'd help do. Once that's done, maybe then I can focus on Hallie and find out why the hell she snuck out of my bed without waking me.

Maybe then I can convince her to rejoin me later.

Hallie's not here.

When I arrived at TD and Ellie's, I was surprised to find Hallie's car gone. Considering she didn't have her keys, that means she was up early and made calls for help. Honestly, it pisses me off a little she didn't ask me. I could have run her to her brother's to retrieve her spare house key, taken her to her condo for the second key to her Jeep, and then brought her back here for her vehicle. Yet, she decided to seek help elsewhere, which is incredibly annoying.

"You okay?" TD asks, stepping up behind me and causing me to startle.

"Yep, good," I insist brightly, tossing the last of the big black trash bags into the outside can.

"You look like shit. I thought you didn't drink much last night," he says, rolling one of the cans to the edge of the driveway to be picked up tomorrow morning.

"Didn't sleep well," I counter, grateful he can't read my mind.

"Heard my sister slept at your place last night."

I almost groan out loud as TD's eyes widen. "What?"

We both turn to face Gabe, who's carrying a box of decorations and putting them in the bed of TD's truck. "She locked her keys in her Cherokee last night, and since she and Logan were two of the last ones here, she said he offered her a place to crash."

My gut churns with anxiety.

TD's eyebrows climb into his hairline. "You only have one bed," he states unnecessarily.

Gabe's eyes narrow just a bit as he stares at me from across the driveway.

That headache I've been fighting all morning starts to pound right behind my eyeballs. "I also have a couch," I reply through gritted teeth. It's not a total lie. I do have a couch and even had every intention of sleeping on it.

Tequila and a gorgeous woman might have changed the plan, but they definitely don't need to know that.

TD holds up his hands in surrender. "I know, I was just messing with you. I know you didn't do anything inappropriate with Hallie. She seemed pretty drunk last night, and if there was anyone I'd trust to protect and help an intoxicated woman, it's you."

Christ. Dig the knife in a little deeper, why don't you.

"She was definitely having a good time last night," Gabe says, walking over and joining us. "Glad she had somewhere to go when she locked her keys in her vehicle."

"See? You're a hero," TD bellows with a laugh, slapping me on the shoulder.

Hero. Right.

A hero wouldn't know what she sounds like riding his cock.

"Anyway, she's home, hopefully sleeping off her hangover. She doesn't drink too much, and I'm guessing she didn't have enough food in her stomach for the amount of wine she was consuming. When she called me this morning, she sounded a little rough and certainly looked it when I picked her up here to run her to her condo."

Well, at least I know it was her brother who grabbed her and took her to get her keys. I'm still a little annoyed she didn't just wake me up so I could do it, but I'm not going to complain too much since the one she called for help was Gabe. And no way am I going to tell him she had a few shots of tequila on top of the wine she consumed.

Fuck, I'm a terrible friend.

Needing a redirect, I turn to Gabe and ask, "How's Blair?"

A wide grin spreads across his face. "Fine. My unofficial diagnosis is morning sickness, and we'll confirm that tomorrow morning at the clinic."

"No shit?" TD says, stepping in and giving him a one-handed bro-hug. "Congrats, man."

"A wedding and a baby?" I ask, slapping him on the shoulder and giving it a squeeze. "Happy to hear."

Again, he has a big, cheesy grin spread across his lips. "Keep it quiet for a bit, if you would. We haven't confirmed anything yet, but we're both pretty sure that's what caused her dizziness and upset stomach. Fortunately, she didn't have much to drink, so we're pretty certain that wasn't the cause. Plus, she has a few other symptoms, but there's no reason to get into that. Once we do the test, we'll figure out when to tell our families. This may put a rush on the wedding, though. Well, not that I care. I'd marry her today if I thought she'd agree."

"I mean, we can throw the decorations back up," TD offers with a chuckle.

"It wouldn't take much to get the tables and chairs out of the trailer," I add, smiling.

"Appreciate the offer. It'll happen soon, and when it does, I'm hoping both of you will agree to stand up with me."

"Yeah? I'd be honored," I tell Gabe. He was a couple years older than us in school and was gone for several years while in medical school, but these last few years he's become a good friend. I know I can call him if I need anything, just as I would TD, so to be asked to stand up with him at his wedding is an honor.

"Me too," TD adds.

Gabe nods. "Good. Okay, that's done. Don't say anything yet to my sister or Ellie. I'm not asking you to keep it from them, just don't offer up the info until Blair has a chance to ask them too."

"Mum's the word," TD says just as Ellie comes around the side of the house with Morgan and Brody, all three of them carrying a box.

"Why are you all hiding up here? The rest of those boxes won't move themselves," Ellie quips as she approaches the truck.

"I got that, wife," TD states, bending down and giving her a kiss as he takes the box filled with the twinkle lights that hung from the trees.

"Thank you, husband," she replies with a giggle.

Even though I want to roll my eyes at their cuteness, I shake my head and smile. "Let's go get the rest of the boxes so they can be returned," I tell Gabe, who follows me around to the back of the house.

Once everything is loaded and the backyard is put back the way it was prior to last night's celebration, my phone rings. I'm a bit too eager pulling it from my pocket. Hope swells in my chest at the thought of Hallie calling me, so I'm sadly disappointed when I see my ex-wife's name on the screen. I tap the silence button and return the device to my pocket.

That's when it rings again.

Sighing, I pull the phone from my pocket, knowing she won't stop calling until I answer. Shay's persistent as hell when she wants something, so I might as well get this over with. I step aside to give myself a bit of privacy and answer, "Hello?"

"Oh, Thank God, you finally answered! You have to get over here right away!" she bellows into the phone.

"What's wrong?" I ask, refusing to get worked up. For all I know, she broke a nail, and the salon is closed on Sundays.

"A pipe burst and there's water everywhere!"

I exhale loudly and rub my throbbing temple. I definitely didn't take enough pain reliever to deal with Shay today. "Call a plumber, Shay."

"I called you!"

"And I'm not a plumber."

"But you used to live here. Same thing."

I bark out a humorless laugh. "Hardly. You need a licensed plumber to help you. That's not me."

She huffs out an annoyed breath. "I distinctly remember you plumbing when you lived here."

"Changing the kitchen faucet is hardly plumbing."

She goes quiet, and after a few seconds, I glance at the device to see if the call is still connected. That's when she bursts into tears and starts wailing through the open line. "You promised to always help me! Till death do you part!" she demands.

"Are we really bringing vows into this conversation right now?" My annoyance is reaching peak limits for the day.

"All I'm saying is you said you'd always be there, and here you are...not." She sounds bored. She's probably sidetracked by a chipped nail.

"I'm not because we're divorced. Call a plumber, Shay. I'm not coming over to fix your damn water leak."

She huffs dramatically. "I can't believe you're refusing to help. This was your family home. And it's flooding with water right now. Those hardwood floors your grandma picked out? Going to have to be ripped out, all because you wouldn't come help me deal with a water leak. Nice, Logan. Real nice."

Teeth gritted, images of my grandparents' house filling with water and ruining the hand-sanded hardwood floors, I mumble a quick, "Fine. I'll stop by and shut off the water, but you're going to have to call a plumber, Shay."

"Yay! See you soon!" The line disconnects immediately, and as I stare down at the device, I somehow feel like I've been bamboozled and used all over again.

"I'm gonna head out," I holler to where my friends are standing.

"Everything okay?" TD asks, a knowing look in his eyes.

"Shay has a water leak. Said the house is flooding," I state, not really believing it even as I say the words.

"Do you need some help?" he offers, ready to jump into action.

"Let me run over and see the extent of the damage, and we'll go from there." I really don't want to call my friend for help, less than twenty-four hours since getting married.

"Sounds good," he replies with a nod.

"I'm available to help this afternoon too," Gabe adds. "Just give me a call. I'm gonna run home and check on Blair."

I wave at my friends before heading back to my own house to jump in my truck. The drive across town to my ex-wife's house is familiar, as is every road in this small town. I grew up here, riding around on these streets on my bike first, then driving in my own vehicles. I love this little town; always knew I'd come back here after the professional football career I never got to have was finished.

Pulling into the familiar driveway, I slowly exit my truck and sigh. I rarely come back here, choosing to stay as far away from my ex as possible. Well, you know, besides the six days a week I am forced to work with her.

"Thank God you're finally here!"

I look at the front door I painted the summer before I moved out and my jaw drops open. Shay is standing on the porch wearing a tiny little pink bikini that leaves little to the imagination. Her enhanced double D's are spilling out of the triangles meant to cover your boobs and the bikini bottom covers about the same amount of skin.

"Why the hell are you wearing a swimsuit, Shay?" I ask incredulously, my feet refusing to walk toward her.

"It's so hot out here," she sings, fanning her perfectly made-up face with her manicured hand.

"Where's the water?" I glance around her bare feet toward the floor, not seeing any rushing water flowing from the open door.

"Come on, it's this way," she insists dramatically, waving me to follow her inside.

Exhaling slowly, I head that way, up the front steps and through the door. I don't look around. I don't care what she did with the place after I moved out. It's hers now. But my eyes definitely start looking for all the water ruining my grandparents' hardwood floors.

"This way," she coos, motioning for me to follow her.

I run my hand through my hair, not wanting to go. Something feels off about this. Shay is...well, Shay, and I don't trust her in the slightest.

"Come on, slowpoke!"

With heavy legs, I start walking down the hallway toward the back of the house to where the bedrooms are located. I thought the two extra rooms would be filled with little ones by now, but here we are.

Pushing those memories aside, I move to the master bedroom, keeping my eyes straight ahead where I walk, and enter the en suite bathroom. My ears are open as I listen for the gush or drip but hear nothing. Well, that's not true. I hear Shay's annoying voice.

"I heard Nancy and Bernie were caught in the alley behind the bakery. Rumor has it, they were supposed to be on their lunch breaks, but snuck off to make out where no one could see."

My jaw clenches. "What?"

"Nancy from the bank? And Bernie who runs the insurance agency, who left his wife last week. I'm sure that's not a coincidence," she adds, smiling and shaking her head.

"Shay. Where's fucking water leak?"

My ex-wife blinks at me a few times. "Oh! I almost forgot! It's right here," she says, pointing to the sink and the puddle beneath it in the vanity cabinet.

I get down and check out the drip, noting where it's coming from. "Go get a bucket."

"A bucket? Like, from the hardware store?"

"From the garage, Shay. There should be a bucket or two somewhere."

She blinks with a dead stare. "Umm, I think I gave that stuff away."

I run my hand through my hair and reach to the back of the vanity, shutting off the water to the sink. "Gave it away?"

She nods. "Yep, all that stuff was in the way, so I just had someone come in and get it out of there."

Standing up, I know I'm going to regret asking, but I can't help it. "You gave it all away? Everything in the garage?"

"Sure did. Now there's plenty of room for my Cadillac," she tells me proudly.

I left her a few things in the garage to ensure she had a few necessities, despite knowing she'd just call someone to help her whenever she needed. I didn't want to be accused of leaving her high and dry, even though she couldn't care less about anything left in the garage. "Call Owen Hansen. He'll come and fix this."

"Can't you?" she asks, slightly panicked.

"I'm not a plumber, and since it's not flooding the house, like you said it was, it'll be fine until he can get here to look at it. But a bowl underneath it and use one of the other bathroom sinks until it's fixed." With that, I turn on my heels and head for the front door, ready to get the hell out of here.

"Wait!" she hollers behind me, following me right out the door.

I pause when I reach the bottom of the steps but shouldn't have. As soon as I stop, Shay throws her arms around my shoulders, pink bikini covered boobs pressed against my chest, and slams her lips against mine. I'm so stunned, I just stand there, unable to move until she pulls her mouth away.

Then, she says three words that make the hairs on the back of my neck stand up and my balls take a defensive stance and draw up into my body.

"Oh, hi, Hallie!"

CHAPTER
seven

Hallie

My eyes have to be playing tricks on me.

After spending the entire morning tossing and turning and thinking about Logan and the way he made my body sing just hours ago, I had to get out of my condo. Sleep wasn't coming to me, so I opted for a little exercise and decided to go for a walk. Even then, my brain kept conjuring up memories. So many memories, I'm walking around wet and achy, desperate for his touch.

Then, I found him standing in front of his ex-wife's house, her arms thrown around him as she kissed him. Hours ago, those magical lips were plastered to mine. Now, they're pressed against Shay fucking Johnson's, the biggest bitch in town and the woman he was once married to.

"Oh, hi, Hallie!"

I didn't even realize I had stopped and was just standing in the middle of the sidewalk, gawking, until she hollered my name.

Logan tenses, his wide eyes turning my way. They're dark and full of a mixture of shock and embarrassment as he steps back, shaking off her embrace. "Hallie," he says, a hint of a smile on those kissable lips.

Unfortunately, the last lips pressed to them were Shay's.

"I was just...walking."

"Oh, exercise! So good for you," Shay states, coming up beside him and slipping her arm around Logan's waist. Her eyes trail up and down my body, a devious smirk on her lip as she adds, "It will definitely help with..." she points to my lower half "...you know."

My big ass.

I get it.

Thanks.

"Shay, call the plumber," Logan states pointedly, trying to put an end to this encounter before Shay decides to comment back.

"Yes, you better call the plumber, Shay. I know how much you support those *laying pipe*. I'm sure you've got a whole list of numbers on speed dial. You know, for plumbing emergencies." I smile sweetly, as if I didn't just insinuate Shay is a ho.

Shay's eyes narrow, and I can sense the claws coming out.

"Come on, Hallie, I'll give you a ride home," Logan blurts out, walking straight for me and practically dragging me toward the passenger side of his truck.

"Have a great day, Shay!" I holler as I'm lifted into the truck. "Choke on a dick, you egotistical cow," I mutter as Logan shuts the door.

Logan doesn't acknowledge his ex anymore and walks around to climb behind the wheel. The moment he shuts the door, his woodsy scent wraps around my nose and tickles my clit.

Pushing that tingling thought aside, I shift in my seat and say, "What a twat. Why the hell were you locking lips with that she-devil right smack dab in your front yard?"

Steering toward my condo, he replies, "Not my yard. And I wasn't kissing her. She kissed me, and I'm pretty sure she only did it because she saw you."

"She's such a piece of work," I grumble, looking out the window.

After a beat, he agrees, "That she is."

We're both silent, lost in our own thoughts, as we move through the streets of town and head to my condo. He pulls into the driveway and puts the truck in park, drumming his thumb against the steering wheel, almost as if he's trying to decide if he's going to get out or not.

The last thing I need is for him to walk me inside. I'm liable to strip off my clothes and throw my feet in the air, and that's not going to happen. "Thanks for the lift, though it wasn't necessary. I could have walked."

He gives me a crooked grin. "I know, but I didn't want to hear you got arrested for fighting Shay in her front yard. Can you imagine the rumors?"

I flash him an appalled look for a second, but it's quickly replaced by a Cheshire Cat grin. "She'd deserve it," I agree with a shrug.

"True." Logan clears his throat and dives into the elephant in the room—or in the truck cab—that needs to be discussed. "Listen, about last night…"

"Let's not do this, okay? We were both drunk. End of story."

He slowly nods. "Yes, I agree, alcohol played a part in what happened…"

"See? There you go. Case closed. There's no need to rehash it. What happened, happened, and we won't do that again."

"Drink?" he asks, the corner of his mouth curling up in a slight grin.

"Well, that too, but I was referring to…you know. The other part."

His dark eyes watch me, studying my every move. "The other part," he repeats, a hint of desire dripping from his voice, as if he's recalling exactly what *the other part* entails.

"So, we'll just pretend it didn't occur and leave it at that." I reach for the door handle and push. "Thanks for the lift."

Logan nods, and I can feel him watching me climb from his truck. Just before I close the door, he hollers, "Hey, Hal? Shay was wrong, you know."

I pause, standing sideways as I gaze back into the cab. "About what?"

His eyes drop to my ass, and he licks his lips. "Your ass is perfect the way it is."

My throat goes dry, and my heart begins to pound a little harder in my chest. Unable to find the words to reply, I step out of the way and shut the door. I can feel his eyes on me like a caress as I make my way onto the front porch of my condo and pull my keys out of my pocket. His truck still idles behind me, but I refuse to turn around. Once the lock is released, I slip inside, the ache between my legs so intense, I feel it move up my torso and land in my nipples.

"You need to forget all about what happened. We're never doing *that* again."

But as I head for my bathroom to shower away the light sweat from my walk, I argue with myself every step of the way. It doesn't matter how amazing it was, we're never getting naked again. It was a mistake. One I won't be making again anytime soon.

Keep telling yourself that.

My phone buzzes later that afternoon, and I smile the moment I spot a text from my best friend on the screen.

Blair: How are you feeling?

Me: I should be asking you that. You left not feeling well.

Blair: It's passed. I'm good.

Me: Happy to hear.

Blair: I'm getting ready to leave the grocery store. Mind if I stop by?

Me: Of course not. I'm here.

Blair: On my way

I glance around my living room and pick up what little clutter is lying around, and by the time I hear Blair's SUV pull into the driveway, I'm already outside with two glasses of strawberry lemonade.

She smiles as soon as she spots me. "Is that what I think it is?"

"It is. I just made it earlier this afternoon," I tell her, handing over a glass as soon as she joins me on the small porch.

My best friend takes a hearty drink of the cold, pink liquid. "This stuff is heaven. I've tried to make it at home with Gabe, but it never turns out just like yours."

I grin. "It's the love I stir into it," I quip, knowing she's unsuccessfully tried to duplicate the recipe, but never gets it just right.

Blair snorts.

"Wanna come inside or head out back to sit at the patio table?"

"Out back is fine. I don't have too much time, but it's too nice of an afternoon to not be outside and enjoy it."

We move through my condo to the kitchen and out the back door where my patio furniture is located. "Not that you're not able to stop by whenever you want, but what brings you by?"

She meets my gaze across the table. "I wanted to check on you. You had quite a bit to drink last night. I figured you'd be pretty hungover today."

"This morning was a little rough. I didn't go over to TD and Ellie's to help clean up," I state, still feeling bad for that, but Gabe assured me they would have plenty of help.

"He mentioned he had to run you home to get your spare key and back to get your Cherokee, and that you were feeling crummy."

"Yeah, I was pretty queasy at that point still," I tell her, taking a sip of my lemonade. "Then I went for a walk to get a little fresh air and have felt much better since."

"And you spent the night with Logan."

Not a question. My brother clearly told Blair about the fact I couldn't get into my place and had to crash at Logan's. I just don't think she realizes exactly how accurate her statement was. "Yep," I reply, popping the P.

"Wow, and you two didn't even kill each other."

He killed me with orgasms.

Does that count?

I clear my throat and push that thought from my head. "We were both pretty exhausted," I say, sticking to the truth.

"Yeah, but how awkward was that? I mean, you two don't always get along and there you were stuck sleeping at his house. Gabe said he was a gentleman and gave you the bed."

Okay, so clearly my brother talked to Logan. Apparently, he left out the part about him sharing said bed with me, to which I am very grateful. The last thing I want is the man I slept with last night to be discussing anything about our night together with my brother.

"What was that look?"

I blink, meeting her curious eyes. "What look?" I ask.

"The look of guilt. What aren't you telling me?"

I swallow over the sudden lump in my throat. "Nothing," I insist, hoping I sound way more casual than I feel. I'm sure I fail.

Her eyes narrow, the wheels inside her beautiful head starting to spin. She's trying to work something out, and all I can do is pray she doesn't succeed.

I clear my throat again and take another drink. The cold liquid doesn't seem to quench my thirst, not in the least. I'm sure that has something to do with the slight onslaught of panic racing through my veins. I'm not a very good liar. I have tells, plenty of signs that give it away for me, but try to hide them behind sarcasm and quick wit. I've managed to perfect them over the years as a way to hide my attraction to Logan.

Just the thought of him has me squirming in my seat.

Suddenly, she gasps and covers her mouth with her hand. "Oh my God! You had sex!"

"What?" I ask. "No!"

"Yes! Holy shitballs, you had sex with Logan!"

"How could you have possibly gotten that from my silence? I was just sitting here," I argue, refusing to confirm her suspicions.

"You may not have said anything, but it was written all over your face. First, when I mentioned his name and you sleeping there, you blushed. Then, you started to wiggle and get fidgety. Holy crap, Hal. You slept with Logan?"

"Shhhh," I whisper-yell. "Keep your voice down. I don't want my neighbors hearing you."

My oldest friend leans in. "That wasn't a denial."

Exhaling loudly, I close my eyes and realize I'm not getting out of this conversation. When I meet her gaze, I confirm, "Fine. Yes. I slept with Logan."

She makes this high-pitched squeal noise and leans in even closer. "Tell me everything! Who came on to who? Was it good? How many times did you do the nasty with him?"

"Do we have to do this?" I grumble.

"Uhhh, yeah! You better start talking, missy."

"Fine, but once I tell you the details, that's it. We're not talking about it ever again."

70

"What? Why?"

"Because it shouldn't have happened," I tell my friend. "It was a mistake."

"So it was bad?" she asks, clearly disappointed.

"Well...not exactly."

She gasps loudly. "So it was good?"

I nod in confirmation. "Definitely," I whisper.

Blair shakes her head and takes a small sip of her lemonade. "Wow, I wasn't expecting this." After she takes a few minutes to collect her thoughts, she says, "So? Tell me all the details. It's not every day one of our friends sleeps with another."

My eyes narrow across the table. "TD and Ellie slept together."

She waves off my comment. "Yeah, but that was destined to happen sooner or later. They've been in love with each other since forever."

"You slept with my brother, or did you forget about that?"

Blair blushes a dark shade of pink. "How could I forget?" she asks with a mischievous grin. "Though, technically, we weren't friends."

"Potayto, potahto. And we promised never *ever* to go into any details where he's concerned," I state, making a disgusted face.

"I would never do that to you," she insists. "Wait, I might tell you all about this thing your brother does with his tongue if you don't hurry up and share the deets about last night with Logan."

"Uhhhhh! So gross," I mutter, shaking my head. "Fine. He took me to his place when we realized my keys were locked in my Jeep and put me in his bed. I'm not sure how long I was out for, but I woke up incredibly uncomfortable in my dress and decided to change. I stole his clothes and then went to see where he was sleeping. He was standing in the kitchen taking shots of tequila, so I joined him. Next thing I knew, we were both naked."

"And?" she encourages, knowing there's more.

"And…we stayed up half the night having sex. Really, *really* good sex," I tell her, feeling a blush creep into my cheeks. I don't usually blush, but when I think back to my night with Logan, I can't help it.

She grins widely. "Excellent. Now what?"

"What do you mean?" I ask, taking a sip. "It was a one-time thing. It shouldn't have happened at all, but did, so we move on. Case closed."

A look flashes across her face as she brings her glass to her mouth and takes a drink, a smirk dancing on her lips.

"What? What was that look for?"

Still smiling, she replies with a quick, "Nothing."

My eyes narrow across the table. "I don't believe you."

"And I don't believe you," she states, a big grin on her lips.

I gape at my friend. "What's not to believe?"

She shrugs, her green eyes full of mischief. "That it was a one-time thing."

Gasping, I sputter my reply, "Wh-what? Of course, you know, once. One time. Never ever again. Like ever."

"Mmmhmm," she practically sings, that annoying smirk on her face still.

"You know what? Whatever, I'm done talking about this," I counter, shaking my head in disbelief.

"All right, done."

"And we won't ever have sex again!" I practically shout.

Hiding her knowing grin, she nods in agreement. "Never again."

Never again.

That's what I keep telling myself over and over.

Unfortunately, I don't think the rest of my body concurs with my brain. I'm just going to have to prove to myself—and Blair, apparently—I can hold steadfast and resilient when it comes to Logan.

One and done.

That's it.
Keep telling yourself that...

LOGAN

The bell over the door chimes, so I look up from the counter to greet the customer. A smile spreads across my lips as she approaches the counter.

"How's my favorite son today?"

"Pretty good. How's my favorite mom?" I ask, pushing aside the packing slips from today's truck delivery to give her my complete attention.

"I'm great. Have a hair appointment up the block in fifteen minutes, so I thought I'd drop by and say hello. How was the wedding reception?"

That one question triggers rapid-fire flashbacks, things I don't need to be thinking about in the presence of my mother. Clearing my throat, I quickly reply, "It went well. Everyone seemed to have a great time."

She nods. "I wish I could have stayed longer. I was just so tired from traveling," she states. Mom returned from a week-long trip to her sister's house in northern Iowa. She had just returned home on Saturday in enough time to get ready for the wedding and drive over to TD and Ellie's house. Even though they would have been perfectly fine with her skipping the ceremony, Mom wouldn't hear of it.

TD practically grew up at my house, and likewise, me at his. We became friends in third grade and never looked back. Where one went, the other was right beside him, and anytime I found myself in trouble, he was usually along for the ride and in just as much trouble as me. He has always been my sounding board and the person I went to when my life turned upside down.

"Understandable. I know they were just happy to have you there," I tell her.

Mom nods and glances around. "He found a good one. Ellie is such a kind woman and a wonderful mother. She's going to make a delightful wife to Thomas."

"That she will," I agree.

"They're so perfect for each other." She glances around. "Speaking of wife, and I use that term loosely, is Shay here?" A look of hesitation passes through her eyes.

"No, she's off today. Hair and manicure day in Hudson," I state with an eye roll.

"Oh, good," Mom replies, relaxing where she stands. "I don't have to pretend to like her right now or worry about running into her at my appointment."

A bark of laughter slides from my mouth. "You never have to pretend to like her."

"I try to keep the peace, for your sake. I know she likes to push your buttons, so if I can be polite when I see her, then she's less likely to cause you problems."

I appreciate her reasoning, but I'm not sure that really helps. If Shay wants to be a pain in the ass, she will, despite who was nice to her. "Well, don't feel required to do that for my sake. I can handle Shay."

She snorts in reply, shaking her head. "I'm not sure anyone can handle that woman."

I flash her a knowing grin.

"Anyway, the other reason I stopped by, I wanted to see if you were busy tonight. I thought we could swing by the diner after you get off and have dinner."

"I'd like that," I reply instantly, knowing I don't have anything to do after work. "Think Gram would want to join us?"

She smiles widely. "I will call her as soon as my hair appointment is finished. I'm sure she'd be thrilled."

Me too. I adore my gram and try to visit or take her to dinner at least once every couple of weeks. "It's a date. Want me to pick her up?"

Mom shakes her head and chuckles. "You're confident she'll join us. Maybe she has bingo at the church tonight."

"That's on Thursdays, and I'm confident because it's me. I'm her favorite grandchild."

She barks out a laugh at my comment. "You're her *only* grandchild."

"Semantics."

"All right, I better get going. Meet you there at five fifteen?"

"Sounds good."

"I'll grab Bernice. There's no reason for you to go out of your way," she replies, walking around the counter. I throw out my arms, knowing what's coming. Mom has always been a hugger, which is fine with me.

"Fine. See you later."

"Love you," she hollers as she moves toward the exit.

"Love you too," I reply with a wave, which she readily returns before exiting the building.

A bubble of warmth washes through my chest as I reach for the packing slips and prepare to get back to work. I've always been close to my family. We may not be very big, but we're incredibly tight. I grew up with family meals at my grandparents' house and spent a lot of time with my grandpa at their cabin.

When he unexpectedly passed when I was twenty-one, I inherited that small piece of land and what was on it. The two-bedroom cabin sits along the lake in Bluff Preserve National Park and is my hideaway when I need a bit of quiet. After he passed, I went there a lot, even prior to discovering he left it to me in his will. It was my connection to him, to the things we enjoyed doing together. Fishing, camping, spending time in nature.

I told my gram I didn't want the property. It was too much. It should have stayed with her, or went to the next in line, my dad. But my gramps was very clear: he wanted me to have it because he knew I would appreciate what I had.

Shortly after he passed, someone convinced me to use the cabin as a rental. That lasted a few years, but I ended up terminating the contract with the rental company that oversaw the reservations. The main reason was I was tired of people trashing my family's property. You wouldn't believe the shit I've had to repair or replace during that time. And it didn't matter how much we increased the security deposit. People would still tear your stuff up and not give a crap about it in the end, relinquishing whatever deposit they gave at the start of the rental agreement.

The other reason was I simply wanted the place when I wanted it. I didn't like having to check in with someone before utilizing my own cabin. If I had a bad day, I wanted to go fish or sit around the fire at my own leisure, not at someone else's because the cabin was rented. Sure, the extra cash the rental brought was nice, but it's not necessary. My house is small, my truck is paid for, and my divorce is long final and in the rearview mirror. I may not have a lot of disposable cash, but I'm happy and content.

What more do I need?

I push through the front entrance of the diner and smile when I spot Ellie behind the counter. "Hey!" she hollers, grabbing a stack of menus and approaching with a big smile.

"What are you doing working this evening? I thought you'd take some time off after the wedding."

She shrugs as the bell on the door behind me chimes. "We're not leaving for our honeymoon until Sunday, so I might as well get some hours in before we go."

"Don't let her fool you. She worked the morning shift, but when one of the evening girls called off sick, she volunteered herself instead of finding someone else to work." TD steps around me and kisses his wife soundly on the lips, making her blush.

She clears her throat and glances around quickly. "It was the easiest solution for last minute," she insists. Turning her attention back to me, she asks, "Just you tonight?"

"Nope, Gram and Mom are on their way."

"Booth or table?" she asks, glancing around.

"Whatever's available."

"How about that booth over there," Ellie states, pointing to the far right along the windows.

"Perfect."

"And I'll send your mom and gram over when they arrive."

Looking over at TD, I ask, "You want to join us?"

"No, I'm good. Brody and Morgan are on their way. I'm hoping I can convince my wife to take a short break and eat with us." The love reflecting in his eyes makes my chest tighten. Not because I'm jealous—those two deserve so much happiness it's not funny—but simply because, for a short period of time, I thought I had that too.

I nod before heading over to the booth, greeting a few patrons along the way. Just as I slide into the side facing the door, I see it open and two of my favorite women enter. Lifting my hand, I wave when they look my way, smiles on both of their faces.

Gram starts to shuffle my way, but quickly detours the moment she spots TD sitting at a table near the counter. He instantly gets up and wraps his big arms around her small body, laughing at something she says. I watch as Gram steps back and looks down at her outfit, as if he complimented her on what she's wearing. Then, she rubs his cheek in that adoring manner she does with me and steps forward to kiss the spot where her hand just touched.

Finally, she moves back and my mom gives him a brief hug. They only converse for a few seconds before the duo makes their way to the table. As they approach, I slide out to give them both a hug. "Should Ellie be worried you were hitting on her husband?" I quip, knowing it'll make her smile.

"Maybe a few years ago," Gram announces proudly, returning my gesture. "So good to see you," she adds, going to slip into the booth.

"I can go in first," I tell her, but she waves off my comment.

"I may be old, but I'm not crippled. I can get in and out of a booth, Logan Christopher Johnson."

Smiling at the use of my full name, I nod and give my mom a quick hug. Once they're both seated, I take my seat with Gram as Ellie approaches.

"Good evening," she sings as she places three menus on the table. "Bernice, you look so lovely in that color."

Gram grins widely. "Why, thank you, dear. That fine young husband of yours said the same thing."

"Well, that shade of green is definitely your color," Ellie compliments. "What can I get you three to drink?"

"Water for me, please," Mom requests.

"I'll take a lemonade," Gram orders.

"And I'll have water also," I add.

"Of course. I'll give you a minute to look over the menu," Ellie says, turning and heading to fill our drink order.

"What sounds good?" my mom asks.

"I wonder if they have any of Saul's bacon-wrapped meatloaf left from lunch. That stuff is always a delight," Gram states, browsing the plastic dinner menu.

"It's the best, but there's rarely any left. Any time they have it for the lunch special, this place is packed," I say, wishing I would have ordered it for lunch earlier today. Unfortunately, the truck came right before the noon hour, and by the time we had it unloaded, it was well after lunch. I ended up eating a microwave frozen meal of some sort I had stuffed in the freezer in the break room.

It wasn't good.

My mouth waters as I scan the menu. Tonight's special is a grilled chicken salad, and while that sounds good on a hot July day, it's not what I'm looking for as my dinner. I'm going to need sustenance and a lot of it.

"Logan, before I forget, we're getting together for dinner at Shiner's on Friday night for Hallie's birthday. We're meeting at six," Ellie says as she sets our drinks down on the table.

"Oh, Hallie! How is that lovely lady?" Gram asks, practically cooing as she speaks of her.

"She's doing well. I haven't seen her since the wedding, but we texted a little last night. She seemed to enjoy herself quite a bit," Ellie tells my grandma, referring to all the wine Hallie consumed.

My dick, of course, recalls exactly how much it *enjoyed* her Saturday night and starts to get hard. I actually have to direct my attention to the older woman sitting beside me in order to get it to go down. No one sports a hard-on while talking to Grandma.

"Well, that's perfectly acceptable. Weddings are a time for celebration," Gram announces. "By the way, any chance Saul has that delicious meatloaf left from lunch?" She adds a hopeful grin for good measure.

"Actually," Ellie says, leaning over the table and getting closer and glancing from side to side, "There may be a plate or two still in the back."

Gram gasps. "Really? What would an old lady have to do to get one of those plates?"

Ellie beams. "Absolutely nothing. If you want it, it's yours. Just don't tell TD. I just told him I was certain we were out." She winks at the woman beside me.

I bark out a laugh and Gram nods in understanding. "Your secret is safe with me, dear. I'll take the meatloaf special."

"And for you?" Ellie asks my mom after writing down my grandma's order.

"I'll take the grilled chicken salad special with ranch dressing, please."

Ellie writes and asks, "Logan?"

"Chicken fried steak," I reply, setting my menu on the table with the other two.

"Mashed potatoes okay?"

"Yep. And if you throw extra gravy on them, I won't complain."

She chuckles and grabs the menus. "Got it. Your food will be out shortly."

Once she walks away, Gram states, "I've always loved that woman."

I lean back, throwing my arm on the top of the booth behind her. "You only like her because she's bringing you meatloaf."

A wicked grin spreads across her face. "I liked her before that. That just pushes my adoration over the top."

The door chimes with another arrival, and in true small-town fashion, everyone turns to see who it is. Morgan and Brody step in, but when he continues to hold open the door, I realize it's for another patron.

Hallie.

Brody spots me and waves, and when I return the gesture, Hallie turns my way to see who he was waving to. As the young couple heads for the table where TD sits, the woman I spent an unforgettable time with just two nights ago gives us a hesitant, yet polite wave.

"Oh, Hallie, dear!" Gram hollers, signaling her over.

My eyes rake over Hallie as she slowly approaches our table. She's wearing little cutoff jean shorts with a formfitting tank top, and on her feet is a pair of black flip-flops that show off her hot pink toenail polish. Her hair is pulled up in a ponytail at the top of her head, and wildly enough, considering my present company, all I can think about is wrapping that hair around my fist and giving it a slight tug as I slide into her pussy from behind.

My grandma's boney elbow slams into my side, causing me to huff out a harsh breath. When I turn my narrowed eyes her way, she's smiling sweetly at me and waiting expectantly. "What?" I ask, confused by her assault.

"I said Hallie looks so pretty today and asked if you agreed," Gram harps, a glint of mischief in her eyes.

"Oh, yes. Pretty," I reply without even looking at the woman now standing beside our table.

"What brings you into the diner, dear? Meeting someone for dinner?" Gram asks before taking a sip of her lemonade.

"I'm just grabbing some dinner to go and heading back to my condo," she answers.

"Well, you must join us then. We insist, don't we, Logan?"

I glance across the table at my mom, but all I see is her eyes dancing with laughter. "Of course you can join us," I find myself saying.

"I don't want to intrude—" Hallie starts but is quickly cut off.

"You're not. We'd love for you to join us. Please, have a seat," Gram insists, pointing to the booth across from me.

Once she's situated, Ellie returns to take her drink and food order, happily adding it to ours. I move my legs, only to accidentally kick Hallie in the shin. She winces and narrows her eyes at me, the accusation clear. I'm just about to apologize for the unintentional act when my grandma speaks up.

"Hallie, you're glowing. Are you dating anyone?"

My eyes widen and fly across the table to Hallie. She seems confused and taken aback by the comment as she slowly replies, "Umm, no?"

"Well, in my experience, a woman only glows like that when she's having really good sex," my grandma says with a smile before sipping her lemonade.

I choke on air and cough and sputter. "Gram!"

"What? I'm serious. I'm old, but I remember that good-sex glow. Your grandpa, rest his soul, was very good at the sexual stuff."

I groan and shut my eyes, trying not to think about my grandparents having sex. Hallie's giggle fills the diner, making my cock jerk in my pants. My mom blushes with her chuckle, and I suddenly wish the floor would open up and swallow me whole.

"Well, sorry to disappoint you, Bernice, but the last time I was intimate with a man, it really wasn't *that* good." A smug grin slips across her mouth before she takes a sip of her tea.

My eyes narrow because I beg to differ.

I'm pretty sure it was very, *very* good. I mean, I'm not a super religious man, but she seemed to be praising God a hell of a lot.

"Oh, that's too bad."

"I'm sure it's just a sweaty glow from cleaning and organizing the preschool today," Hallie replies casually.

Gram gives a knowing nod. "That doesn't sound nearly as fun. But who knows, the next guy you take to bed may very well knock your socks off. Just you wait."

My chest puffs out as the challenge is laid at my feet. She thinks our time together wasn't that great?

Game on, Cupcake.

CHAPTER
nine

Hallie

"There she is!" Ellie hollers when we arrive at Shiner's Sports Bar. "Happy birthday!"

Smiling, I make my way to the table Ellie and TD have reserved for tonight's gathering they insisted we have. Thirty-six is just another number, and while I enjoy getting together with my friends, a birthday celebration isn't something I need. "Thank you," I tell Ellie, giving her a hug.

"You look so hot," she announces, taking in my cowboy boots and light blue and yellow sundress that hits mid-thigh. It also dips very low in the front, revealing plenty of cleavage.

"Thank you," I reply, doing a little curtsy.

"That's what I told her when she came out to my SUV. She's going to turn all the heads tonight, and not just the single ones," Blair chimes in, looking just as foxy in her white and green dress with nude flats.

"I'm not the only one. Good thing your fiancé is with you. He looks like he's ready to throw down with the first guy who looks your way," I quip, already noticing how my brother's head seems to be on a swivel.

"This is so fun! I'm so glad we decided to do this," Ellie adds, looking positively beautiful in her denim skirt and purple halter top.

When Blair initiated a conversation Monday morning about my birthday, it was decided we'd do something low-key. Dinner with friends at Shiner's. But why stop there? With Ellie and TD leaving Sunday morning for their honeymoon to a resort in The Bahamas, she was digging through her stuff looking for outfits to take, and we all agreed to wear a cute outfit from the back of the closet that never sees the light of day. Even Ava is joining us tonight and agreed to find something out of her normal everyday wear.

"First off," I start, pulling out a chair and taking a seat, "I want to know when you bought that top and when you were planning on wearing it."

Ellie blushes a dark pink shade. "Oh, uh, I thought I might wear it on a date about five years ago, but that never transpired."

TD growls beside his wife and pulls her into his arms possessively. "Now you only wear it for me."

"Yes, husband," she coos, going up on her tiptoes and kissing his cheek. "Only you."

"Okay, enough. No one wants to watch you two be lovey-dovey all night," I tease, grabbing the menu card from the center of the table.

"You're going to have to give us a little time on the lovey-dovey part," TD counters, pulling out Ellie's chair for her before taking his seat. "We're still firmly in the honeymoon phase, and we haven't even gotten to the honeymoon. Plus, we're making up for lost time."

I groan goodheartedly. "Fine, we'll give you some grace, but only because I'm certain she'll come home from said honeymoon knocked up."

TD grins widely. "Hopefully."

"Ava!" Blair greets, getting up from the chair beside me to hug the newest arrival.

"Hey, everyone," she replies, returning the hug before turning my way. "Happy birthday."

I take in her red dress and gasp. "Holy shit, look at you! This dress is fire."

"Thanks. I was worried it was going to be a little too much, but when Ellie texted me a picture of what she was wearing, I decided to just do it."

"It's so beautiful. Red is definitely your color," Blair adds.

"I wore it last year at my cousin's wedding in Florida. I never thought I'd wear this baby again," Ava announces with a chuckle, making us all laugh, considering we're all wearing something we never thought we'd actually wear. "And remember, no photos on social media with me in them."

"Of course," I tell her, reaching over and giving her hand a squeeze.

Several years ago, Ava had old photos of her doing keg stands in college posted on social media. One of her fifth-grade student's parents saw it, and because they were upset at her for failing their son, took those photos to the school board to try to get her fired. It was terrible. Ava hasn't stepped foot in any of the local drinking establishments since, fearful photos of her having a drink—despite being well over the legal age limit and off the clock—will come back to bite her in the ass again.

"I'm just happy you agreed to join us. I know this isn't your thing," Ellie says as we all start to take our seats around the table.

Ava shrugs. "I've decided celebrating the birthday of a friend was worth the risk."

"Well, you're definitely making a statement in that dress. I'm pretty sure Gavin Pierson almost tripped over his own two feet when he glanced this way," I tell her, noticing the local contractor and construction guru continually looking this way.

"What? That's probably because I teach his daughter," she mutters, lowering her head. "Do you think he's going to cause a problem?" Worry mars her beautiful face.

"No way. His interest in you is definitely more of the 'I want to rip that dress off you and do you on the table,'" I state, watching as she turns a dark shade of red in embarrassment.

"I would never date the parent of one of my students," she insists, but there's no missing the way her eyes dart toward the bar where Gavin and his employee, Max Goodman, are sitting.

"Heard there was a birthday celebration tonight."

The hairs on the back of my neck stand up and my nipples pebble against the material of my dress. Slowly, I turn around to confirm what I already know. Logan is here, and he didn't turn ugly or grow a paunchy beer gut since the last time I saw him.

Dammit.

"Cupcake," he greets with a knowing grin.

My clit hums to life.

"Logan," I reply crisply, turning my attention back to the menu.

"What's everyone drinking? I'll go up and order a round," he states, taking the empty chair directly to my right. Instantly, his woodsy cologne infiltrates the thick protective armor I slid into place before coming out tonight.

The table goes through their drink order, and when it finally gets to me, I wave my hand. "Just water for me."

"Come on, Hal, it's your birthday!" Blair encourages.

"I know, but I don't usually drink much, and I'm pretty sure I drank enough last Saturday night to cover me for a while," I tell her, trying to ward off the memories of Logan and me after all the tequila was consumed. "Plus, you're not drinking. Friends drink together."

"Well, we can have a celebratory belated birthday drink in nine months," she says with a small shrug.

"Nine months? Why so? Oh my God! You're pregnant!" I holler, jumping up from my seat and tackle-hugging my bestie in her chair. "I can't believe this! I mean, I can and was really hoping it would happen soon, but I thought you would wait until after the wedding."

"Me too," my brother grumbles, but I can tell by the smile on his lips, he's incredibly excited about becoming a dad.

He stands up when I hug him and squeezes me extra hard when I whisper, "Love you, big brother."

"Love you too," he murmurs.

A few minutes later, a tray of drinks shows up. There are glasses of water, a few bottles of beer, and two margaritas in a sugar-rimmed glass. "All right, so we're doing lots of celebrating tonight," Logan starts, passing out the drinks. He places one of the margaritas in front of me, a drink I didn't order, and holds up the final beer. "To TD and Ellie's marriage, Gabe and Blair's new addition and upcoming wedding, and Hallie's thirty-sixth birthday."

We all clink glasses and take drinks. The tequila in mine instantly starts to warm my blood as recollections start to flit through my mind of the last time I consumed tequila. I'm sure this brand isn't nearly as smooth as the one at Logan's house, but paired with the rest of the fruity concoction, it's still pretty tasty.

Gabe claps his hands together. "All right, everyone. Let's eat!"

"What do you say we make this round interesting?" Logan asks, tossing the ball up in the air and easily catching it in his hand. He steps up way too close for my liking, invading my personal space. His eyes are cast down, and I have no doubt he's looking at my cleavage, which is clearly on full display. I would never admit this aloud, but I might have had him in mind when I chose my flirty dress for tonight.

"You mean more interesting than me beating you?" I taunt, even though we've both technically won a round.

We're at the Skee-Ball machine, trash talking like it's our jobs and having a surprisingly good time. "I believe we've each one a game. How about we make a bet on this game?"

My eyes narrow. "What are we betting?"

His eyes move down to my thighs and slowly caress their way back up to my face. "You pick."

"Hmm," I murmur, reaching for one of the balls. "How about if I win, you have to wash my Jeep?"

His left eyebrow rises toward the heavens. "Seriously? That's what you want?"

I nod smugly. "Yep. Of course, you'll have to wear what I pick out for you and do it in my front yard for all the neighbors to see."

A gravelly chuckle slides from his mouth. "All right, then I choose the same. You'll wash my truck in my front yard wearing what I pick."

"Deal," I boast, reaching out my hand to shake. Electricity zips through my veins the moment we touch, but I'm able to hide any reaction.

"Five throws, alternating players. At the end of the five, we tally the scores. Ladies first," he says, stepping aside and holding out his hand for me to take my position in front of the board.

I let my first ball fly, earning a quick thirty points. Not my best score, but I'll take it. Stepping aside, Logan moves into position and throws his ball down the lane, sending it flying. It hits off to the side and drops into the ten-point hole.

"Aww, too bad," I sing with mock sadness.

"Yeah, yeah, yeah. I'm just getting started." He claps his hands together and slides them against one another like he's warming them up. The sound of his hands hitting together makes my thighs clench and my ass burn, almost as if I can recall exactly what said hand felt like smacking against my bare behind.

By the time I grab my fifth and final ball, I'm only ten points ahead. It's anyone's game right now, and the last thing I want to do is lose to Logan. There's no telling what outfit he'll make me wear to heighten the humiliation, and I have no intention of finding out.

I take aim and launch my ball up the lane. My breath is stuck in my throat as I watch the ball leap into the air, dead center for the holes. It hits the inside of the fifty and falls in with a loud thud. "Yes! Fifty points, loser! You'll never be able to beat me. You need sixty," I boast, doing a little victory shimmy in celebration.

His eyes caress my body as the corner of one side of his mouth curls up. "I can still win."

"What? There's no way."

Logan gives me a confident nod. "The one-hundred-point hole."

My jaw drops as I spin around. "No one ever gets that."

"Well, watch and learn, Cupcake," he states, reaching for his fifth and final ball.

Holding a drink in one hand, he does an extra little squatty bounce as he gets into position. My eyes are glued to his ass in a pair of well-worn denim, and I don't even notice when he releases the ball. I hear the slide as it shoots up the lane and hits the back. I turn just in time to witness that damn ball fall into the small hole at the top left corner of the game.

One hundred points.

"Yes!" he bellows victoriously, throwing his arm straight up in the air. "Winner, winner, baby!" He punches the air, making me want to punch him in the face.

"You cheated," I insist, unable to comprehend how he just got that ball into the one-hundred-point spot. "No one hits that. It's impossible."

"Well, today is my lucky day, Cupcake. I hit the one hundred, *and* I get my truck washed. Now, what am I going to make you wear while you're scrubbing my truck?" He taps his lips in contemplation.

I narrow my eyes and I spin around, heading straight for the table. "Did you win?" Ellie asks through her yawn.

"He cheated."

Logan laughs behind me. "Hardly. She's the world's worst loser," he says, plopping down on his chair with a satisfied smirk across his too-damn kissable lips.

"She is," Gabe chimes in. "One time when we were playing Battleship, she threw her game board at me when I sank her last ship."

"You cheated!" I declare, pointing my finger at my brother.

He just shakes his head and grins. "My fiancée is tired. I'm going to get her home," Gabe announces, standing up and extending his hand toward Blair.

"Are you about ready?" Blair asks me, since they picked me up and brought me up here.

I glance around, realizing TD and Ellie are probably getting ready to leave too, and Ava took off about an hour ago. That'll leave Logan and me, and while I don't exactly want to stay here for him, I do want a bit of redemption, so I'm not stuck washing his truck in a duck costume or something equally as horrible.

"I might hang around a bit longer," I reply casually, walking over and giving my friends hugs goodbye.

"Are you sure? We're happy to drop you on our way," Gabe says.

"I'm sure. Don't worry about me," I reply with a big grin.

That's when I see a look pass between my brother and Logan, as if he's silently communicating with him about making sure I get home safely.

Whatever.

TD and Ellie do leave almost immediately after Blair and Gabe, and after a few hugs and well-wishes for their honeymoon, I turn my attention back to a smirking Logan. "All right, Johnson. Double or nothing?"

"Why would I do that? I've already won," he replies, crossing his arms over his broad chest. I try to ignore the way his T-shirt sleeves stretch across taut muscles and tattooed skin.

"Because you know it was a fluke," I state, hands on my hips.

He chuckles. "Again, why would I agree to a rematch?"

"Because you don't back down from a challenge."

He holds my gaze for several long seconds before asking, "Are we still talking about Skee-Ball?"

Lifting my chin, I reply, "Of course. What else?" I know exactly what he was referring to.

"All right, Miss Rhodes, I accept your challenge, but I get to pick the game."

"Fine," I reply confidently, hoping he picks pool. I'm a pretty decent pool player and would kill him in a game of nine ball.

Logan scans the bar, which has a huge room full of activities to choose from. From pinball machines, arcade games, pool tables, and more, this place is great for unwinding at the end of a day. Plus, it's a big hit with the younger crowd.

Suddenly, a wolfish grin spreads across his face, and I know he's decided. "What are the terms? Are you going to wash my truck a second time?"

"Nope, we'll raise the stakes."

"Okay, and what would those be?"

Thinking for a few long seconds, the perfect idea hits me. "If I win, you not only have to wash my Jeep in whatever I pick, which was the original bet, but you also have to call bingo at ladies' night at the church."

"That's it?" he asks, shocked by such a manageable task.

"In a tutu."

His eyes widen before narrowing. "Wait a minute, this isn't how all or nothing works. If I win, I get both. If you win, you get nothing."

I shrug my shoulders. "Yeah, well, it's my birthday. My rules."

After a beat he finally answers, "Fine. But if I win, I get both too. You washing my truck and wearing a tutu while calling bingo."

"Deal," I agree, extending my hand. "What's your choice?" I ask, looking out at the vast space filled with games. I try not to let my hopeful eyes linger too long on the pool table, hoping he doesn't remember I used to play a lot when I was younger. If anything, I'm pretty decent at most of the arcade games and would definitely kick his ass at pinball. In fact, there's not a lot in here I wouldn't have a damn good chance at winning. Well, everything but one thing.

A wolfish grin transforms his gorgeous face into a work of art. He levels me with a look as he leans in and whispers, "Darts."

Shit.

CHAPTER Ten

LOGAN

"I think I'm just going to walk home. I don't get into vehicles with cheaters."

The easiest bark of laughter flies from my mouth and lightens my soul. When was the last time I enjoyed myself as much as I have tonight? The lighthearted banter, the bets, and the woman herself have combined to make a pretty fun night.

"I didn't cheat. You just suck at darts," I tell her, clicking the unlock button on my fob and opening the passenger door. "Besides, Gabe would beat me up if I left his sister stranded on the sidewalk at the bar."

Her eyes narrow and her arms cross over her chest. The act causes her ample cleavage to spill out of her dress even more. And speaking of the dress, did I mention how fucking edible she looks tonight? I almost swallowed my tongue when I walked into the bar and saw her standing with our friends. "It's Pine Village. I live three blocks away. I'm sure I can manage to get myself home safely without the help of a big, strong man. Go find a damsel in distress elsewhere, Johnson."

My cock roars to life at the sass behind my last name, getting hard and pressing painfully against my zipper. "I see no damsel in distress, only a woman who is a horrible loser." I point inside the cab of my truck. "Get in."

She huffs but does as instructed and climbs inside the cab of my truck. Once the door is closed, I walk around and get behind the wheel. I only had one beer early in the night before switching to water, so I'm perfectly fine to drive. Starting the truck, I pull out of the parking spot and steer toward Hallie's condo.

"I'm not wearing a tutu," she grumbles from the seat beside me.

Hiding my smile, I reply, "I'm pretty sure you would have made me wear one had you won. Stop being a sore loser, Cupcake. You did the crime, now you do the time."

"But it's my birthday," she argues, as if that's reason enough to forfeit the bet.

"Your point?" I ask, turning down the street leading to her place.

"My point is...you know what? Never mind. You're mean."

Again, I laugh and shake my head. When I pull into her driveway, I throw my gearshift into Park and turn to face my passenger. "I'm not mean, Hallie. I just know what buttons to push."

Her blue eyes, despite being dark in the truck cab, turn a deeper sapphire color, one I can associate with her being turned on. "Why do you do that?"

"Push your buttons?" I shrug my shoulders and continue, "I guess because I enjoy getting a rise out of you. And before you argue, it's not because I like seeing you mad or anything, but because you give it right back. If I thought it really bothered you, I wouldn't do it."

"So you like torturing yourself...and me?"

Smiling, I shrug. "Yeah, I guess so."

Her blue eyes bore into me with so much intensity, I feel it down into my soul. There's a hum in the truck cab, a heady mixture of familiarity and sexual tension. Before I can reach for my door handle to walk her to the door, she blurts out, "I'm not sleeping with you," and lifts her chin in defiance.

An eyebrow lifts in question. "I don't recall asking."

"You didn't," she states, shifting in her seat and averting her gaze. "I'm just making it clear."

"It's a good thing you made that crystal clear, Cupcake," I reply, opening my door and sliding out.

When I reach the passenger side, Hallie's climbing out of the truck. "I don't need you to walk me to my door. This wasn't a date."

I shove my hands in my pockets, partially to appear casual and nonthreatening, but also to keep myself from reaching for her, pulling her into my arms, and kissing the hell out of her. "Just being a gentleman, Hal."

With a sigh, she marches toward her front entrance, pulling her keys from her little purse. I almost comment about being glad she has them this time, but I decide it might not be the best time to poke the bear. She does have keys in her hand. It'd be my luck she'd use them to gouge out my eyes.

The moment the lock is released, she turns to me. "Well, I guess thank you anyway, even though it wasn't necessary to bring me home and walk me to my door."

Opting to ignore the last part of her statement, I focus on her thanks. "You're welcome."

We stand here, staring at each other for what feels like a thousand minutes, which in reality, it was probably five. I don't know who moves first, her or me, but we seem to react at the same time. I rip my hands from my pockets in just enough time to catch her as she throws herself at me. Her arms wind around my neck and her legs around my waist. The heels of her boots dig into my body as our mouths collide urgently, our tongues battling for domination.

I step into her home, kicking the door closed behind me, all while deepening the kiss. I spin around, pinning her back against the door and rocking my hips into the apex of her legs. My cock is begging to be let out, screaming to slide into Hallie's sweet pussy as she digs her nails into my scalp in both pleasure and pain.

I reach for the lock but pause. Ripping my mouth from hers, I state, "Tell me to leave and I will."

She growls in frustration, her blue eyes swimming in desire. "Take me to my room."

Flipping the lock on her door, I spin around and stalk straight down the hallway. Her mouth trails open-mouthed kisses down my neck, nipping and licking as she goes, causing my cock to press painfully against my zipper. I manage to get us to her bedroom without slamming into a wall, but the moment we're inside her room, I'm searching for wall real estate to use as leverage.

Hallie's yelp turns into a groan as I cage her to the wall and rock my hips, just as I did against the front door. She moans, squirming to get closer to where she aches for my touch. I wish her panties were already gone and my pants were around my ankles. I'm in the perfect position to thrust, filling her sweet pussy completely in one fluid motion.

"Yes."

"What?" I ask. Did I ask a question.

"Whatever you were thinking. I want that." Her voice is breathless and filled with anticipation. "Now. Hurry."

A chuckle slides past my lips. "So impatient."

"So annoying," she grumps, but I quiet her with my mouth.

Setting her down on her feet, I continue my assault with my lips as I reach beneath her dress for her panties. A loud moan fills the space around us when I connect only with smooth, bare skin. "You're not wearing fucking panties?" I ask.

Hallie shrugs. "I do that from time to time," she says, a glint of pure evil in her stunning blue eyes.

My fingers slide between her lips, gliding through all the moisture as I rub her clit. "Christ, now every time I see you, I'll wonder if you're wearing them."

Her eyes close and her head falls back. "You'll just always have to wonder."

I press a single finger inside her pussy. "You're diabolical."

Her snort turns into a pleasureful groan. "Only with you."

Slipping a second finger inside her body, I whisper, "How do you want it?"

"Exactly what you were thinking just a few moments ago."

My brain replays the way I envisioned pinning her to the wall. "You sure?" I inquire, waiting for her to ask for details.

"Yes, dammit."

Even though I don't want to, I remove my fingers from her body and release my belt. I quickly follow that up with unbuttoning and unzipping the fly of my jeans before pushing them down to my ankles. I should most definitely remove my shoes, but there's no time. All I feel is the urgency to get inside her, to feel her come around my cock.

She reaches out and strokes my dick, sending a flood of pleasure through my blood, while I rip my T-shirt over my head. It feels too good, and if she keeps that up much longer, this party will be over way before it starts. Placing my hands around her hips, I tell her, "Back up you go."

Her eyes widen with a bit of panic. "What? No."

"Yes, Cupcake."

"I'm too heavy, Logan," she insists, a flash of worry dancing across her face.

Sliding my hand along her jaw and up into her hair, I reassure her, "I've held you like this several times."

She swallows hard. "Yeah, but this will be longer than just a minute or two."

"You clearly don't understand how worked up you've got me right now. A minute or two might be all you get," I quip, only joking a little. I'm way too close to the edge, but if she's giving me permission to fuck her against the wall like this, I'm taking it. "Come on, Hal. I've got you. Trust me." Then, I place my mouth against hers, this time in a more gentle, tender kiss.

She reciprocates, sliding her tongue against mine and her hands up my chest. When she wraps her arms around my neck, I lift at the waist, carefully bunching her dress up around her hips. As her legs settle around me, I make sure we're in the best position possible and carefully reach between us. Hallie lifts and shimmies until my cock is nudging her entrance. With her lips pressed to mine, I lower her onto me, filling her completely in one long stroke.

It's euphoric.

Bliss.

Pure fucking heaven.

With her back pressed to the wall, I use my arms and legs to move, but she's having a hard time keeping her legs locked with those cowboy boots still on her feet. Since I have no intention of letting her take them off, I decide to try a different position.

"Hang on," I tell her, even though she's anchored pretty tightly to my body.

Turning, I shuffle toward the edge of the bed, wishing I would have been smart enough to take my shoes and pants off. When I reach my destination, I lay her down on the corner of the bed and stand, my cock still buried in her. This position is perfect. She'll be comfortable on the bed, with me standing between her open legs.

Reaching down, I give the chest of her dress a tug, causing her ample tits to spill out of the material. I slide my cock out, leaving in just the tip, and ask, "No panties? No bra?"

She smiles up at me, a wicked little grin that makes my balls heavy and my cock ache to thrust. "Let's get back to the task at hand," she encourages, the heels of her boots digging into my lower back as she tries to pull me forward using her legs.

Reaching behind my back, I unlock her legs and slide my arms under her knees. It opens her up and gives me one hell of a view. She gathers her dress around her waist to keep it out of the way as I thrust forward. Seeing her lying before me, her legs spread and her tits bouncing free from the top of her dress is like something straight out of my wildest fantasies.

My hips piston forward over and over on their own accord, and my eyes feast on the sight. Hallie groans with each thrust, her internal muscles starting to tighten. "Reach down and touch yourself, Hal. Get there. Now."

One hand moves to her clit as she frantically strokes her index finger over the sensitive nub, while the other goes to her nipples. She rolls and pinches the first one, then the second, before starting over again. Her grip on my cock tightens, and I know she's close. My balls start to draw up, the tingling beginning at the base of my spine. I'm ready to come, but need to make sure she does too.

Just then, she erupts. Her pussy squeezes me like a vise as she cries out, triggering my own release. I follow her over the edge, drawing out every ounce of pleasure our bodies possess, and even when it's over, I still move. My body does it all on its own, savoring the feel of her wrapped around me.

When all that's left are the shudders, I lean forward, covering her with my chest and finding her lips with mine. This kiss is much more leisurely, yet just as pleasurable.

I move my head to the crook of her neck and just breathe her in. Hallie wraps her arms around me and sighs in contentment. I try to ignore how right this all feels. Her legs hitched over my hips, her tits pressed against my bare chest, and my spent cock still buried inside her. It's the perfect end to the night, even if neither one of us wants to admit it.

A warm puff of air tickles my shoulder. "You're not spending the night."

"Too bad. I was hoping for round two. I haven't had my mouth on you yet," I mutter.

I feel her shiver in anticipation, but don't push the issue. If I'm going to stay, it's not because I sweet-talked my way into it. Slowly, I pick myself up off her and slide my cock out of her body, making a huge mess as I do. I quickly grab a discarded shirt and slip it between her open legs. Reaching down, I pull my pants up to my ass, careful not to pinch anything so I can head to her bathroom and clean up.

Inside the space, I grab a washcloth and wet it with warm water. Once I've taken care of my mess, I retrieve a second washcloth so I can do the same for Hallie. Returning to the bedroom, I find she's moved up to where she sleeps, having kicked off her boots and tossed them onto the floor. Her dress is there too, which leaves her completely naked, except for a balled-up T-shirt between her legs. It's hard not to notice how incredibly beautiful she is in this moment.

"I brought you a washcloth to clean up," I tell her.

She reaches out, so I place the material in her hand. Trying to give her a bit of privacy, I finish righting my boxers and jeans before fastening the button and zipper. When I'm done, I look up and find her watching me.

"It's awfully late," she says softly, holding my gaze. "You might as well stay."

The corner of my mouth ticks. "Is that an invitation?"

"No," she blurts out quickly, curling on her side. "Just an idea," she adds through her yawn.

Unable to contain my smile, I unbuckle my pants once more, kick off my shoes, and remove my jeans. When I'm down to my boxers, I climb into her bed and reach for her. She flips over, throwing an arm over my bare chest and a leg over my thigh. I keep my hands to myself, even though I long to slide my hands across her naked skin.

I close my eyes and exhale, fully relaxing enough to fall asleep. Reaching over, I run my finger across her shoulder and feel her shudder beneath my touch. "Happy birthday, Hallie," I mutter.

"Night, Logan." She wiggles against me, getting closer, and then promptly falls asleep.

And me? With her tucked into my side once more, I sleep like a fucking baby until she wakes me up two hours later sucking my hard dick in her mouth.

CHAPTER
eleven

Hallie

I've intentionally avoided Logan for the last three weeks. Why? Because, honestly, I have no clue what to say to him.

The sex was outstanding. The kind that reaches into your bones and tattoos the memories into the marrow of your being. I've thought about it way too much to be considered normal. Well, at least in the evenings. And at night. And when I wake up in the morning.

I'm good throughout the day, though, since I stepped back into the classroom the first of the week. The students don't actually start until the upcoming Monday, but I've hosted two backpack nights, so my next group of preschoolers can come in, meet me, and see their classroom. It's always an incredibly nerve-racking, yet exciting time for the students—and me—and I've learned bringing the kids in with their parents helps ease the magnitude of the transition they're about to make.

Today, I'm finalizing my lesson plans for the first day of school and making sure my space is ready to go. I'll have a morning three-year-old class and an afternoon four-and-five-year-old class, with a small period of time to myself in between. Most of the time, I just stay here, in the small school attached to the Lutheran church. I love this little place and the support I receive from the community, which is why I spend so much of my summer making sure this preschool is the best it could possibly be for the upcoming school year.

My stomach rolls, reminding me I haven't eaten lunch yet. It's just after noon, and I'm at a standstill. Everything is ready to go for Monday, and really, it has been ready all week, so there's no reason for me to hang around on this Friday afternoon just for the sake of preparation. There's nothing more I can do.

I head over to the cabinet where I keep my purse and feel my stomach flop. That queasy feeling settles in, and I start to sweat. Forgoing my purse, I move quickly to the bathroom down the hallway. I barely make it inside the stall before dropping to my knees and throwing up. Everything I had for breakfast this morning reappears, leaving me exhausted and disgusted at the same time.

What a terrible time to get the flu!

Once I've finished and am certain nothing else is coming up, I flush the toilet and exit the stall. I wash my hands and wet a paper towel, using it on my face and neck. I don't feel fevered, just flushed from exertion. I bend down and rinse my mouth out before exiting the bathroom and returning to the cabinet in my classroom. I find the new package of toothbrushes and pull one out, along with the travel packet of toothpaste, and return to the bathroom.

When my teeth are clean and my stomach calms again, I finally grab my purse and prepare to leave. My stomach growls, and even though a big, juicy cheeseburger sounds like heaven right now, there's no way I'd risk eating something that heavy. Instead, I'll stop at the diner and see if they have any soup available, despite being mid-August.

I turn off the lights, lock the door, and set the alarm. Finally, I'm out at my Cherokee and ready to head out. It's hot, but thankfully, not sweltering heat. I crank up the air-conditioning and back out of my parking spot before driving toward the main street through town.

Since it's during the noon hour, the downtown square is packed. I contemplate just going home and finding something there, but the prospect of some of Frannie's homemade chicken and noodle or creamy broccoli soup has my stomach begging loudly. Fortunately, I get lucky and find a car pulling out of their parking spot right in front of the diner. I throw on my turn signal and parallel park into the spot, super excited to have secured it. With purse in hand, I head inside to place my order.

Stepping inside is almost too much on my senses. The seating area is loud and packed with patrons, no doubt thanks to Saul's meatloaf special on the menu. I wave and say hello to those I know but keep my feet moving toward the counter. As I approach, I see Ellie stepping out of the kitchen, carrying a big tray of food. "Hey, I'll be right back," she says as she walks by to deliver the mouth-watering food to the customers.

My stomach growls once more, a little louder than I would have liked, catching the attention of a man sitting at the counter beside me. I divert my attention to the specials board, grateful to see chicken and rice soup listed for today.

"Sorry 'bout that, Hal. What can I get ya? It might be a few minutes before a table opens up," Ellie says as she approaches.

"No, I'm not staying. My stomach is a little queasy, so I thought I'd grab some soup and head home."

"You pregnant? That seems to be going around," she states with a laugh.

My eyes widen. "What? I'm not pregnant." Then something else hits me. "Are you?" I whisper.

She shakes her head, a flash of sadness in her eyes. "Not yet, but we're definitely trying."

"It'll happen soon, I know it," I reassure her.

"Yeah, when it's time, it's time, right? Do you want crackers with your soup?"

"Yes, please. If you have a few extra packets, toss those in. I'll pay for them," I insist, digging my wallet out of my purse. "Oh, and a Sprite too, please."

She nods and types into the cash register. "Six fifty-seven."

I dig a ten out of my wallet and hand it over. "Keep the change."

"Thank you," she replies, tossing what's left into a jar behind the counter. "Give me two minutes, and I'll have it ready." With that, she spins around quickly and heads off to the kitchen, leaving me standing where I am.

The bell sounds behind me, but I don't have the desire to turn and see who has entered. Pine Village is at peak tourist season, meaning the cabins and campgrounds are all full of out-of-towners here to take advantage of the national preserve. Between fishing, trail riding, and hiking, there's plenty to do all summer long.

"Fancy meeting you here," Blair says, stepping beside me and pulling me into a hug.

"What are you doing here?" I ask, even though I don't need to. There's only one reason she'd be here. Waving my hand, I add, "Never mind. Stupid question."

"Your brother is finishing up with a patient who is talking his ear off, so I decided to run over and see if they have any meatloaf left."

"You may be in luck. I've seen plates of it coming out of the kitchen, so they must still be serving it."

"Oh good." She places a hand on her flat belly. "This baby is craving it like no other. I begged Gabe to make it for me last night. It was nothing like Saul's," she states with a chuckle.

"There *is* something magical about it," I say, just as Ellie returns from the kitchen with a bag.

"Hey, Blair!" she greets eagerly. "One second." She grabs a Styrofoam cup off the shelf, scoops a little ice into it, and fills the cup with Sprite. "All right, Hal, you're all set."

Blair glances down at my small bag. "No meatloaf for you?"

"No, my stomach has been a little funny today. Probably all the nerves from starting a new school year on Monday," I tell her.

She nods in understanding, but the look in her eyes is skeptical. "We've seen a few cases of summer upper respiratory infections, but no flu yet. Usually that doesn't rear its ugly head until mid-fall."

"I told her she was probably pregnant," Ellie chimes in, making Blair's eyes widen.

"She's kidding," I mutter.

Blair nods as Ellie asks, "What can I get you, Blair?"

"Two meatloaf specials to go, if you still have some."

"We do," Ellie informs her while making the note on the order pad. "Anything to drink?"

"No, thanks."

"All right, let me get this in. It will only take a couple of minutes," Ellie assures her before she buzzes back to the kitchen to place the order. When she returns a minute later, her tray is piled with more food as she heads out to deliver the plates.

"You don't look fevered," Blair states, her observing eyes focused on me.

"I don't think I have one. Just a little upset stomach is all. I ate a fast breakfast on my way out the door this morning and have been finishing getting everything ready for Monday. I'm sure it was a combination of eating too fast, stress, and having lunch later than normal." I shrug my shoulders, hoping she realizes this isn't a big deal.

"All right," she replies with a slow nod. "Your brother is going to Hudson this afternoon to see a patient and the schedule isn't too heavy, so if you want to come in, just text me."

"Thanks," I tell my oldest friend as I grab my soup and cup of Sprite. "Have a great afternoon. Tell my brother I said hello."

"I will. I'll check on you later," she replies as another to-go bag comes from the kitchen and is placed in front of her.

I want to tell her it's not necessary, but her attention is turned to Ellie, who approaches the counter and starts to ring her up. I wave goodbye to a few patrons before slipping out the front entrance and making my way to my Jeep. The soup smells amazing, and it takes all my self-control not to just rip into it right here and now. My stomach is growling, my mouth watering, but since there isn't a spoon in the bag, I decide to hold off until I get home.

The drive home is short, and as I pull into my little driveway, I press the button for the garage door to open. Not even bothering to close the door behind me, I make my way inside my condo through the garage entrance and practically race to the drawer for a spoon. Dropping my purse on the counter, I pull the contents from the bag out and remove the lid. The chicken and rice goodness fills my senses and makes my mouth water once more. Lifting the spoon, I dive into the warm soup and take my first hearty bite.

"Oh my God," I groan in happiness, just as my stomach lets a hard jolt.

Definitely not happy right now.

I push the soup away and cover my mouth with my hand. *What the hell is going on?* Closing my eyes, I count to ten and slowly inhale and exhale. It takes the second round of counting before my stomach calms down again and the unsettled feeling passes. Unfortunately, my appetite has passed too, and the soup no longer sounds—or smells—appealing.

Sighing, I push away from the counter, grab my Sprite, and head for the living room. I take a small drink of the cold liquid, grateful it doesn't make my stomach uneasy, and curl up on my side. I definitely don't feel like I'm sick, despite the upset stomach, but perhaps Blair is wrong and I have a rare case of the flu. Stranger things have happened, especially for teachers who are around kids all day long.

But...I haven't exactly been around the kids yet, outside of the backpack nights.

Keeping my eyes closed, I relax and decide a nap would probably do the trick. When I was younger and not feeling well, there was something magical about napping that seemed to make everything better.

But as I lie here, my mind won't settle enough. The truth is, while I'm a little drained, I'm not really tired. My mind is going from one direction to the other, spinning with all the things I want to get done this weekend before school starts. I need to mow, clean out the refrigerator, and go grocery shopping. Plus, dust, vacuum, and wash a few loads of laundry. There's just too much to get done, and no time to be under the weather.

Then, something else hits me.

My period.

That's what this is. I'm getting ready to start. Sure, the symptoms are slightly different. Instead of the cramping and discomfort, it's nausea and fatigue. Ugh, this is going to be a rough week if I'm dealing with my period on top of starting the school year.

As I lie here, trying to relax, my brain starts to do the math. Suddenly, I sit up and swing my legs over the couch. My mouth drops open moments before I scramble from where I sit in search of my phone. I dump my purse onto the counter and find the device right away. It takes me three tries to input my passcode, but finally, I'm granted access.

Pulling up my calendar, I slowly walk toward the couch once more. I scan the prior weeks of August, searching for the info I need. When I don't find it, I flip the month to the one prior and continue my hunt. When I finally see the date, I start computing the weeks since. The moment I hit five...

"No. Oh my God, no," I whisper, going back to July and doing the math once more, coming up with the same result.

Five weeks.

It's been five weeks since my last period.

I'm officially late.

I flip over to the message app and pull up Blair's name.

Me: What time is Gabe leaving to go to Hudson?

It takes her a few minutes—minutes where I fret and fidget and try not to freak the fuck out—but eventually, my phone dings with a response.

Blair: He leaves at three. Why? What's up?

Me: I may stop by.

My heart is pounding like a galloping racehorse in my chest.

Blair: No problem. Still not feeling well?

Me: Not really.

Blair: All right. I'll tell the front desk to send you back to my office when you get here.

Me: Thanks, Blair. See you around 3:30.

She replies with the thumbs-up emoji, and I feel like I might have a heart attack when I toss my phone on the couch. *How can this be happening?* I know my period can be somewhat wonky and is often heavy, which is why I always log it in my calendar to help keep track of it. I should have started last week, and while I've occasionally fluctuated a day or two early or late, I've never been seven days late.
Never.
Three thirty can't come soon enough.

With a shaky hand, I open the front entrance door to Pine Village Medical Clinic and step inside. Thankfully, there is no one in the waiting area to witness my arrival, not that they'd know why I'm here, but still.

"Hi, Hallie. Blair mentioned you were stopping by. Go ahead and go back to her office. She's just wrapping up with a patient," Stella Stabler says with a smile, pointing to the doorway.

"Thanks, Stella," I reply brightly, hoping it doesn't come off too fake.

I bypass the doors on both sides of the hall until I get to the end, just past the employee break room. On the left is my brother's office, and on the right is Blair's. It used to be her father's, but when he decided to take a step back following his heart attack, he passed it to his daughter to use.

Inside, I keep myself busy by looking at the framed photos on her credenza. There's one of Blair and her mother at her college graduation, one of her and her younger half sister, Aggie, another of her father, stepmom, Patience, Aggie, Blair, and Gabe from this past Christmas, and finally, a larger one of Blair and Gabe together. I still can't believe my brother hooked up with my best friend, but I'm glad it happened. They're incredibly happy, getting married, and having a baby.

"Hey, sorry to keep you waiting," Blair says from the doorway behind me.

"No worries," I state, spinning around to meet her gaze.

She steps inside and moves to the mini fridge in the corner of the office, grabbing a bottle of water. "So what's up?"

"Umm," I start, my stomach churning a bit from anxiety. "I need you to run a test for me." Her eyebrows pull together in question. "A pregnancy test."

The bottle pauses halfway to her mouth as she gapes at me. "A pregnancy test?" she whisper-yells.

I nod, unable to find the words to confirm.

"Holy shit," she states, setting her bottle on the desk and reaching for my arm. "Come on," she demands. She drags me down the hall to the nurses' station and promptly retrieves a urine sample cup. "Pee."

Numbly, I take the cup and move across the hall to the bathroom. It takes only a few minutes to do my business and wash my hands, and the moment I crack open the door, my best friend practically barges inside and takes the cup from my hand. On wooden legs, I follow her back across the hallway and watch as she conducts the test.

In my heart, I already know what it's going to say.

"I don't even know what to say," she mutters, doing her thing with my cup of pee before taking it across the hall and disposing of it in the toilet. Once she removes her gloves and washes her hands, she returns to where I pace. "Is this from the night of the wedding?"

My face flushes and I avert my gaze.

Blair gasps. "You slept with him again? When?"

"My birthday?" It comes out a question.

"You didn't say anything!" she accuses, keeping her voice down so no one overhears.

"I know," I declare, leaning back against the wall. "It wasn't supposed to happen, but there were a few drinks, we made some bets, he took me home, and one thing led to another."

Blair grins. "Holy crap, I can't believe this. What are you going to do if it's positive?"

I shake my head, unable to truly wrap my head around it. "I don't know."

"You're going to tell him, right?" There's a touch of accusation in her question, but I know it's because she's protecting both him and me.

"Of course I will. I'm not heartless. Plus, I'm pretty sure he'd figure it out."

"True," she replies before a timer dings. Blair holds my gaze and asks, "Ready?"

I nod, even though I'm not.

She picks up the test and hands it over without looking at it, even though I'm sure she wanted to. I close my eyes, my heart racing as it climbs into my throat, making it hard to breathe. With one more deep breath, I open my eyes and look at the test results.

CHAPTER
Twelve

LOGAN

What a day.

Not only was the hardware store busy from open to close, but I had to deal with my ex-wife for a big chunk of that time. Despite being with customers, she chattered nonstop about absolutely nothing, never once contributed to assisting customers or anything productive to the business. She fucked with her nails, her hair, and her makeup, all while talking and driving me absolutely crazy until I told her to go home.

Then, when I finally got home, TD texted me to let me know someone called in a report that the door to my shed at my cabin property was kicked open. He was at the high school, preparing for the football scrimmage night, and unable to come by until after he was done. Unless I needed someone right away, then he'd radio for county to help.

That's why I'm in my truck, driving down the lane toward my grandpa's cabin. *My* cabin. As soon as I pull up the short dirt lane that leads to my property, I can tell something's not right. There's a ton of tracks from a four-wheeler or side-by-side, letting me know someone has been here recently. The moment the shed comes into view, I see the door standing open and slightly crooked on the hinges.

"Son of a bitch," I grumble, turning off my truck and sliding out. With quick steps, I head straight for the small structure that's normally secured with a padlock. I realize it's been cut, and the door practically ripped from the top hinge. I don't touch anything but take a few minutes to look around. The first thing I notice is my gas cans are missing. The four-wheeler and lawn mower are both still here, which tells me the thief wasn't here to completely rob me.

Deciding to go inside to check the cabin, I find the key for the lock and enter slowly. My eyes scan the windows to see if any are open or broken and the décor in case anything is out of place. It only takes me a few minutes to check over the entire place, and I'm pleasantly surprised to find it undisturbed. The back door is still secured, as was the front one before I came inside. Everything is fine too, and I'm extremely grateful.

Knowing I don't have new hinges here, I jump back into my truck and return to town. Instead of heading home like I want, I drive toward the hardware store to get the supplies I need to fix the shed door. I grab two new hinges, as well as a new lock. I'm hoping I won't have to build a new door for it, considering I don't have a lot of free time right now. After jotting down the part numbers so I can enter my purchases into the computer tomorrow, I set the alarm for the door and make sure it's locked as I go.

My stomach growls, reminding me I haven't eaten since breakfast, but now isn't the time. I'd much rather get the shed secured and then go home for a bite. I'm not big on fast food, so I avoid it as much as possible. The diner, on the other hand, is a staple in town and for me. If I don't feel like cooking, I grab something from Frannie's, which is sometimes better than anything I can make at home.

Returning to the cabin, I get to work fixing the little damage the thief caused. Once the door is straight once more, I take another peek around the shed before closing it up and securing the new lock.

Nothing else appears missing, thankfully. It was just some asshole looking for gas. Still pisses me off someone felt the need to break into someone's property and steal what they needed instead of waiting for the gas station to open.

Finally, I slide the new lock onto the door and latch it. Maybe now is a good time to check into cameras. The only problem is having a strong enough Wi-Fi signal to maintain them. During the summer months, the signal isn't terrible, but once the snow and ice show up, it's practically nonexistent.

I head back to the cabin and close the screen door. It's warm and stuffy in here, so I open both doors and a few windows and let the breeze blow through. This place has air-conditioning, but I only run it if someone's staying here. Otherwise, I get by with opening the windows and letting the place air out a bit.

A car pulling into the lane catches my attention. TD probably sent someone over to take my statement regarding the breaking and entering, since he's one of the local police officers, so I head for the door to meet them outside. As I push through the screened door, I'm pleasantly surprised to see Hallie's Cherokee parked beside my truck. She's sitting in the driver's seat, staring at me, but has yet to exit. I decide to wait her out, reaching my arms over my head and grabbing onto the frame of the small porch. I'm not tall, so it's a stretch, but it feels good in my shoulders and back to do it after the day—and early evening—I've had.

There's also a tightness going on in my pants, but I ignore it at the moment.

It takes a few minutes before the driver's door finally opens and Hallie slides out. She keeps her head up, but I can tell something's bothering her. There's turmoil swirling in her stunning blue eyes, and it makes my gut clench. Something is clearly wrong, and if she's come all the way out here for help, it must be something big.

"Hi," she says after clearing her throat.

"Hey."

She glances around and spots the tools I used to fix the door. "Making repairs?" she asks.

It feels like she's searching for something to talk about, but I don't call her on it. "Yeah. Someone broke into the shed and stole my gas cans. I had to fix the door and replace the lock."

Her mouth falls open in shock. "That's terrible! Did you catch them?"

"Naw, someone spotted the door open and called TD. They were long gone by the time I got out here." When she doesn't say anything right away, I finally ask, "Wanna come in for a minute?"

She nods instantly, without giving me any sass. That's a huge red flag something's definitely bothering her.

We walk into the cabin and move to the couch. "Want anything to drink? I don't know what's in there, but there should be some bottles of water. Maybe a few Mountain Dews."

"Water would be great," she says, taking a seat on the couch. She's perched at the edge, not getting too comfortable, which makes me shake my head in confusion.

After grabbing two bottles, I join her, sitting beside her on the couch, but not too close. I don't want to crowd her but am ready to be her friend if she needs one. A few incidents flash through my mind. Could one of her parents be sick? Is something wrong with Blair or Gabe? Their baby? Problems at work? Maybe she lost her job? All these questions flit through my brain as I watch her take a small drink of the cold liquid.

"Thank you," she whispers before setting the bottle on the wooden coffee table in front of us. She sits up straight and clears her throat again, shifting in her seat as if she can't get comfortable.

"Are you okay?" I ask, reaching out automatically and covering her hand with my own.

Her eyes meet mine. There's a mixture of fear, worry, elation, and confusion all churning together like one giant storm cloud. "This is the hardest thing I've ever had to do," she whispers, almost absently, as if she wasn't talking to me.

Deciding to lighten the mood, I quip, "Are you breaking up with me?" I add a little laugh, knowing she'll probably find my joke funny. You know, considering we're not dating and all.

She stares up at me without cracking a smile and blurts out, "No. I'm pregnant."

Her words take several seconds to infiltrate my brain. They just sort of float out there without making any impact on me. Until suddenly, they do. They impact hard, like a wrecking ball slamming into my gut, knocking me on my ass.

I stand up and open my mouth, only no words come out. So I try again, this time a gargled noise slides past my dry throat. With my hands on my hips, I take a few deep breaths and try to calm my racing heart. "Okay," I finally say, tapping my foot on the hardwood floors. "All right. So..." Deep breath. "Pregnant? You're pregnant?"

She nods numbly, her eyes wide in disbelief.

"How?" I find myself asking. As soon as that single word is out of my mouth, I recognize the stupidity in the question. I'm pretty sure I know exactly how.

Her eyebrows pull together as she makes a face at me. "Really?"

"I know *how*, I guess I'm just..." I run my hands through my hair and down my face. "I'm messing this up, I'm sorry." I take another deep breath and drop back onto the couch beside her.

"It's okay. I've been a little out of sorts since I found out this afternoon," she mutters, reaching for the bottle of water and taking a drink.

I don't ask her for confirmation that it's my baby. She wouldn't be here if it weren't, and I've known Hallie my whole life. She's not one to lie about something like this. Hell, I've never known her to lie about anything. She's usually blunt and straightforward, one of the qualities I've always liked most about her besides her loyalty, empathy, and grace.

"I'm sorry," I find myself saying, realizing this is all my fault.

"What? Why?"

I turn a little in my seat and reach for her hand. "I didn't protect you. I should have thought with my big head, not the little one."

"Logan—"

"No, this is on me, Hal. I should have kept a cool head long enough to realize I wasn't using a condom."

The corner of her mouth ticks up in a grin. "Every time?"

A parade of dirty images filter through my mind, and as much as I try to push them away, they won't leave.

Shaking my head, I reply, "Every time. It was my responsibility to make sure we were protected from disease and pregnancy."

"No, it was both of our responsibility, and I was just as...caught up in the moment as you."

I lean over and bump my shoulder against hers as I say, "There were some pretty good moments."

She snorts in reply but smiles as she leans into my shoulder with hers. "Yeah, maybe."

We sit here, her hand still tucked inside mine as I run my thumb over her knuckles. Everything flashes before my eyes. I'm going to be a dad. Holding my child for the first time, rocking him or her to sleep at night, 2:00 a.m. feedings, baths, and giggles. I see it all so clearly, even if this wasn't exactly how I thought it would happen.

"What now? I'll follow your lead, Hal."

She exhales and leans her head against my shoulder. I try to ignore how good it feels to have her beside me like this. "I'm not really sure yet. I guess, I knew I needed to tell you, though I wasn't sure when I was going to do that. But after Blair confirmed it this afternoon, I went home and just...I don't know. Didn't want to be there by myself, so I went to your house, but you weren't there. I thought about going to the football scrimmage, but I wasn't really in a people-y mood. I started driving around and just sort of ended up here. I don't know why, because I actually thought you'd be at the football field with everyone else."

"I was planning on it, but then TD texted me, so I changed my plans."

We sit together in silence for another minute, both lost in our own thoughts, before she says, "I'm not ready to tell everyone yet. I'd really like to give it a bit just to wrap my head around this."

"All right, I'm fine with that. We won't tell anyone right now."

"Except Blair knows, but she said she wouldn't tell my brother unless she absolutely had to. I'd never ask her to lie to him, so if something has to be said for whatever reason, she has my permission to tell him."

I squeeze her hand.

Suddenly, she pulls away enough so she can turn and face me. "Okay, so I need to say this, so just wait until I'm done before you respond, all right?" When I nod, she continues, "I'm keeping this baby. This wasn't the way I thought I'd become a mother, but what's done is done. If you want to be involved, you can. If not, I get it. I won't ask anything of you ever, but I also won't sit there and beg you to be involved. I know what Ellie went through, and although being a single mother wasn't planned, it's happened. I'll be okay."

Even though I know she has more to say, I interrupt anyway, needing to say my piece. "I'll be there every step of the way, Hal. You won't ever be alone in this. We made this baby together, and we'll raise him or her that way."

The corner of her mouth slips up for a flash. "But we're not together."

"Not in the traditional sense, no, but I'll still be there for you and the baby." I toss my arm around her shoulder and hug her. "We'll figure it out, but it doesn't have to be today, all right? We both were dealt a pretty big blow, so let's just take some time to process and then we can talk again."

"Yeah, okay," she replies with a sudden yawn. Just as she does, her stomach growls angrily, making me chuckle.

"Come on," I insist, standing up and extending my hand to her. "Let's go feed my baby."

When she stands, I can't help but notice a blush on her cheeks. I'm not sure exactly what caused it, but I do like seeing the coloring return to her beautiful face. I didn't realize it until just now, but she was a little pale when she pulled in and walked toward me.

"I'm not so sure that's a good idea. This baby doesn't seem to like food."

I can't help but chuckle. "You mean my baby?"

"Yeah, your baby. Causing me grief and nausea already," she jokes, elbowing me in the gut as she passes by and walks toward the door.

"Like father, like son," I mutter as I move around the cabin and secure the windows I had opened earlier to help air the place out. I make sure the back door is locked and return to the front where Hallie waits.

"I should probably just head home. I'm not sure I want to be around food right now," she tells me, sticking out her tongue and making a face.

"Come on, Cupcake. You gotta eat. I'll even buy," I tell her, placing my hand on her lower back and guiding her toward her Jeep.

She pauses halfway and narrows her eyes. "This isn't a date. I can buy my own dinner."

"Fine, you buy yours. I'll buy the baby's," I state, trying to fight off my cocky grin and failing.

She sighs loudly and opens her driver's side door. "You're impossible."

"It's one of my many charming qualities, Hal. Now let's go. I'm starving."

Once she's safely tucked in her vehicle, I grab the tools from the small porch and toss them in the bed of my truck. Then, I climb in and follow her down the lane and toward town.

My mind spins. In the last thirty minutes, my life was flipped upside down. I'm suddenly a man who's going to be a father. A jolt of excitement races through my veins. I've always wanted kids and pictured myself as a dad for a long time. Of course, this isn't exactly how I pictured it happening. Even though we argue all the time, I still consider Hallie a friend. We're not in a relationship, despite the amazing sex we've had. Those two nights were based off tension, chemistry, and a bit of necessity, not love.

Things have definitely changed, and surprisingly, I realize I'm not afraid of it. Despite the most shocking news ever being dumped in my lap just a short time ago, I won't run or hide. Not from Hallie or our child.

I'm going to be a dad, and I couldn't be happier.

CHAPTER Thirteen

Hallie

My stomach has been fine, despite the nausea-inducing anxiety I've felt since finding out I was pregnant. I had every intention of going home and trying to figure out my next step, but the next thing I knew, I was in my vehicle and looking for Logan. Well, I wasn't looking for him per se, but I was trying to find some clarity when my world was flipped upside down, and that clarity came in the form of Logan.

Still, it was incredibly difficult to tell him I was pregnant. This wasn't how I pictured this moment happening. You know, hunting down the guy you slept with to tell him you'd both made the mistake of not wearing a condom? Definitely not on the list of ways I pictured this going down. And even though he seemed out of sorts and shocked at first, he took the news really well. I also have no doubt that he'll be one-hundred-percent involved moving forward. Logan is that type of man. Loyal and good, and he'll be a wonderful dad to my little peanut, even if the circumstances in which he or she was conceived were less than ideal.

Oh my God, what are my parents going to say?

As I hit the main street through town, I find it somewhat deserted. Everyone appears to be at the football field, enjoying the scrimmage night and kickoff to the season. Part of me wants to drive right past Frannie's and head home, but there's nothing in my fridge that sounds remotely appetizing, despite having several options available for quick meals. The thought of Frannie's fluffy strawberry and banana pancakes actually makes my mouth water, and I find myself pulling into the first spot adjacent to the diner and parking.

When I get out, Logan is there, having parked behind me. "Ready?"

"I guess," I reply, worried the scent of what's inside might make this visit a bad idea.

"Come on, Hal. Let's feed my baby," he replies, placing his hand on my lower back to escort me inside the diner. I try not to think about the zip of electricity racing through my blood at the slight touch, especially since it's not meant to be sexual in any way.

It's also hard to ignore the tingle I get every time he says *my baby.*

I glance around to make sure no one heard his comment before we enter the diner, finding it fairly empty. There are a few tables occupied by out-of-towners, but otherwise, we have our pick of the booths. "How about that one?" he asks, pointing to one of the back spots, farthest away from the other patrons.

"Sure," I reply, heading in that direction.

I take the closest bench and slide in, knowing Logan prefers to be facing the room. He's always been like that, dislikes having his back turned. I don't know why I just thought of that, but it's definitely something I've picked up on over the years.

"Hi, guys. What can I get you to drink?" Susie, one of the servers, asks as she sets two menus down on the table.

"Ice water for me," I reply after Logan waves for me to go first.

"Same. Thanks, Susie," Logan says, glancing at the menu.

"Sure thing. Be right back."

"What sounds good?" he asks when we're sitting alone once more.

"What sounds good and what my stomach will allow me to eat appear to be two entirely different things," I reply, recalling the late lunch I really wanted to eat but couldn't.

He nods, scanning the familiar listing of meals available. If he's anything like me, he probably has the entire thing memorized.

"Are we ready to order?" Susie asks, setting two glasses of water down in front of us.

Logan looks up, waiting for me to go first. While the pancakes still sound good, I decide to avoid it at the moment and go for something a little heartier. I mean, if I'm going to throw it back up, I want it to be something I really enjoyed eating, right? "I'll have the country-fried steak with mashed potatoes and gravy. Green beans if you have them."

"Yep, we've got them tonight," she states as she makes notes on the order pad.

"I'll have the double western cheeseburger with sweet potato fries," Logan says, sliding both menus across the table toward Susie, who collects them before offering a fast, "It'll be out shortly."

As soon as she walks away, my brain circles right back around to the reason we're even here together. "I'm sorry I'm making you keep this a secret. I promise you can tell your mom and whoever soon," I blurt out, tearing off the corner of my napkin and rolling it into a ball.

A soft smile instantly spreads across his lips. "My mom and Gram are going to be very excited."

A zip of nervousness slides through my veins. "Really?"

"First grand and great-grandbaby? Hell yes," he informs me with a chuckle, leaning forward on the table so our conversation remains private.

I notice the tattoos on his arms. Logan has several, and while I've never thought of them as sexy, I definitely changed my tune after seeing him naked. Clearing my throat and forcing those images out of my brain, I mutter, "They're probably going to hate me."

"What? Why?" He seems genuinely perplexed by my statement.

"Well, we're not dating or anything. They'll assume I did this on purpose."

He's already shaking his head in disagreement before I even finish speaking. "Nope. No way. Both my mom and Gram adore you. They'd never think that, especially about you. Shay, on the other hand, they'd believe it was a trap."

I jump over his comment about me and focus on the latter part. "She would totally do that, wouldn't she?" Then something else hits me. "She didn't ever do that, did she?"

Logan snorts. "No. Shay didn't want kids."

My eyes widen as I stare back at him. "Seriously? And you still married her?"

"Well, she didn't tell me she didn't want them until *after* we were married. The first time she told me, I assumed she might change her mind over time. You know, realize our lives would only be enriched with a few kids running around," he says, his kissable lips curling upward as he speaks. "But over time, she became more and more insistent, and that's when I realized she was firm on her decision."

"I'm sorry. I can totally see you as a dad," I speak honestly. "You were always so good with Brody, especially when he was a little guy. I'm surprised you didn't have that conversation with her before you guys got married."

"We did. She lied and said she wanted kids."

My mouth drops open. "Seriously? What a bitch."

He snorts. "No arguments there."

"I knew she was conniving, but I guess I didn't really understand the full extent. That's terrible. I'm sorry you had to deal with that."

He shrugs. "I'm over it, but at the time, I was devastated. It was right after my dad passed, and I found out he left the business to me *and* her. I felt trapped."

I remember Logan's dad, Ed. He was this big, happy man who greeted you with a smile no matter where you saw him. It's the exact same way with his wife, Logan's mom, as well as Ed's mom, Gram. They're glass half-full kind of people, and even though I find myself more annoyed with Logan than not, he's really the exact same way. Everyone loves him, which is maybe why I goaded him as much as I did.

Or do?

I guess I still do it, right?

"But you got out," I say, just as our plates of food are delivered. I take one look at my country-fried steak and my mouth waters. "Oh my God, this looks amazing." Then, she sets Logan's double western cheeseburger down, along with a separate platter of sweet potato fries.

I practically drool down my chin.

"Yes, I got out, but it wasn't easy. I tried to talk to her about everything, hoping to save the marriage, even if I wasn't sure I really wanted it saved," he tells me, squirting a large blob of ketchup onto the platter and moving it into the center of the table. "Help yourself. Anyway, my dad had just passed and there was all this tension at home and we were both miserable. When I finally decided I was done and told her I was filing for divorce, she told me she was filing first," he says with a snort.

"Shut up," I reply, taking one of his fries and dipping it in ketchup.

"I shit you not. She ran to the highest-priced divorce attorney in the state and attempted to break it off in my ass from day one. Pardon the expression," he says, cutting his massive cheeseburger in half with a knife and holding it out to me.

My tongue practically hangs out like a dog as I look at what he's offering me. Even though I have a perfectly good, delicious meal in front of me, I have a sudden craving for his juicy burger.

But I won't eat his food. That's rude and completely unfair to him.

These fries, however, are fair game. He did put them in the middle of the table.

I shake my head at his offering and take another fry dipped in ketchup. As I chew, I cut into my chicken-fried steak, but my eyes remained glued to the half of his burger he left on his plate. "She's always been a petty bitch, so nothing shocks me anymore where she's concerned," I state, scooping a small bite of my gravy-covered meat with a dollop of mashed potatoes. The moment I put my food in my mouth and start to chew, it sits heavy on my tongue and takes several long seconds of chewing before I swallow.

It's not the food.

I'm certain my meal is delicious. In fact, I know it's a fairly popular menu choice, but for some reason, it's just not right.

Setting my fork down on my plate, I reach for my glass and take a sip of water as Logan asks, "So, what's the deal with the douchey ex? He still bothering you?"

I shrug, replacing my glass. "He just thinks I should give him another shot. He's wrong."

Logan chews his burger, nodding one time as he swallows. My eyes drop to his plate once more, and I can't help but wish I would have ordered a burger. Though the mashed potatoes and gravy sounded really good, it's just not hitting the spot the way I anticipated.

"Here." Logan hands over the second half of his burger once more.

I open my mouth, prepared to decline again, but my stomach growls, a loud noise triggered by the amazing aroma floating from the food in his hand. Reaching out, I snatch the burger and take a huge bite. "Oh my God. This is amazing," I state, my eyes practically rolling back in my head as I chew and swallow. I don't even care I was talking with my mouth open.

"Not bad, huh?" he asks, the hint of a smile on his lips.

After I consume my half of the burger, we end up sharing the rest of his fries, and he munches on my chicken-fried steak, all while I try not to notice how comfortable and easy this feels. Meals were never like this with Curtis, mostly because he was on his phone the entire time and only half listening to anything I said. When we first started dating, I could appreciate his determination and drive, but over time, his main priority remained his work. It became evident I was second to his job, and that's not where any woman wants to be in a relationship.

"Thank you," I tell him, feeling stuffed and oddly satisfied, while still waiting for the other shoe to drop.

"You're welcome," he says, pulling his wallet out of his back pocket.

"I can get it. You bought that time I joined you and your mom and Gram," I insist, reaching for my purse.

"Get used to it, Cupcake. I plan to keep feeding my baby."

A blush creeps up my cheeks as Susie drops off the check and grabs our empty plates. "How was it?"

"Delicious, as always," Logan answers, giving me a knowing grin.

My thighs clench together, even though I'm certain that's not what he meant. "Yes, very good, thank you."

"I'll be right back with your change," Susie announces.

"Keep it," Logan offers, sliding out of the booth. "Ready?"

We exit the diner together with farewell waves to the staff and step out into the warm August evening air. "Thank you, again, for dinner. You really didn't have to. And...I'm sorry I ate half your burger. That was rude."

He grins this boyish, sexy smile that makes my heart do weird things in my chest. *I'll blame that on the pregnancy hormones.* "It's fine, Hal. As long as you're carrying my baby, you can eat whatever you want off my plate," he tells me with a shrug.

"You may live to regret that statement," I quip. I've never been one to pick at food on someone else's plate, but in this case, I might continue to make an exception.

A heavy, slightly uncomfortable air hangs between us. I can feel his eyes on me, even though I don't glance up to confirm. Instead, I toe at a rock on the sidewalk with my foot.

"Will you call me if you need anything?" he asks, breaking the silence.

I glance up again, finding nothing but sincerity in his dark eyes. "Okay. When I have my first appointment, I can let you know."

He nods. "Yeah, that'd be great. I'd love to be there. Well, if you're okay with it."

"I'm okay with it," I confirm.

"Okay."

"Yeah, okay," I parrot unnecessarily.

He walks toward my Cherokee, and the moment I click the fob to unlock the door, he has it open for me. I climb inside, placing my purse on the passenger seat and secure my seat belt. "Drive safely," he says, stepping back so I can close the door.

It feels like more should be said, but I have no clue what it is. Instead, I give him a small smile and close the door. Logan steps back but stands on the sidewalk while I start my Jeep and carefully pull out of my parking spot and head for home. A quick glance in my rearview mirror confirms he's still standing there, hands in the front pockets of his jeans, watching me drive away.

Warmth spreads through my veins as I head home, the memory of his kindness and the intensity in his dark eyes with me every step of the way.

Here we go again.

I'm curled around the toilet, having just thrown up everything I consumed at dinner tonight. The wave of nausea has finally passed, and my stomach slowly starts to settle once more. I'm flushed and exhausted, covered in a nasty sheen of sweat, and with a gross taste in my mouth that makes me want to gag all over again.

After several minutes, I finally climb off the floor and move to the sink to brush my teeth and wash my face. I'm pale, a ghostly shade of gray that does not complement my blue eyes, so I ignore the mirror and keep my gaze down. I should run through the shower, but I just don't have the energy right now.

This is going to be a very long nine months, if the first day is any indication. I just found out I was pregnant, and I'm already miserable with the worst case of morning sickness imaginable. How in the hell am I going to work like this? I'm supposed to be teaching a classroom of nine students come Monday morning. Will I be able to make it through the two-hour class without having to throw up, or will I be spending half the time in the bathroom? And what will happen to my classroom of three-year-olds? I can't exactly leave them to their own devices for more than a few seconds.

Man, this sucks donkey balls.

Flipping off the light, I walk on jelly legs to my bed and fall face-first onto the bedspread. I reach for my phone on the nightstand and pull up the text app.

Me: I hate you.

The bubbles appear immediately.

Logan: What's new? *insert cheeky grin*

Me: I'm throwing up again. It's your fault.

Logan: I'm sorry. Anything I can do?

Me: Yeah, you can do all the throwing up from this point forward. I relinquish that task to you.

Logan: Cupcake, if I could, I would.

Me: Night. I'm going to sleep. Just wanted to tell you I hate you.

I hear my phone chime, but I'm too exhausted to check his reply. I don't even get up to turn off the bedroom light. Instead, I curl up on my side once more, this time on my soft, comfortable bed, and fall into a deep sleep.

CHAPTER *fourteen*

LOGAN

When I pull into her driveway, it looks like Grand Central Station. Every light in her condo appears to be on, and even though it's barely after eight and still somewhat light outside, it looks like she's trying to land planes. Shaking my head, I grab the bags on the passenger seat of my truck and climb out, heading to her front door.

My initial knock goes unanswered, as does my second. Uneasiness washes over me, and I start to worry something is seriously wrong. Why wouldn't she answer the door? Reaching down, I give the knob a turn, both grateful and incredibly disappointed at the same time. Grateful because I don't have to break in, but also annoyed she'd risk her safety by leaving it unlocked. Not that Pine Village has a high crime rate, but she's carrying my child now, which means I want to ensure both are safe at all times.

With a sigh, I push open the door. "Hello? Hallie?"

I get no response as I step inside and close the door behind me. The TV is on, some reality television program playing, so I walk over to the remote and flip it off. She's not on the couch, so I head toward the hallway. After a quick peek in the kitchen to confirm she's not in there, I move down the short hall. The bathroom door is open, lights on, so I quickly flip them off on my way by. The guest room is the only space without the light on, but my eyes are drawn to the master room. Specifically, to the beautiful woman lying across the bed.

Hallie is face down, sleeping peacefully. Finally setting eyes on her calms my racing heart a bit. I walk over and run my knuckles over her cheeks, just to feel her soft skin and make sure she's all right. She leans slightly into my touch and sighs in contentment, and for the first time since she stopped replying to my texts, I relax.

Spinning on my heel, I return to the kitchen and place the bags on the counter. I place a few items in the fridge and keep the others out. I take what I need and return to where Hallie is resting.

Setting them on the nightstand, I have a seat on the edge of her bed and lean her way. "Hallie," I say gently, placing a hand on her back.

"Logan?" she asks without opening her eyes.

"It's me, Hal. How are you feeling?"

"So tired," she mutters.

"I brought you something for your stomach."

"My stomach doesn't want anything," she mumbles, turning on her side and facing me. "How did you get in here?"

"I broke down your front door," I say, the lie rolling off my tongue easily.

"What? What the hell is wrong with you?" she chastises, her pretty blue eyes narrowing.

A chuckle falls from my lips. "I'm kidding, Cupcake. You left your front door unlocked. You're lucky I'm the only one who came in here."

"I'd welcome them killing me right now," she mumbles, clearly feeling miserable.

I bark out a laugh and reach for her, helping her sit up. "Come on, Cupcake. Time to get up and eat."

"Don't say the E word!" she bellows, flopping around and making it difficult to get her in an upright position.

"It won't be so bad, Hal. And just think of the end result. A little puking every now and again will be worth it, right?"

"Says the man who can eat whatever the hell he wants without throwing it up thirty minutes later," she grumbles, eventually sitting upright.

"Here," I offer, opening a can of ginger ale and a sleeve of saltine crackers. "I was reading online that ginger can help with morning sickness, and so does bland food. Toast, crackers, fruits like bananas, pears, and applesauce."

She grabs a cracker and takes a small, tentative bite. "Why do they call it morning sickness? It should be called all-day sickness."

"Your guess is as good as mine," I reply, holding out the can of ginger ale.

Hallie sighs, takes the can, and sips the cool liquid.

"Oh, try this," I say, grabbing the small box and ripping it open.

"What's that?"

"It's a motion sickness wristband," I reply, taking the band out and reaching for her wrist. "Some of the women on the websites I read swore by them." I place it on her arm and glance up.

She's staring back at me, mouth slightly agape as she watches me. "You read websites?"

Shrugging, I feel my cheeks heat a bit. "Just a couple, you know, on my way to the grocery store. No big deal."

Nibbling on the cracker again, she gives me a very small, grateful grin. "Thanks, Logan."

"Yeah, well, I'd hate to mess up the perfect streak I have going on, but I figured you could go back to hating me when I leave."

She snorts and finishes the first cracker, taking a few small sips of the soda before consuming a second one. "What else did those websites tell you?"

I lift my left leg up on the bed, careful to keep my boots off the bedding. "Well, I know it feels like forever away, but the morning sickness usually only lasts through the first trimester. That means about two more months, and you should be past the worst of it."

"Easy for you to say," she mumbles, continuing to nibble crackers like a rabbit.

"Oh, there's some peppermint candies in the kitchen too. I know you're not a fan of mint, but if it helps you not get sick as much, I figured it would be worth dealing with a few mints every so often."

When I look her way, there's a faint smile on her lips. "Every now and again, you have a few redeeming qualities."

"Don't tell anyone," I tease, leaning over and lightly elbowing her side.

She snorts and elbows me back, much harder. "Oh, don't worry. I won't."

It feels good to laugh, in spite of the situation we're in. "I'll let you get some rest." When I stand, I add, "Oh, the website also said to keep that stuff by your bed. When you wake, eat a few crackers and take some sips of the ginger ale."

"Stop it or I might actually start to like you," she mumbles, shaking her head and glancing down at the sleeve of crackers.

"Noted. I'll lock the front door when I leave. Anything else?"

"No," she replies. "Thanks again."

With a wave, I slowly exit her bedroom, trying not to think of all the dirty things I did to her in this very room. Of course, that's why we're in this predicament, and that thought alone should be enough to stop the parade of memories, but it doesn't. In fact, some primal caveman part of me I didn't know I possessed roars to life at the thought of her carrying my baby. It's arousing, honestly, but I'll keep that to myself.

I walk into the kitchen and make sure everything she could need is ready to go and flip off the overhead light, but leaving the one over the sink on in case she gets up in the middle of the night. Finally, I head for the front, turning off the living room table lamp on my way by. At the door, I give her space one last glance, wishing I had a reason to stay. Part of me wants to crash on the couch in case she needs me, but I know she wouldn't be a fan of that. While I like riling her up, I'm not looking to piss her off.

With a sigh, I flip the lock and make sure the door is closed and secured behind me. The sun has finally set and the streetlights are on. As I walk to my truck, I feel that sense of calm once more. I'm not freaking out the way I expected I would after finding out I was going to be a dad with a woman I wasn't in a relationship with.

It's Hallie.

Sweet, feisty, beautiful Hallie.

I can do this.

We can do this.

Together.

Hallie: I scheduled my doctor's appointment. I go in 2 weeks.

It's Monday, half past noon, and I'm behind the counter at the hardware store. I haven't heard from her since she texted a quick thanks on Saturday morning, and I've been a little anxious since. She started school this morning, so I've been doing my best to respect her boundaries and not text her unnecessarily. That doesn't mean I don't think about her or wonder what she's up to.

Me: 2 weeks? Why so long?

I mean, it's Pine Village. It can't take that long to get an appointment.

Hallie: They usually do the first appointment at 8 weeks.

Me: Ahh, okay.

Hallie: Do you want to go? It's at 4 in Hudson.

Me: Yeah, I'll be there. Want me to drive?

I pull up the schedule and make a note that I'll be off that day at three thirty. It's not often I leave before the end of the workday, but I have a good team here to keep the business going in my absence.

Hallie: Ok. I can meet you at the hardware store when I get off.

Me: Sounds good. How are you feeling?

Hallie: Not terrible, but not 100%. The crackers and ginger ale definitely seem to help.

Me: I'm glad. Have you had lunch?

Hallie: Just finished. Bland is the key right now. I had some applesauce and a peanut butter sandwich.

My stomach growls, as if on cue, reminding me I have yet to grab lunch myself.

Hallie: My afternoon class starts at one fifteen, so I tried to eat a little early. You know, just in case...

Me: I'm getting ready to run and grab a sandwich. Need anything while I'm out?

Hallie: No thanks.

Me: All right. If you change your mind, let me know.

Hallie: Will do. Have a good one.

I fire off a quick reply and place my order for a sandwich pickup. Just as I turn to start pulling an order for a local contractor, the bell over the door chimes.

"Honey, I'm home." Like nails on a chalkboard, my balls draw up into my body as my ex-wife enters, the clicking of her expensive heels echoing through the building.

"Weren't you supposed to be back at noon?" I ask, checking the time on my watch.

She snickers, flipping her long, blond hair over her shoulder. "Are you kidding? I own the business."

"Lead by example," I reply, taking the list Gavin Pierson dropped off an hour ago and a basket before walking around the counter. I'm really hoping she'll head back into the office she claimed for herself, leaving me in peace, but unfortunately, that's not what happens.

Ignoring my comment, she scurries down an aisle, trailing behind me. "Whatcha doing?"

"Working," I state, looking for the right length of truss wood screws. "You should try it."

She sighs dramatically. "Why so testy? Did you have a bad weekend?"

"No. My weekend was fine," I reply, grabbing what I'm looking for and dropping them in the basket before walking to another aisle.

"Are you mad at me?"

I scan the electrical supplies and take a dozen white outlets and the blue outlet boxes. "Why would I be mad at you?" I ask, even though I don't want to know. I should have just said no and left it at that.

"You're short and tense." Suddenly, her hands are on my shoulders. "Remember what I used to do when you were tense?" she coos, squeezing my shoulders gently. And no, she's not referring to a massage.

"Not happening, Shay," I state bluntly, stepping away from her eagle claws before she can dig them into my skin. I grab the terminal connectors and throw them in the basket too.

"You sure?" she sings, batting her overly blackened eyelashes at me, as if flirting has any effect on me anymore.

"Yep." With most of the stuff needed, I walk with purpose toward the register, start scanning the items and tossing them into a bag.

"Why is Hallie texting you?"

I glance up, realizing I left my phone sitting on the counter, and now Shay is holding it, staring at the screen. I'm not worried about her reading the message. It's password-protected, and as nosy as she is, I'm certain she doesn't know the number sequence. It's not any of the important dates she'd think I'd use, not that she'd remember any of those anyway. She's too self-involved for that.

"None of your business," I tell her, reaching for my device and grabbing it out of her hand.

"Geez, you're so pissy," she counters, crossing her arms over her fake tits and pushing them up and out the neck of her tank top. As much as I want to pitch a fit about her attire, I know it won't do me any good. The last time I complained about her not wearing a company shirt, she went and had the logo printed on the ones I bitched about.

"I'm not pissy. I'm private. There's a difference."

I realize my mistake immediately.

"Private? About what? About Hallie? Are you seeing her? She's totally not your type. That would be, just no," she spits out without taking a breath.

"It would also be *none of your business*," I repeat, this time with a clipped tone, leaving no room for discussion. I'm not talking about Hallie, especially with Shay.

"Fine, whatever. Do your thing," she replies, flipping her hair once more. "Just don't come crying to me when—"

"No worries, Shay. I won't," I state, punctuating each word in hopes she understands this discussion is closed.

"Okay, whatevs. Don't get your panties in a twist."

My eyebrows pull together. "My panties?" What the fuck is she talking about?

She smiles sweetly and winks. "Well, yes, silly. It can't be my panties in a twist. We both know I don't wear them." And with that, she flips her hair and disappears down the short hallway leading to the offices.

I run my hand down my face, wishing with everything in me I didn't have to deal with her on a daily basis. I've moved on since our divorce but working side-by-side with her—if you can call what she does work—is its own brand of hell. She's always up in my business, and not just the one we own together. She thinks co-owning this place gives her the right to pry into my life, especially my relationships—or lack thereof.

The only easy day was yesterday, my dad used to say.

When I'm certain she's not coming back up front, I flip my phone around and tap on the screen. The newest message from Hallie pops up, bringing a smile to my face.

> **Hallie:** Good news. So far, lunch has stayed where it's supposed to. Maybe you found the cure-all for morning sickness and it's over!

Smiling, I send her a thumbs-up emoji and slip my phone back into my pocket so nosy, pains in my ass can't snoop. My foot taps to the classic George Strait song playing on the radio, and an even bigger grin spreads across my face that Shay hasn't noticed yet. I know the moment she does, she'll play Taylor Swift from her phone. Nothing against Taylor, but it's not the vibe I'm going for here, nor my personal preference.

When I send the guys out to collect the lumber for Gavin's order, I head out to retrieve my lunch. Just before I climb into the truck, I feel my phone vibrate and pull it from my pocket.

Hallie: Nope, not over. I hate this. All the points you earned are wiped away. *insert middle finger emoji*

A bark of laughter flies as I stare down at that single bird flying at me.

Some people might be offended to receive her message, but not me. I know it's part of the game, the tease.

The foreplay.

That's how it feels every time she snaps at me for something silly or inconsequential. A dance we've been taking turns leading for years. Every time she pushes, I push back just as hard, just to get a rise out of her.

Why?

Because she's sexy as fuck, and I don't think I'll ever get enough of her spunk, that fire.

It's what makes her *her*, and I hope she never changes.

Not for anyone.

Myself included.

CHAPTER *fifteen*

Hallie

Today's the day.

My first doctor's appointment to check on the baby.

I've been anxious all day, constantly watching the clock. Of course, like any other watched pot, time seems to slow down, the second hand ticking by at a snail's pace. Usually spending the afternoon with a rowdy group of four-and five-year-olds will fly by, but not today.

I leave work at three fifteen and head for the hardware store. There's a parking lot in front of the storefront building, but I pull into a spot along the side where Logan's truck is, and park. I wait a few seconds, wondering if I should go inside, but then I consider the fact Shay is probably in there, and realize that's the last thing I want or need.

Text it is.

There's no need for either, because a few moments later, Logan appears out the side door and approaches my vehicle.

"Hey," he greets, somewhat awkwardly, when I climb out.

"Hi."

"Ready to go?"

When I nod, he opens the passenger door on his truck and I get in. Fastening my seat belt, he pulls out of his parking spot and moves toward the road. I glance toward the building and spot Shay standing there, arms crossed over her fake boobs and finger tapping on her bottom lip. I can practically see the wheels in her head spinning, and most likely, about to give us trouble.

"Gabe and Blair set a wedding date," I announce, even though he probably already knows.

"Yeah?"

I nod, settling into the comfortable seat as we head to Hudson. "December twenty-third. It's the three-year anniversary of when she got stuck in the snow and he picked her up for me," I state, recalling that weekend very well.

Of course, at the time, I thought my brother just picked my friend up from the snowdrift she got stuck in. Little did I know, they did the nasty too, and even though she spent the next couple of days at my condo with me for the holidays, she never said a word about it. Until the next year, when she returned to town to help work at her father's medical practice while he recovered from a massive heart attack. Little did she know, my brother Gabe also worked there.

Small world and all that.

Now they're in love, getting married, and having a baby.

"They're waiting until December? I figured they'd run off and elope on some Caribbean Island with white sandy beaches or something."

"Me too, honestly," I state, turning slightly in my seat to face him. "But it's all about the date for them. She'll be about six months pregnant then, and probably cute as a freaking button in her wedding dress. I'm insanely excited for them."

"A snowy, Christmas wedding. Good for them," he says with a decisive nod.

We arrive in Hudson and make our way to the medical clinic I've been a patient at since I was sixteen. I went to the local clinic in town for general appointments and illnesses, but there's no way I was going to either my oldest friend's father or my brother for gynecology. Once Blair returned to town, she took over the younger patients through the practice, since she's a pediatrician, so it's not like she could be my obstetrician. Hence, seeing a wonderful physician in Hudson for all my womanly appointments.

"This one?" Logan asks, slowing down in front of a large brick building.

"Yep. Park anywhere in the big lot," I tell him, a wave of excitement coursing through me.

The truck is parked a few seconds later, and we're both climbing out. As we walk toward the building, Logan places his hand on my lower back. He opens all the doors as we enter and hangs back just a bit when we step up to the counter.

"Hello, Hallie Rhodes," I tell the receptionist.

She types on her computer and asks questions to verify my information and insurance. "Sign on the pad," she instructs me, pointing to the small box attached to her computer. "You're all set. Have a seat, and you'll be called back shortly."

"Thank you," I reply before turning and searching for a place to sit.

There are several people in the waiting area, and knowing Logan prefers to see the room, I head for the back wall where a love seat is available. "This okay?"

"Sure," he says quickly. The moment he sits down, he wipes his hands on his jeans, as if his palms are a little sweaty. He's also bouncing his foot, a sign he's a little anxious.

"You all right?"

"Yes," he insists quickly, his eyes scanning the individuals in the room. All but one is female, and the only other male is a younger child here with his mom. "What should we expect? The internet had some thoughts, but every office is different."

His curiosity and research are really endearing, just don't tell him I said that.

"Well, I'm not entirely certain, but I think it'll start with vitals, and I know there will be an ultrasound," I explain, a smile easily spreading across my lips at the thought of seeing the baby for the first time.

"Really?" he asks, eyes wide and equally as eager.

"Yep."

"Cool," he says, sitting beside me and continuing to smile. His foot still taps on the floor, but not as frantic as it was a minute ago.

Our wait doesn't take too long. We're called a short time later and lead through the door toward a small room. "I'm Gina, and I'm going to take some vitals first. Would you step on the scale?"

I do as instructed, glancing over my shoulder and telling Logan, "Don't look."

He holds up his hands and replies, "I wouldn't dare." Then, he crosses his arms over his chest and turns to the side, giving us a profile view. I'm pretty sure I hear the older nurse sigh in appreciation.

After she takes my blood pressure, she steps out of the small room. "There's a restroom directly across the hall. We'll need a urine sample, which we'll do at every appointment."

When that part is complete and I've handed my sample off to the waiting nurse, she gives me a smile and says, "All right, follow me, please."

We head down the hallway to an available room. We step inside and Gina points at the empty chairs. "Go ahead and have a seat. We'll run through your medical history and then get to the good stuff. Today's appointment will be the longest one. The rest after this will take half the time, I promise," she says apologetically, sitting down at the counter and typing on her tablet.

It takes a little time to run through my medical history, but when we're finally done, she stands up and goes to a cabinet. "Okay, everything off from the waist down, the opening in the front."

My mouth falls open. "What?"

"Yeah, sorry, but we do a pelvic exam at the first appointment too." She gives me an apologetic smile. "Dr. Bergman will be in shortly."

And then I'm left alone.

With a thin gown.

And Logan.

"Uhh, I take it you weren't anticipating this part?"

I turn and narrow my eyes at the other occupant in the room.

"I'll just…go in the waiting room," he says, the disappointment evident in his voice.

Logan opens the door, but just before he steps out into the hallway, I find myself blurting out, "Wait." I close my eyes for a brief moment before meeting his gaze. "You can stay. *But* you have to stay at my head the whole time. Understand?"

He gives me a fast nod and moves to the head of the table.

"Wait, I need to get undressed. Turn around."

"I can step out into the hallway," he offers, letting me know he's trying to respect my boundaries as much as he can.

"It's fine. Just don't sneak a peek," I state, standing up and grabbing the gown.

He snorts, facing the wall. "I've already seen all the goods, Cupcake."

"Yes, but this is different," I argue.

It's not different.

Not really.

"Whatever you say. Would you like me to step out into the hall while you strip?"

"Just turn around."

I don't even care he already has and is facing the back wall. My eyes are drawn to his arms and back, to the T-shirt stretched tautly across both. Sighing, I peel my eyes away from the spectacular view, knowing my time is somewhat limited before Dr. Bergman knocks on the door, and I'd rather not be mid-change when that happens. With lightning speed, I slip my sandals from my feet and strip off my capris. Usually this is when I'd fold them neatly and place them on the chair, but time is of the essence here. I take another glance at Logan to ensure his eyes are facing the wall still and slip my panties off, shoving them beneath my crumpled pants. Then, I practically throw the gown on, crossing it in front of my abdomen, and hop up onto the table.

"Okay, you can turn around."

When he does, he stays at my head, the way he was instructed. It's hard to see him from this vantage point, but I can tell his hands are now shoved into his pockets as he rocks back and forth on his heels. I wish I knew what to say to him, but no words come.

Fortunately, the silence is short-lived when a knock sounds at the door. "Ready?" Dr. Bergman asks, poking her head into the room.

"All set," I confirm.

"How are you feeling today, Hallie?" she asks as she enters the room.

"Pretty good right now. Lunchtime was a different story," I reply with a chuckle.

"I hear you're having quite a bit of morning sickness," the doctor states.

"Unfortunately, yes."

"The good news is that usually levels out by the second trimester." Dr. Bergman looks at Logan and smiles, offering her hand. "I'm Dr. Mona Bergman."

"Logan Johnson. I'm the father."

"Nice to meet you, Logan. We'll take great care of both mother and baby." She grabs a seat at the counter and types on the tablet. "All right, so I see the first day of your last period was July fifteenth. That puts your due date at April twentieth."

All I can do is smile.

We go through a few more questions and discuss what to expect at today's appointment and the ones that follow. When the basics are covered, she stands up and says, "I'm going to do a pelvic exam, and then we'll get to the good part and take a look at the baby."

I take a deep breath and lie back, hating this part any other time it's done, let alone with Logan in the room too. I know what's coming next, so I place my feet in the stirrups as Dr. Bergman drapes a paper sheet over my legs. With my eyes closed, I pretend I'm not in this exact predicament, lying on a table with my legs spread for my OB-GYN, all while Logan looks on from his place behind me. I know he can't see anything, but it's still incredibly mortifying.

"All right, all done with that part. Now, we're going to take a peek at the baby," she informs us, pulling the ultrasound machine over to the table. "We're doing a transvaginal ultrasound today, since we get a better picture of the baby this way at this stage of the pregnancy. This will be a little cold at first," she informs me, prepping the wand.

Exhaling, I close my eyes once more as she starts to do her thing. I feel a warm hand rest at the side of my head, his fingers dancing along my hairline. I don't know what it is about his touch, but it instantly soothes and calms me.

"I'm going to take a few quick measurements," Dr. Bergman announces, drawing my attention back to her. I hear her tap on the keyboard and feel her move the wand as my anticipation grows wildly.

Finally, she turns the screen toward me. "Okay, let's have a look. This is your uterus," she says, running her finger around the circle on the screen before pointing to a small little bean, "And this...this is your baby."

A gasp spills from my lips as my eyes blur. I stare at the screen, to the human growing within me, and let a few tears fall. The feeling in my chest is instant, the love growing showing no bounds. I fall in love with that little spot on the screen immediately.

I feel Logan's hand wrap around mine moments before his other hand wipes away the moisture seeping from my eyes. I risk a glance his way as he moves to stand at my shoulder and am shocked to find his own eyes a little misty. He holds my gaze and smiles, the sweetest and sexiest grin I've ever seen in my life.

Together, we return our sight to the screen and watch as the doctor captures a few pictures for us to take home. The ultrasound doesn't last nearly as long as I'd like, but only because I think I could sit and stare at the screen for hours on end.

"Okay, everything looks really good. We'll see you back here in four weeks. I'm going to send a prescription to your pharmacy on file for some prenatal vitamins, and if the morning sickness becomes too much, call the office. Do you have any questions?" she asks after standing up and moving the ultrasound machine back over to the corner of the room.

"I don't think so," I say, glancing at Logan for confirmation.

He shakes his head also, and it's in that moment I realize he's still holding my hand.

"All right, well, congratulations to you both. We'll see you back in four weeks."

When we're left alone, I drop my legs from the stirrups and try to sit up. Logan is there, helping me, before moving back to the head of the table and turning around. "I'll give you a few minutes."

Quickly, I redress, tossing the paper sheet in the trash can and the gown on the table. "I'm all set."

He turns back around and smiles. There's a lightness in his dark eyes I didn't see before, exhilaration mixed with eagerness, and it makes my heart happy. We leave the room, taking the ultrasound photos Dr. Bergman left for us on the counter, and head for the front reception area, where I make my next appointment. I choose a late afternoon timeslot, so I don't have to miss school and it's easier for Logan to attend too. Something tells me he's going to be by my side at every single one, and I'm surprised to find I'm okay with that. In fact, I *want* him here.

The drive back to Pine Village is filled with chitchat. "When do you think you want to tell everyone?" he asks as he pulls onto the highway that leads us home.

"Well, originally, I was thinking of waiting until I'm past the first trimester, when the risk of miscarriage is less, but now that we've had that appointment and I've seen the baby, I kinda want to tell everyone now," I reply honestly.

He glances over and smiles. "Me too."

"Okay, so what about this weekend?"

"I'm fine with that. I'll go with you to visit your parents."

"You don't have to do that," I tell him, but one look my way lets me know it's not up for negotiation.

"I want to be there, Hal. I want them to know I'll be there every step of the way, and that includes telling them they're going to be grandparents."

"Times two. I'll be due a little over a month after Gabe and Blair."

"That's right. Your parents will be on cloud nine."

"Oh, I'm certain they will, but if you go with me, will it give the wrong impression? We're not together."

"No, it'll give the right one. It'll tell them I'm there for you, whether we're dating or not. We're going to still be a family, even if it's not conventional."

I nod, understanding what he's saying. "Right. We'll be in two households but co-parenting and doing what's best for the baby."

I notice he hesitates, but eventually nods in agreement. "Yep."

"Okay. I'll go with you to tell your mom too."

He glances over and grins. "Sounds good. I'll text her and find out when a good time is, and just let me know when you're going to see your parents. I work Saturday, but we close at noon, so I'm available after that."

We make our way back to Pine Village, and within a few minutes, are pulling into the lot for the hardware store and drive to the side of the building. My Jeep is still sitting there, as is Shay's SUV. I didn't notice it the first time I pulled in, but now that it's the only other vehicle sitting in the lot—and it's right next to mine—you can't miss it.

Logan sighs, parking on the opposite side of my Cherokee. "She's going to start digging for dirt," he states, putting the truck in park.

I glance at the fancy, sporty car sitting on the other side of mine. "You're probably right. That's why we should tell our family this weekend."

"Agreed." He opens his mouth like he wants to say something else but doesn't. Instead, I open the passenger door and climb out. We've had a decent afternoon together, with no bickering, and the last thing I want to do is jinx it.

"I'll let you know when I talk to my mom about this weekend."

Logan climbs out of his truck and walks me to my vehicle. "Thanks."

It turns awkward again, as we both just stand here, staring. Part of me wants to invite him back to my condo, to hang out and have dinner, but I don't. We've never been friends like that. Sure, we hang out while we're with our friends, but never one-on-one.

Unless there's sex involved, apparently.

"Bye," I blurt out, trying to push the thoughts of sex with Logan from my brain.

"Talk to you later, Hal."

I climb into my Jeep, start the engine, and pull from the parking spot. As I prepare to merge onto the street, a quick glance in my rearview mirror confirms Logan's still standing there, watching me go. A flutter of butterflies takes flight in my stomach, and even though I'd like to think it's related to the baby, I know it's not.

It's Logan.

He's making me feel things I haven't felt in a long time, and as disconcerting as it is, I don't hate it.

In fact, it's quite the opposite.

Logan Johnson is growing on me.

Dammit.

CHAPTER
sixteen

LOGAN

I can't stop staring at the ultrasound.

It's been two days since we saw Dr. Bergman, and I've kept the images of the baby close since Hallie shared them with me. One is at home on the fridge and the other tucked safely in my desk drawer at work. Both will be put into a frame as soon as we tell our family and friends and our secret is out. Until then, I pull this one out while I'm at work and gaze down at the most magnificent sight I've ever seen before tucking it back into my drawer for safekeeping.

"Hey, Logan?" Chip asks from my doorway as he knocks. "Donald Smith is here and looking for a little direction on that new line of hand tools we just got in. Can you come out and help him?"

"Of course," I reply, and follow Chip out of my office. Chip has worked for me for about six years and is a vital part of the company. He helps me with the resale side of the business but can also maneuver around the lumberyard with ease and knowledge.

I move to the large counter and find the old man waiting. "Good afternoon, Donald. I hear you're in the market for some new hand tools?"

"Well, I've heard good things about this brand and wanted to check it out, especially since it's made right here in Wisconsin," Donald says as we walk together toward the display of Loyalty Tools.

We chat for about twenty minutes, while I demonstrate a few different pieces. He ends up choosing the basic tape measure, level, and square set, promising to come back and get more soon.

After ringing him up, I holler at Chip. "Going back to my office for a bit. Holler if you need help."

"Sounds good," he replies as I round the corner and move down the short hallway.

As I breach the threshold of my office, I stop in my tracks. Shay is sitting at my desk, but it's what she's holding in her hand that causes my heart to seize in my chest. "What the hell are you doing?"

My ex-wife's eyes slowly move from the ultrasound photo she's holding to me. "Well, isn't this interesting," she practically sings, a wicked grin spreading across her bright pink lips.

"Can I help you with something?" I ask, crossing my arms over my chest.

"Oh, don't go all caveman on me. I came in here to leave you a note."

"Notepads are on the desk," I counter, blowing holes in her bullshit the size of the Grand Canyon.

"Yes, but I needed a pen," she adds sweetly.

"Coffee cup by the phone," I reply, pointing to where there were a dozen pens directly in front of her face.

"Oh, I didn't see them." Her laugh is excessive and over-the-top, a telltale sign she's lying.

I stand here, waiting her out. I'm going to make her ask about what she's looking at. I won't bring it up first, mostly because the first person I talk to and tell about the baby isn't going to be my ex-wife.

"This is why you've been hanging out with Hallie?"

Again, I don't say a word.

"Wow, I can't believe it. You and Hallie? I didn't see that one coming."

"Why?" I blurt out before I can think better of it, but she's always had a negative opinion where Hallie's concerned, and frankly, I want to know the reason.

"Well, you're so different," she starts, tossing the ultrasound photo onto my desk like it's nothing, and I suppose to her, it is. "You have a type, and she's not it."

Anger swirls in my gut as I continue to stare at her. "What type would that be?"

"Oh, you know. Blonde with a skinny waist and boobs," she states matter-of-factly with a shrug.

"Actually, that's not my type. Well, it was, back when I was young, dumb, and only thought with my dick. Now that my actual brain is involved, she's very much my type."

She seems stunned by my comment and sputters a response. "Wh-we-well..."

"My *type* is none of your concern, but I assure you, Hallie Rhodes checks every box on my list," I reply, watching as my ex's cheeks turn an unnatural shade of red. It's not necessarily out of embarrassment but most likely out of anger. Shay has never liked Hallie and hates being second to her for anything.

Me included.

The fact I could be in a relationship with her—even if only in Shay's mind—would be enough to send my ex into a tizzy of pettiness and spitefulness.

Shay clears her throat and stands. "Well, I'm glad you're happy."

"Thanks," I reply, a fake smile on my lips.

She glances down at the ultrasound once more before sauntering around my desk and heading right for me. I step aside, giving her plenty of room to pass by me, but of course, in true Shay fashion, she rubs against me with her tits and hands. "You know, if you ever get bored, you can give me a call."

"*Never* going to happen, Shay."

Continuing to stare at me under heavily made-up eyelashes, she bats them a few times before smiling. "If you say so," she replies with a shrug, running a finger across my chest. "Just know the offer stands. We had a *lot* of good times, Logie. If you get tired of watching your girlfriend's already big ass grow even larger, call me."

Before I can mutter a word in outrage, she struts out of my office, the clicking of her obnoxious heels on the floor grating on every nerve I have. I step farther into my office and shut the door with a little extra force. I'm pissed. Pissed she found the ultrasound. Pissed she insulted Hallie the way she did. Pissed she had the fucking gall to think I'd ever stoop so low as to sleep with her again. I let my dick make my decisions back when we got together, and I'll be damned if I let that happen again.

Except I kinda let that happen with Hallie...

But this is different.

Hallie and Shay are night and day different.

I move to my desk and pick up the picture of our baby. A smile moves my lips as I scan the image of our tiny bean. Taking my seat, I can't help but wonder if this little one is a boy or a girl. My gut tells me boy, but honestly, it doesn't matter either way. He or she is going to be loved so fiercely by both Hallie and me, and that's all that matters.

Knowing what I need to do, I pull my phone from my pocket and type her a message.

Me: Houston, we have a problem. Shay found the ultrasound.

She's wrapping up the end of her workday, so it takes a few minutes before she replies.

Hallie: Seriously?! How the hell did she find it?

Me: I had it in my drawer at work and she went snooping.

Hallie: Can't you fire her for that? What a nosy bitch!

Me: I could try, but she does hold half the company in her greedy little paws.

Hallie: She's such a nasty cow. Now what do we do?

Me: Well, chances are, she's going to run her mouth. I know we decided to tell our parents this weekend, but we may want to move that up.

Hallie: I agree. Man, I really dislike that woman.

Me: I know.

Hallie: You married her…

Me: I'll see if my mom is going to be home tonight. We can stop by before or after your parents if you want.

Hallie: Ok. Give me a few minutes to call my parents.

Instead of putting my phone away, I pull up my mom's name and give her a call.

"Well, hello there, Son. To what do I owe this mid-afternoon phone call?" she greets pleasantly.

"Just thinking about my favorite lady," I tell her, returning the smile I hear in her voice.

"Stop bullshitting me. I'm too old for that," she quips with a chuckle.

"You're far from old."

"Yeah, well, tell my knees that."

"You should call Gabe and see him if they're bothering you," I suggest.

"I will, honey. So? I'm sure you didn't call in the middle of the workday to discuss my knees. What's up?"

"I was wanting to stop by tonight for a visit. Will you be home?"

"Actually, yes. Gram is coming for dinner tonight. Would you like to join us?"

My mind flashes to Hallie. "Uhh, let me get back to you on that part."

"Okay. There'll be plenty of food for you if you want to join us."

"Sounds good. I'll let you know for certain shortly."

"All right, dear. See you later," she replies.

"Bye, Mom."

I switch apps and fire off a text to Hallie.

Me: My mom and Gram are having dinner together at Mom's and we're invited.

I leave out the part where they don't know she'd be attending too.

Hallie: My parents are bowling tonight and won't be home until late. Tomorrow is better for them.

Me: Ok. Just tell me when and I'll be there.

Hallie: Thanks. What time should we head to your mom's?

Me: Is 5:30 ok?

Hallie: Yep.

Me: I'll pick you up. See you then.

Hallie: *insert thumbs-up emoji*

Shaking my head, I finally place my phone on my desk and run my hands through my hair. What a fucking mess. I can't believe Shay snooped through my desk like that. No, wait. I can, really. She used to pull that shit when we were still married. Always looking through my phone—which I had nothing to hide—and through closets and drawers.

I need to get her away from this company, but my repeated offers to buy her out are fruitless. Maybe I'll reach out to my lawyer once more and try again. It's been about a year since I made my last offer, so it's time to try again. I can't exactly afford to keep upping the offer too much more, but what's a little more debt when it comes with some peace of mind that I wouldn't be dealing with my ex-wife six days a week anymore.

That would be heaven.

A pipe dream at this point, but heaven nonetheless.

"Ready?" I ask as I pull into the driveway of my childhood home.

"Not really," she mutters, looking a little pale.

"Are you feeling okay?" I ask, quickly stopping and throwing my truck into Park.

She glances my way with those pretty blue eyes of hers. "I'm not nauseous, just nervous."

"Don't be," I insist, grabbing my keys. "My mom and Gram love you. They're going to be thrilled."

Hallie sighs. "I hope you're right."

Climbing out of my truck, I head around to the passenger side and help her out. "I'm always right," I quip, knowing it'll get her mind off her anxiousness.

She rolls her eyes dramatically. "Whatever, Johnson. You're so full of shit."

"Is that Hallie?"

I didn't even realize my mom had opened the front door, and now she's standing on the porch, a wide smile on her face the moment she spots Hallie.

"Hi, Mrs. Johnson," she replies, walking to where my mom stands and giving her a hug.

"Enough of that Mrs. Johnson stuff. Mrs. Johnson is my mother-in-law inside. Call me Patty, please. Come inside. I'm so happy Logan brought you," she says, wrapping an arm around Hallie's shoulders and guiding her onto the front porch.

The moment they step inside, I hear her stomach growl. The aromas are a mixture of freshly baked bread and rich marinara with a touch of spice, and I know exactly what my mom made for dinner. Definitely not the bland diet Hallie's been going for, but I don't think she's going to complain.

"Look at you," Gram says, getting up from the table and moving straight for Hallie, arms extended. She's pulled into a tight hug immediately, squeezed hard for several long seconds. When she pulls back, she adds, "You're glowing, dear. Simply beautiful."

I watch Hallie blush with her smile. "Thank you. It smells so good in here."

"I hope you brought your appetite," Mom says, walking around the kitchen island and stirring a large pot on the stove. "I made Logan's favorite."

"You didn't have to do that, Mom," I state, joining everyone in the kitchen and giving my grandma a kiss on the cheek. "Hi, Gram."

"Hello, sweet boy. I'm so happy you're joining us this evening, *and* you brought this beautiful woman with you," Gram announces, offering us both a smile.

"I appreciate Logan extending the invite to me," Hallie says with a tight smile. "Otherwise, it would have been something quick and simple at home and not nearly as delicious smelling as what we're having here."

"Have a seat at the table," Mom announces. "Dinner is ready."

"Let me help you," I offer, moving to the stove to help carry the food to the table.

"If you haven't had Patty's Italian shells and cheese, you're in for a real treat," Gram says to Hallie as she takes a seat.

"Her garlic bread is the best too," I chime in as I place the dish on the potholder in the middle of the table.

"It's the butter," Mom replies, setting a bowl with chunks of hot bread beside the dish. "Everything is better with real butter," she adds with a wink, taking her seat.

We all dive in, scooping up big helpings of the Italian dish. I watch as Hallie takes a small bite of food, slowly chewing and swallowing. Her eyes widen immediately. "Holy crap, that's amazing."

We all chuckle as Gram reaches over and pats her hand. "You're not wrong." She takes her own small bite before asking, "So, what's been happening with you two?" There's a twinkle in her eyes that causes me to pause. It's a knowing little gleam, making my heart pound a little harder in my chest.

Hallie's wide eyes hesitantly glance up from across the table, waiting for me to take the lead. I clear my throat and set my fork down. "Actually, there is something we wanted to talk about, but it can wait until after we eat."

Mom gasps. "Are you two finally dating?"

"What?" Hallie asks, a look of shock on her face.

"I've been secretly hoping this would happen forever," my mom confesses, making me want to hide under the table.

"No, no. We're not dating," I reply, breaking my mom's heart with just a few words.

"Oh. I just thought..."

"We're not dating, but we do have something else going on," I say, trying to figure out the right words. I've been imagining this conversation for the last few hours, but now that it's happening, I have no clue what to say.

"What's that?" Gram asks. Again, the meaningful look on her face is suspicious as hell.

Hallie sets her fork down and drops her gaze to her plate, while I decide to just rip off the Band-Aid. "Hallie and I are having a baby."

My mom gasps, covering her mouth with her hand. "What? Really? A baby?" she asks, instantly smiling before her eyes narrow at me. "You're not messing with me right now, are you?"

"Of course not, Mom. I'd never joke about something like this," I insist.

She relaxes and nods. "Wow, a baby. I'm going to be a grandma," she whispers, as if trying that word out for size. Then, her chair scrapes on the linoleum floor as she pushes back and stands. She reaches for Hallie and pulls her into a big hug. Hallie somehow stands and returns the gesture. "I'm so excited," my mom whispers, sniffling and wiping her eyes.

"I know this is a little unconventional," Hallie starts but is waved off.

"Don't worry about any of that. I couldn't think of anyone better to share a child with Logan than you," my mom says, causing Hallie's eyes to get a little misty.

She turns to me and approaches, arms extended. I prepare for the hug and am rewarded with a fierce one that reminds me of the ones my dad used to give. "Love you," she whispers in my ear, making my throat tight.

"Love you more," I tell my mom, giving her a few extra seconds of squeezes.

When we finally release our embrace, I turn to Gram, who's still sitting in her chair, smiling. "You don't seem very surprised," I find myself saying.

Gram shrugs her dainty little shoulders. "Well, if I hadn't already heard, I definitely would have figured it out when I saw Hallie. She has that pregnancy glow."

The hairs on the back of my neck stand up.

Hallie must miss it, because she replies, "That glow's not from the pregnancy. It's from puking."

"Wait, you already knew?" I ask, glancing over at Hallie, who finally realizes what was said.

Gram shrugs her shoulders. "I might have heard about it before I arrived here."

Hallie's mouth drops open. Considering no one else knew before three or four hours ago, that's pretty telling as to who opened her big fucking mouth.

I sigh and drop onto my chair. "Where did you run into her?" I ask, unable to hide my irritation.

"At the bank. I'll be honest, at first, I didn't believe it. No way would my grandson be expecting a baby and his ex-wife know before me," Gram says with a chuckle. "But then I took one look at this lovely woman when she walked in, and I realized it was true."

"Shay knows?" my mom asks as we all return to our seats.

"Unfortunately," I mutter, reaching for my fork. "She went nosing through my desk this afternoon and found the ultrasound."

My mom's eyes brighten. "There's an ultrasound?"

Hallie nods. "I'll get it for you."

"After dinner. Let's all enjoy a meal together," Mom replies, picking up her fork once more.

"That's right. We're not letting that ungrateful cow spoil our evening," Gram says, lifting her glass of water. "To Logan, Hallie, and my little great-grandchild. May the pregnancy be smooth and healthy, and may what I assume was a drunken night together be the start of something amazing and forever."

I groan, while Hallie chokes on the air she breathes.

"Let's eat!"

CHAPTER
seventeen

Hallie

The moment we get into Logan's truck, my phone rings. I pull it from my purse and spot my mom's name on the screen. Fearing something's wrong, I quickly tap the answer button. "Hello?"

"Hallie Marie Rhodes!" she bellows into the phone, causing me to pull the device away from my ear. "You're pregnant?!"

All I can do is sit here, silently.

"I take that as a yes," she mutters.

"In my defense, this is why I called you earlier, but you weren't going to be home. It's why I told you I would be coming over tomorrow night after work."

Mom sighs. "I just hate having to hear something like this from Jeanie Long."

I close my eyes and take a deep breath. "I'm sorry. It wasn't supposed to happen like that. We had every intention of telling you before the rest of the world found out."

"Your parents know?" Logan whispers, a look of horror and resolution on his face.

I nod at him and continue talking to my mom, "Shay found out by snooping in Logan's desk drawer. She found the sonogram and apparently told everyone before she even left work."

There's a short pause on the phone line. "Logan Johnson is the baby's father?"

"Uhh, yes?"

"I didn't know you were seeing him!" she proclaims. "Roger, Roger! It's not Curtis's baby, it's Logan's!"

"Logan Johnson? I wasn't aware they were dating," I hear my dad say in the background.

"Look, it's a long story, and one we don't really need to get into it right now."

"Yes, of course. Your father and I stepped outside at the bowling alley to call you. When that nosy Jeanie and her stick-in-the-mud husband, Truman, came in, they started telling everyone about your pregnancy. The wretched woman even smirked at me, as if she knew she was speaking out of turn and announcing something before I even knew."

"Sounds about right. The apple doesn't fall too far from the tree," I grumble.

"Well, now that I've had a few minutes to absorb this shocking news, I'm elated. Two grandbabies. Of course, I thought my children would both be married before making us grandparents, but I suppose that's just how today's society is. It's so common to have three kids with three baby daddies these days."

I groan. "Stop, Mom."

"What? I'm just saying, we can be young and hip like the rest of you. Anyway, we need to get back inside. Our game is about to start."

"Okay, good luck tonight. I'll stop by tomorrow still so you can see the ultrasound."

I hear my dad speaking, but don't quite hear what he's saying. "Dad says to bring Logan with you. He'd like to have a word with him."

I swallow hard. "Will do. Oh, Mom? Why would you think the baby's Curtis's? We've been broken up for two years."

"Well, he called me not that long ago to see how we were doing. He mentioned you two were talking and probably getting back together."

"What? That's not true," I insist, anger coursing through my veins at my ex going behind my back and calling my mom like that.

"Well, to be honest, we're both glad. Curtis never put you first the way you deserved. He will always be married to his job," Mom says.

"I know."

"All right, well, you have a good evening, honey. See you tomorrow," she says before we both sign off.

"So, your parents know," Logan confirms once more unnecessarily.

"Yep. You can thank your ex-wife for calling her equally nosy mom and telling the entire town before we could."

It's in that moment, my phone starts to blow up.

Blair: Everyone knows. Your brother just got a text message from his friend, Hunter.

I moan and shake my head. "Shit."

Ellie: The rumors are running wild. Please tell me I didn't have to find out one of my best friends is pregnant from Shay freaking Johnson.

Ava: Whoa! Why am I hearing you're pregnant while I'm buying apples at the grocery store?!

Then, as if on cue, Logan's phone starts to chime with incoming text messages. He glances at his phone. "Your brother would like to have a word with me. Now."

"This is a mess," I whisper, firing off messages back to my friends. I tell them all the same thing, that I had every intention of telling them all this weekend and I'm sorry they had to hear about this from someone like Shay. They all seem excited for us, even if there's the lingering question about the status of my and Logan's relationship.

"I put your brother off until tomorrow," Logan tells me when he sets his phone down on the console and backs his truck out of his mom's driveway.

"You have nothing to be afraid of where he's concerned," I find myself saying. My brother is a big teddy bear. He's firm when he needs to be, but one of the most caring, empathetic individuals I've ever known. It's what makes him a remarkable physician.

"I'm not worried about that. He has a right to be a bit flustered, but not angry. What happens between you and me is just that. Between us. We're both adults."

"I know, but he's still my big brother. He's protective."

"And I respect that about him, but I won't let him disrespect you."

"Or you," I say, sliding my own phone back into my purse, ignoring more text messages for now.

Logan shrugs. "I'm not worried about me. I can handle Gabe's wrath, but I don't think it'll come to that. Once I tell him I'm committed to being by your side throughout the pregnancy and our baby's life, he'll back down. He's just irritated I slept with his sister," he says with a smirk.

A warm tingle slides through my veins, landing firmly between my legs at his words. The memories of our two nights together come flooding back, despite my best efforts to brush them aside. "What are we going to do about Shay?" I ask, looking to change the subject.

"Nothing. Continue to ignore her like always. Though, I'm definitely going to be reaching out to my attorney to ask him to present an offer one more time. She wants nothing to do with the business. She just refuses to let go because she knows it pisses me off."

We head for my condo in comfortable silence, both lost in our own thoughts. When he pulls into my short driveway, I release my seat belt and give him a quick, "Thanks."

He turns my way and gives me a gentle smile. "We don't have to have everything figured out right now. It's going to take time."

I nod. "I know."

"Do you need anything? More crackers or ginger ale?" The corner of his mouth turns upward in that sexy way I can't help but notice.

"No, I think I'm okay," I insist, opening the door and sliding out of the truck.

"All right. If you change your mind, just text me."

"Night, Logan."

He looks like he wants to say something else, but only offers me a soft, "Night."

I walk toward my front door and release the lock. Logan doesn't move until I'm inside, door securely locked behind me. Only then do I hear his truck backing out of the driveway and heading down the street.

As I get ready for bed, I start to feel that familiar heat rush through my body. I go quickly, moving to the bathroom with determined steps. Just as I drop to my knees, tonight's dinner makes a reappearance. And that really sucks, because it was so, so good. Way better going down than coming back up.

When the sickness has passed, I climb off the floor, brush my teeth, and wash my face. Just as I'm turning off the bathroom light, there's a knock on the front door. I consider ignoring it, but it could be something important. Instead of going to my bed like I'd prefer, I make my way to the door and peek through the peephole.

"Logan?" I ask, releasing the lock and pulling open the door. "Is everything all right?"

He takes one look at me in my frogs reading books pajamas—sans bra, mind you—and pale complexion. "Did you get sick?"

I lean against the door and offer the smallest smile I can muster. "I'm sad to report the baby does not like your mom's Italian shells and cheese."

He pushes past me without waiting to be invited.

"Please, come in," I mutter, closing the door behind him.

"I brought you ice cream from Molly's."

My ears perk up, and even though I probably shouldn't risk eating something milk-based right now, the thought of ice cream has my mouth watering. "Ice cream? What kind?"

"Vanilla and peach swirl," he replies, referring to my favorite flavor.

I dive for the bag, ripping it from his hand. "Gimme!"

Logan laughs, releasing the goods before the bag can rip. "You're vicious when you're pregnant."

"You're dangling ice cream in my face, five minutes after I threw up everything in my body like an exorcism."

He makes a disgusted face. "Sorry to hear. Ice cream may not make it better."

I roll my eyes and head straight for the kitchen to grab a spoon. "Said no one ever. Ice cream makes everything better, Johnson," I holler behind me.

"Noted, Rhodes."

When I turn, he's standing in the walkway between the kitchen and living room, blocking my progress. I shoulder bump him, surprising him a bit, and move past. I head straight for my bed, because there's nothing better than ice cream in your comfy bed, while watching some trashy reality TV show.

I climb into bed, getting myself comfortable, and dig into the fresh homemade ice cream. "Oh my God, this tastes like heaven," I groan, mouth full.

He steps into my room, crosses his arms over his chest, and glares. "You're really not going to share that?"

"Why would I?" I ask, taking another bite and licking the spoon.

His eyes narrow and track the movement of my tongue. A wave of excitement rushes through my veins. "I bought the large bowl so we could share."

I snicker and shake my head. "I never share ice cream, Logan."

Just as I dip the spoon back into the creamy, peachy goodness, I catch movement out of the corner of my eye. I glance up to see him approaching, the look of a lion stalking his prey in his eyes. "You won't even share one bite?"

My nipples pebble against the cotton of my pajama top and my throat goes Sahara dry. Unable to speak, I shake my head slowly, watching as his eyes move down to my chest. No doubt he caught sight of my excited nipples. Bringing the spoon back up to my lips, I hold it out and let my tongue do all the work, all while holding his gaze.

His nostrils flare and his cock goes hard in his jeans. He does nothing to try to hide the fact. Logan takes one more step closer until he's standing directly in front of my bed. "Not even a taste?"

I could practically orgasm right now from the husky timbre of his voice, mixed with the insinuation of his words. "Nope," I challenge, popping the P and shoving the entire spoonful in my mouth.

Just as I pull the spoon from between my lips, he pounces. I let out a squeal and try to get away, but he's too fast. He's on top of me, pinning me to the mattress before I even know what's happening. With his mouth hovering over the top of mine and my wrists trapped in his big hands, I have no choice but to just lie here.

And wait.

"You're not nice when it comes to ice cream," he whispers, his warm breath tickling my lips.

"You should have brought your own," I tease, trying to move my hand to bring the spoon to my mouth, but being unsuccessful.

"I brought this one," he states, shifting his weight so he's holding himself above me. It's in that movement I feel his erection brush against my leg.

"Hmm, too bad for you," I reply, continuing to poke the bear. Mostly because I want to see just how far he's willing to take this. He's clearly aroused, much to my complete enjoyment.

"Yes, I suppose it is. I guess I'm just going to have to *take* a little taste, since you're so unwilling to share with me."

I lift my chin, the challenge clear. "Do your worst."

I don't know what I was expecting, but it wasn't for him to steal his taste from my lips. He brushes his mouth across mine gently at first, before coaxing my lips apart and sliding his tongue between them. There's a heady mixture of peach ice cream and pure Logan as he deepens the kiss. I'm very aware he's kissing me and I make no attempts to stop the kiss. If anything, I willingly let it happen, curling my body against his to get closer.

Before I'm ready for it to end, he pulls his mouth from mine and licks his lips. "Delicious."

I'm left breathing heavily, my clit swollen and tingling. I want more, just like I did on my birthday. You know, the night that got us into our little predicament.

Logan releases my hands and pushes himself up and off the bed, careful not to squash me. "I suppose that'll just have to do for tonight."

My skin is hot, my blood swooshing rapidly through my veins. The ice cream is all but forgotten, thanks to the hum of desire helping fill my brain with inappropriate thoughts.

"Thanks for the taste, Cupcake."

And then, he's gone, exiting my room without so much as a single glance back. I hear the door open and close, knowing without a doubt he flipped the lock on his way out. Sitting up, I reach for the ice cream and take a hearty bite of the melting treat. Once I take a couple more bites, I reach for my phone and pull up the text app.

Me: Tell me why I slept with Logan Johnson? He drives me bonkers.

Blair: Great abs and a killer smile?

Me: That has never been my thing before. Why is it so attractive now?

Blair: What did he do now?

Me: He brought me ice cream.

Blair: The asshole!

Blair: Great, now I want ice cream.

Me: My brother still mad?

Blair: He's not mad, just concerned. He thinks Logan took advantage of you.

I can't help but snort as I chuckle, recalling how everything played out. I'm certain I was the one who initiated our night together. Well, both nights.

Me: I just LOL'd.

Blair: He'll get over it.

Me: There's nothing to get over. We're not together. We'll co-parent. It'll be fine.

Blair: As long as the big jerk stops bringing you ice cream?

Me: Exactly.

Blair: You're weird. How's the sickness?

Me: Still there. I'll probably be throwing up this vanilla and peach swirl he brought me in thirty minutes, ensuring I hate him all over again.

Blair: Your brother is going to get me ice cream.

Me: Hahahaha! My brother is so whipped. *insert whipping motion gif*

Blair: *insert smirking emoji*

Me: Okay, I'm going to finish this ice cream and try not to think about Logan's abs.

Blair: Good luck with that.

"No shit," I grumble, picturing those very abs. Then, because my brain is particularly evil tonight, I recall what it was like having his erection pressed against me. The attraction and chemistry we felt several weeks back is still there, alive and well, just below the surface. All it will take is one little spark to light the fuse all over again.

But that can't happen.

The last thing I need is to let my overactive hormones take charge. Logan must remain tucked firmly in the friend zone, where I don't think about stripping off his clothes and doing dirty things to his cock. We're having a baby. That alone adds an incredible layer of complication, which is exactly why there will be no more sex.

But that doesn't mean I can't think about it.

I just need to limit how much I picture his naked body. You know, like how adults limit television time to young children.

I can do that. I just need to come up with some sort of schedule.

Logan and his magical cock are only allowed time in my subconscious on Saturdays, between the hours of seven and nine in the evening.

See? Easy-peasy.

I can do this.

My subconscious starts to laugh.

CHAPTER
eighteen

LOGAN

By the time Hallie hits twelve weeks, the morning sickness has all but stopped, thankfully, because I hate seeing her miserable. Now that we've hit the three-month milestone, she seems to have a regular appetite again, and the fatigue seems to get better with each day that passes.

Today, we're headed back to the doctor for our second check-up. The internet says we could hear the heartbeat on a Doppler now, and a big part of me is hoping that's accurate.

Hallie and I have fallen into a routine. As the weather has slowly started to change from the heat of summer to the cooler days and nights of fall, we get together one or two nights a week and share a meal. Turns out, we are perfectly capable of having an enjoyable time with conversation, as long as I'm not being too bossy and all up in her business.

Her words, not mine.

We've also gone to the football games together on Friday nights. It's weird not seeing Brody out there, but he's joined us in the stands most weeks this season. Morgan too. I really like them together, and I can tell by the way he looks at her, he's completely smitten. I think there might be something there long term, and I see him making it official with a ring someday.

I pull into Hallie's driveway for our trip to Hudson, and before I can put the car into Park, she's exiting her condo and heading for my truck. With the temperatures falling and the days growing shorter, she's been complaining about the temperatures. It's cool in the mornings, warms up in the afternoon, and then starts to get cold again once the sun sets. Perfect football weather, but not so great for a woman with raging hormones from pregnancy.

And speaking of pregnancy, it's looking great on Hallie. She's not showing yet, but her body has definitely filled out. From her boobs to her hips, everything screams woman right now. Maybe it's the fact I haven't had sex since our last night together in July, or perhaps it's the fact it's this particular woman who seems to check all my boxes right now and has for a while.

"Hey," she says when she slides into the cab of my truck.

I throw the car into reverse and start to back out. "How was work?"

"Good," she says with a grin. "I'm getting ready for the classroom Halloween parties at the end of the month. It's one of my favorite events to do with the kids. That and the Christmas book exchange. Plus, the parents are amazing, and we have some of the best treats and play games."

"Sounds like fun," I reply.

"It is. How was your day?"

"Decent. Shay was off, so that helped." I chuckle, loving how easy the day goes when she's not there to throw wrenches into everything we do.

"I bet. I don't know how you do it, working with your ex every day. If I had to work with Curtis, I'd definitely quit."

"Well, I don't have that option," I say, pressing down on the accelerator as we reach the city limits and head for the neighboring town. "I'd never let her have my family's business. She'd kill it in under six months and both my grandpa and dad would be rolling over in their graves."

"Speaking of, can I ask you a question?" She turns a little so she can see me easier.

"Shoot."

"You don't have to answer, but I was curious as to why you gave Shay the house when you divorced. It belonged to your grandparents."

I sigh, going back for a brief moment to that time in my life. I don't mind talking about it now—it's been long enough—but at that point, I was pretty torn up over everything transpiring. "I was done arguing," I tell her honestly. "The house, we hadn't been in it that long, and even though it was my grandparents', I didn't have the sentimental attachment to it I once had, so it was easy for me to give in and let her have it."

"It doesn't surprise me she wanted it," Hallie states, shaking her head. "That house was gorgeous with all the original woodwork."

"She only wanted it because she thought I did, not because of the beauty it possessed. But when I gave in too easily, that's when she stuck her claws in the business and refused to sell her half. In fact, after I moved out, she updated a lot of the woodwork. She only kept the floors because she didn't want to move furniture, but all the cabinets in the kitchen were ripped out and thrown in a tattered pile along the road for someone to pick up within a year after I moved out."

Even though I'm looking at the road, I catch Hallie's mouth falling open in shock in my peripheral vision. "What a bitch biscuit."

I chuckle. "No arguments there."

"Your place is nice though."

I shrug. "It's a place to sleep and hang after work. It's a tad small, but really, I don't need a lot of room. Plus, it was within a very short walking distance from TD, so I'd just cut through the backyards that separate us and crash his bachelor pad. Well, before he married Ellie."

"I don't mind small," she says casually. "My condo has been perfect for me. Now, with the baby coming, I'll have to make the second bedroom into a nursery." She pauses a few seconds before asking, "Are you going to make your guest bedroom into a nursery?"

"Yeah. It's a blank canvas since I never got around to putting a bed in there. I'll probably wait though until we find out what we're havin'," I reply.

"You want to know what we're having?" she asks, sitting up straight in her seat.

"Well, yeah. Don't you?"

I glance over in time to see her shrug. "I don't know. I like the idea of being surprised."

"I get that, but I'm more of a planner. I think I'd like to know what we're having so we can buy accordingly," I tell her, feeling her start to tense beside me. Before I even realized what I'm doing, the hornet's nest is kicked.

"You buy gender-neutral items, like greens and yellows." There's a bite to her tone, one that makes my dick twitch in my pants.

"That just seems silly. Why not just find out so you can buy the blue or the pink?" I risk another quick glance over to see her eyes narrowed and smoke practically billowing out of her ears.

"There are only a few real surprises a person can enjoy in life. This is one of them. Why not be truly surprised when the baby is born?"

I fight the grin threatening to spread across my lips. "Wouldn't it be just as big of a surprise to find out at the ultrasound? Then you can do one of those gender reveal things in the backyard with fireworks and balloons like everyone does on the internet."

She practically growls when she huffs out a deep breath. "You *really* don't want to be surprised? *Really?*" Her agitation is evident in her questions.

I let her sit on it for a few seconds before I finally shrug my shoulders. "Actually, I think we should just wait and be surprised when the baby is born. I mean, we have so few real surprises in life, so why not take advantage of this one and just wait?"

Her hands fly up in the air before one swings around to whack me in the arm. "You're such a dirty asshole." She crosses her arms and turns to face the window.

A bark of laughter flies from my lips. "Oh, come on, Cupcake. That was funny."

She turns her glare my way once more. A lesser man would cower, but all it does is turn me the fuck on. "I was trying to have a normal, real conversation with you, but you had to ruin it," she pouts, keeping those arms crossed.

I slow with traffic as we approach Hudson, doing my best to maintain the speed limit. I follow the now-familiar route to the doctor's office. I crack another smile as Hallie rants from the other side of my truck, calling me a plethora of names, each one a little more colorful than the last.

The moment I pull into the parking lot, I turn off the ignition and say, "My baby is listening, you know. His first word is going to be dirty asshole."

"*Her*. And if the shoe fits, wear it."

Grabbing my keys, I slide out of the truck and shut the door. As soon as I walk around and hold her door open while she slides out, I say, "I kinda like shit biscuit."

Hallie pauses and holds my gaze. I swear there's desire mixing with that annoyance she feels for me, and if it were another time and place, perhaps I would try to draw it out of her a bit. But getting ready to walk into the OB's office isn't exactly the right moment, so I'll table that discussion for another time.

She lifts her chin and states, "Maybe that'll be what I call you then. Instead of Baby Daddy, you can be Shit Biscuit."

I laugh so hard my stomach hurts and I have tears in my eyes. "That's going to be my boy's first words. Shit biscuit."

"*Daughter,*" she replies, walking right past me and heading for the physician's office's front door.

I shut the truck door and make sure it's locked before hurrying to catch up to her, the entire time, wearing a smile on my lips. I reach her just as she's ready to open the door, so I do the honors, meeting her gaze for a brief second. Something passes in that moment, an electrical charge of some sort, a heaviness that makes my heart skip a beat.

We step inside the warm reception area and move toward the front desk. Hallie answers a few basic questions before being told to have a seat. She walks over to the same spot we sat in last month, me trailing behind a step or two. Neither of us speaks as we wait, and fortunately, it's a short one. Within five minutes, we're called back.

The nurse goes through the same drill with Hallie. First, getting her weight and blood pressure before handing her the small cup for a urine sample. "You can step across the hall and wait in room three if you'd like," she suggests to me while Hallie goes into the restroom.

I walk around the small room, taking in the posters on the wall, only to realize I'm gazing at a woman's reproductive system. Yeah, I went through health class, so it's not like it's completely foreign to me, but it's not something I thought I'd be staring at on a random Monday afternoon.

"Okay, Hallie, have a seat," the nurse announces from behind me.

I quickly move to the single chair positioned along the wall and drop my ass into it, while Hallie sits on the table. I remain quiet as they speak about Hallie's pregnancy over the last month, the nurse making notes in the chart.

When she stands, she says, "Dr. Bergman will be here in a few minutes. Go ahead and open your button and zipper, but you don't have to take your pants off."

"Thank you," Hallie replies, glancing around the room, at anywhere but my direction, the moment the door closes, and we're left alone. She does as instructed, leaving her pants open while she lies back on the table. "Are you always this annoying?" she asks, crossing her arms and looking my way.

"I'm just sitting here," I reply sweetly.

"Exactly!" she whisper-yells, waving her hand in my direction. "You're just sitting there, acting like everything is fine."

My eyebrows creep toward my hairline. "Everything isn't fine?"

"No." Her reply is instantaneous.

"What's wrong? Is it the baby? Are you feeling like you're going to get sick?"

She huffs out a frustrated breath. "No, everything with the baby is fine."

I wait for her to elaborate, but when she doesn't, I finally ask, "You're going to have to help me here, Cupcake. Are you mad at me?"

"Yes."

"Why?" I ask, incredulously.

"Because!"

I throw my hands into the air. "Women. No, wait. Pregnant women!"

"Knock, knock," Dr. Bergman announces as she raps her knuckles to the door and pushes it open. "Hi, Hallie." She glances at me and nods. "Logan."

"Hello, Dr. Bergman," I reply at the same time Hallie mutters, "Hi."

She glances from Hallie to me, as if she can tell we're both surrounded by tension. "Well, all right. How have you been?"

Hallie gives her a wide smile. "Great. We're both anxious to hear the heartbeat."

"Okay, we shouldn't have a problem hearing it on the Doppler this week. Usually by eleven or twelve weeks it can pick up the sound, so go ahead and lie back. I'll measure your stomach, and we can take a listen."

I move to the edge of my seat and watch as the doctor tucks a paper towel of some sort into Hallie's underwear before she runs a small tape measure across Hallie's lower stomach. I'm not exactly sure what's she's measuring, so I make a mental note to check the internet when I get home.

"All right, Hallie. This gel might feel a little cool," she informs her right before squirting a small blob onto Hallie's belly. Then, she reaches over and grabs this little joystick looking device from the counter and places one end onto Hallie's stomach. She moves it around, and within a few seconds, the sound of a swooshing thump echoes through the small speaker in her other hand.

"Is that—" I'm standing up and moving toward Hallie before I realize it.

"Yep. That's your baby's heartbeat."

"It's so fast," I say unnecessarily. I know one of the websites I was on talked about the heartbeat and how much faster it is while in the uterus.

"One hundred forty-five beats per minute. That's a perfect heartbeat," she announces with a smile.

I have no clue when I reached for Hallie's hand, but when I look down, I find her much smaller, warm fingers entwined with my own. "Wow."

Together, we listen until the doctor removes the Doppler and wipes away the gel. "Any questions for me?" Dr. Bergman asks, extending a hand to Hallie and helping her sit up.

"No, I don't think so."

She nods. "All right, we'll see you back in four more weeks. After your next appointment, we'll order some labs. A lot of patients use the walk-in clinic on Jefferson Street for lab work. It's a fraction of the cost, and you don't have to schedule through a hospital."

"That would be helpful, thanks."

"No problem. See you in four weeks," she says before exiting the room.

I'm still standing here, holding Hallie's hand even after she used the other to sit up on the table. She just watches me, a smile on her lush lips. Helping her off the table, I invade her personal space, standing directly in front of her. "Still mad at me?" I ask quietly, sliding my thumb over her knuckles.

"Always," she murmurs with a crooked grin and a gleam in her blue eyes.

"Good to know nothing has changed." I match her smile. "Ready to head out?"

"Yep," she says, walking to the door and stepping out into the hall. Another couple is approaching, so begrudgingly, I release her hand so she can walk in front of me.

We stop by the front reception counter and schedule her next appointment, and as I push open the glass door taking us to the sidewalk, we're hit with a cool breeze that escorts us all the way to the truck. When we reach my vehicle, I click the fob to unlock the door and prepare to pull it open. Just as I reach for the handle, my cell phone rings. I pull the device out of my pocket as I open the door. When I spot Gabe's name on the screen, I stop and click to answer the call.

"Hey, what's up?"

"Are you with Hal?"

I glance at the woman beside me, who's watching me intently. "Yeah, we're just leaving her doctor's appointment. What's wrong?"

"Her condo. There's a fire."

Fuck.

"How bad?" I hold her gaze, dreading having to tell her this news.

"It looks like it's the condo beside hers mostly, but I'm not entirely sure. They're trying to put it out first."

"Shit. All right, we're on our way," I tell him, barely hearing his "Hurry" as I click the screen to disconnect.

"What's wrong?" she asks without getting into the truck.

"The condo beside yours is on fire. We need to go. Now."

"Oh my God." Her complexion goes pale as she hops inside my truck and reaches for her seat belt. I have her door closed and am jogging around to the driver's side, jumping in the truck, and turning over the engine fast. Then, I'm pulling out of the lot, pressing the accelerator a little harder than I should.

I glance over, noting her worried expression, and reach for her hand. "It's going to be okay, Hal. It's going to be okay."

Sadly, by the look in her eyes when she glances my way, I can tell she doesn't believe me.

I'll just keep the faith for the both of us.

CHAPTER
nineteen

Hallie

When Logan rounds the corner for my street, we're met with lights. I can see smoke, but no flames, which I pray is a good sign. Realizing we can't go any farther, Logan pulls over and parks the truck. We both jump out and meet at the front of the truck, his hand extended toward me. The moment my hand is secured in his, we take off jogging toward my condo.

We reach the barricades and an officer standing post. He's an older man I've known my whole life, and he holds my gaze as I approach.

"What can you tell us?" Logan asks Dwayne before we're stopped.

"I can't tell you anything," he replies sadly, "And I can't let you pass."

"But that's my place," I tell him even though he already knows that. Everyone knows everybody in this town, including where they live.

"I know, Hallie. I can radio for the fire chief, but he's busy right now extinguishing the blaze. Why don't you go across the street. I think Gabe and some of the others are gathered on the sidewalk. I'll send someone over as soon as they have more information for you."

All I can do is give a short, wooden nod.

"Thanks, Officer Simmons," Logan replies on my behalf and escorts me over to the sidewalk on the opposite side of the street.

My eyes are glued to the structure I call home. There's a massive hole in the roof of the condo alongside mine with smoke billowing out, and from what I can see under the bright lights from the fire department, my roof seems fine. But I'm not naïve either. There's only one wall separating the condo beside me from mine. While I don't see damage to my roof, that doesn't mean my condo isn't affected.

"There's your brother," Logan says, guiding me past my neighbors and toward Gabe.

Ignoring those around me calling my name, I keep my focus ahead on my brother's worried eyes and run straight into his extended arms. The moment I catch a whiff of his familiar scent—a combination of his bodywash and some sort of antiseptic smell that comes from the clinic—I burst into tears. "Shh shh shh, don't cry, Hal. It's going to be okay."

I sniffle and turn my face into his arm.

"Did you just wipe your nose on me?" he asks with a chuckle.

"Yeah, get used to it. Your kid will do the same thing," I tease my brother as I step back. He makes a disgusted face as he glances down at the wet streak across his arm, but I've already moved on. I throw myself at my best friend, who is crying. "What's the matter?" I ask, wiping my own tears.

"Hormones," she replies, waving me off. "I can't believe this is happening."

I turn and face my condo and view the activity. Volunteer firemen move around, spraying water onto the place beside mine. All I can do is stand here, in complete shock, and watch. I feel a warm, strong hand snake around my hip, and when Logan draws me closer to his side, I go willingly. The comfort he's offering outweighs any logic in my head that says we shouldn't be touching. All this touching is liable to put other ideas into my head. Ideas that involve a lot fewer clothes, and frankly, that's the least of my concerns right now.

"I called Mom and Dad so they wouldn't worry when they heard about the fire. They offered to come, but I told them there was no reason for it. All they'd be doing is standing here and watching with the rest of us, but Mom did ask you to call her soon and let her know you're okay."

I nod, my eyes still glued to the scene in front of me.

A few people come over, but I'm not in a chatty mood. Logan and Gabe take care of that part, accepting condolences on my behalf and thanking them for their kind words and support. My mind races. Even if my condo doesn't sustain fire damage, the water and smoke alone will be enough to destroy it. What will happen to my belongings? Is anything salvageable inside? My Jeep is still in the driveway, covered with a mixture of ash, soot, and water. It'll probably smell like smoke.

But I'm okay. I'm alive. I wasn't home when the fire started, and from what I've gathered, neither were my neighbors. They're a sweet young couple named Lilly and Jason Smithers, and from what I've gathered from our brief chats since they moved in a few months back, he works for the railroad and is gone throughout the week and she's a registered nurse at the hospital in Hudson.

As if thinking of her conjures her up, Lilly comes running toward where we stand. "Oh my God, that's my place," she hollers, trying to get someone's attention on the opposite side of the barriers.

"Lilly," I yell, moving toward her.

She's crying and throws her arms around my neck. "What happened? I just got off work and saw the lights."

"I don't know what happened," I tell her. "Someone is supposed to let me know more soon."

"I just can't believe this," she cries, wiping at her tears.

"I'm sorry," I find myself telling her, squeezing her arm in support.

"I need to call Jason. He's down in Illinois working this week," she mumbles, digging for her cell phone.

"Go make the call. I'll be here and let you know if someone has any info for us," I tell her.

While she walks away to call her husband, I find myself leaning against Logan and resting my head on his shoulder. "What am I going to do?" I whisper to no one in particular.

"Baby steps, Hal. We'll take it day by day, minute by minute. Don't get yourself stressed out. It's not good for the baby," Logan murmurs, kissing the top of my head and holding me close.

I exhale. "I know I should probably tell you you're right, but I'm not gonna," I retort, a touch of sass evident in my voice.

"That's more like it."

While we wait, TD and Ellie join us, as does Marcus, another friend and former classmate who is the local mechanic. Lilly returns, letting me know her husband has left work and is driving home to be with her. One of the neighbors brought bottles of water out to us, but I'm too hyped up and worried to drink anything. Logan won't have it, however, and keeps holding the bottle out to me, encouraging me to take small drinks to keep hydrated. I want to yell at him that a few hours without a drink of water isn't going to make me dehydrated, but I just don't want to fight right now.

Plus, it's kinda sweet how he keeps trying to take care of me.

"There's Gary," Gabe announces, pointing to the fire chief. "He's coming this way."

I stand up straight and prepare for what he's about to tell us. Lilly moves closer and is standing directly beside me.

"Are you the other occupant?" he asks Lilly when he approaches.

"I am. Lilly Smithers. My husband is on his way home from Illinois."

He nods. "I'm Chief Franklin. We don't know all the specifics right now, but we do know the fire seems to have originated in the second unit, the one occupied by the Smithers. Once we're sure we've taken care of the major flames, we'll go inside both units and take a look around and see what kind of damage you're looking at, but for now, you both need to make arrangements for a while. The fire marshal will come tomorrow and be able to hopefully determine the cause of the fire. The Red Cross is also here, over by the ambulances, as is your landlord, Mr. Fitzgerald. You're both welcome to go over and speak with them."

"Thank you, Gary," I reply, trying to comprehend what he said.

"Thank you," Lilly adds before he returns to his post to continue his job. "I'm going to go over and talk to Mr. Fitzgerald."

"I'll be there in a minute," I tell her, taking a few deep breaths. "I can't stay here tonight."

"You can stay with us," Gabe pipes up and offers.

"Yes, we have a nice guest room," Blair chimes in with a nod.

"I don't want to impose," I start, though I have to admit, staying with them would be better than moving back in with my parents.

"You'll stay with me."

My eyes narrow as I turn to glare at the owner of that voice. "Excuse me? I don't take orders from you."

He rolls his eyes and crosses his arms over his chest. "Today you do."

A buzzing sounds in my ears and everything around me just fades away. I can no longer hear the conversations nearby, nor can I see anything other than this infuriating, stubborn man in front of me. "I don't recall giving you any authority over my life, Logan."

"Actually, you did. The day you told me you were pregnant. That gave me the *authority* to do whatever it took to protect both you and my baby, and this qualifies. You need a place to stay, and I'll be that place." His tone is serious with a touch of an edge, like he's leaving no room for discussion.

My clit actually aches. There's something incredibly hot about him right now, but I refuse to acknowledge it. No way will I let him win so easily, nor will I let him know how sexy I think he is when he's standing his ground and bossing me around.

I take a deep breath and dig down deep for a reason. "Logan, you only have one bed. I'm not taking your bed. Who knows how long I'll be out of my place."

He shrugs, softening just a bit. "I don't mind. In fact, the thought of having you and the baby under my roof and getting to be a part of your day-to-day where the baby is concerned is pretty exciting."

I swear I hear Blair sigh and swoon. "I understand that, but I can't let you sleep on your couch. It could be weeks. Hell, it could be months!" I proclaim, trying to get him to understand my point.

"Okay, so not my house then. We'll go to the cabin," he states, as if he's not insisting we live together for the foreseeable future.

"The cabin? Logan, we can't."

"We can." The brown in his eyes seems to darken even more. "And we will. I'm not trying to be a dick, Hallie, but that's my baby," he states, pointing to my abdomen. "I will do everything humanly possible to protect my child, and that includes you. Where my baby goes, I do."

I throw my hands up in the air in frustration. "You've got to be kidding me. You won't even let me go stay with my parents? My *brother?* I can go stay at the cabin by myself. I'm a big girl."

He smirks a naughty grin. "I know," he whispers. "And you're not going to the cabin alone. Not with someone breaking in and stealing."

I huff out a frustrated breath. "That was two months ago, and they broke into your shed to steal gas. It's not like they were in the cabin."

He lifts his broad, muscular shoulders. "That's the deal, Cupcake. We go together or not at all. If we don't go to the cabin, we're going to my house. Take it or leave it."

We're in a stare down, neither wanting to concede first. To be honest, it might not be so bad staying with Logan. We've gotten along much better recently, and he has a point, this is his baby. The whole caveman routine, while annoying as hell, is understandable.

Crossing my own arms to mimic his stance, I lift my chin. "Fine, but we'll go to the cabin so we each have separate rooms. I'm not letting you sleep on your couch, and we're *not* sharing a bed."

The corner of his mouth ticks, as if he's telling me a simple door and lock has a slim chance of keeping him out.

I kinda hope it doesn't.

"You two are so cute."

I narrow my eyes and turn to face my best friend, who's standing with Ellie, watching the show. "You're not helping."

Blair grins widely. "You're welcome to stay with us, but I completely understand choosing another option. I don't think I'd like living with my parents or big brother after being on my own for so long."

"No, she's right. Staying with Logan is clearly the better option," Ellie chimes in, a pleasant smile on her lips. However, I can see the mischief there, and if I had to guess, she's matchmaking. I realize it's because I'd do the same thing if I were in her shoes. Hell, I *was* in her shoes a year ago, trying to encourage her to take a chance on TD, friendship be damned. I saw something there—we all did—and Ellie just needed a little coaxing.

Logan and I aren't like TD and Ellie though. We're not like Gabe and Blair either. We don't have a future like they did. We're having a baby, and with that will come compromise, teamwork, and mutual respect. That's the main reason I've agreed to go stay with him at the cabin. We're a team and the sooner I realize it, the better off we'll be.

"I'm going to need clothes," I mutter, mostly to myself. My brain starts listing off all the things I'm going to need sooner rather than later.

"I've got stuff you can wear," Logan replies.

"I do too," Blair says.

I don't have the heart to remind her we're not the same size and whatever she has is unlikely to fit me.

"I'm off tomorrow so I can grab whatever you need. I can run to the big chain stores in Hudson for you too," Ellie offers.

My mind spins a little, realizing I'm going to have to deal with a lot of stuff in the next few days, all while maintaining my job. "I should probably take tomorrow off, but I'm not sure I can find a sub on such short notice." There are a few names who are retired teachers willing to fill in for me on the off chance I take time off or use a sick day. It rarely happens though. Any vacation I take is done during the summer when the preschool is closed, and I've been very fortunate to remain healthy in the last handful of years.

"I'm sure you can find someone to help, especially under the circumstances," Blair adds.

"Yeah, okay. I'll call one of them shortly. Let's go over and talk to Mr. Fitzgerald." I'm suddenly exhausted and ready to lie down.

This day started off well and ended in disaster.

I just hope staying with Logan doesn't have the same fate.

"Let me get a fire going," Logan suggests when we're finally inside the cabin.

It has been the longest evening ever. Between talking to the authorities about the fire, calling my parents to assure them I'm fine, and then going to Logan's to pack up a few bags, it's almost nine by the time we arrive at his cabin. My feet are killing me and I'm starving, despite having food handed to me while we were talking to the Red Cross.

The scent of burnt wood and plastic is tattooed in my nostrils, and to be honest, I'm not really a fan of fires right now. But I'm also freezing and have been for a while, so adding the warmth a fire would offer doesn't sound so bad.

I take a seat on the couch and watch while he builds the small fire and lights it easily. My entire body is chilled, so I draw my legs up on the couch and wrap my arms around them protectively. The flames dance in front of me, growing larger and filling the room with heat. I continue to watch them as the sadness of what I've experienced washes over me once more. It's an odd feeling, a numbness really, and I don't really know how to handle it.

I've taken the rest of the week off from work. Once the pastor of the church that houses our small preschool heard about the fire, he insisted I take the time. He helped me secure a substitute through Friday, with the understanding I can have more time if needed. I don't think I'll need it, but it's nice they offered.

"Here."

I startle, not realizing Logan had gotten up and gone to the kitchen. He was in there long enough to heat up some water and make me a cup of tea. The warm mug feels amazing against my fingers and the calming scent of chamomile floats smoothly to my nose. "Thank you."

"I'm going to heat us up some of the food Frannie brought over," he says, referring to the bags of food she delivered to the firemen and first responders. She also had a large white bag she personally brought over to where we were standing after talking to the Red Cross.

I sip my tea and continue to watch the flames move. Considering the cabin is probably seven hundred square feet and there's a large walkway between the living room and kitchen, I can hear everything Logan does as he prepares to heat up whatever was in the bag. My stomach growls angrily, reminding me it's been hours since I've eaten anything.

Fortunately for me, he returns a minute later carrying a tray. "We've got two grilled cheese sandwiches and bowls of tomato bisque soup."

"Oh my God, Frannie's tomato soup?" I ask, reaching for the closest bowl. "This stuff is the best."

"The sandwiches are probably a bit on the soggy side, since I had to use the microwave to reheat them, but if you dip them in the soup, I'm sure it won't matter."

Already on it. I have one of the triangles in my hand and dunking the corner into the warm soup before he even finishes his sentence. My senses explode as the combination of soup and cheesy sandwich settle on my tongue. "Oh God, this is so delicious."

Logan laughs and makes sure the tray is closed. "Eat, Hal. Then, we'll get showered and ready for bed."

My throat goes thick at the thought of showering and going to bed together, and no matter how hard I try to push it aside and focus on my dinner, I can't seem to evict those ideas, especially when I look down and see the rug in front of the fireplace. It looks comfy and cozy, perfect for lying down with someone and making love in front of the fire.

Yeah, this was a terrible idea. Unless I can shut off my brain and my hormones—and fast—this is going to be one hell of a long night.

CHAPTER Twenty

LOGAN

She fell asleep almost immediately.

The moment her soup was devoured, and her tea mostly consumed, she curled up on the couch, her head on my leg, and promptly passed out. I could tell the fire made her uneasy but being the quickest way to heat the small space, I took the chance it wouldn't completely freak her out. Plus, I don't want her to be scared of fire, especially since it's a big aspect of life in the northern part of the country throughout the winter.

Now that she's sleeping peacefully, I feel like I'm able to fully relax for the first time since Gabe called me. Tomorrow, we're hoping to find out a little more about the fire and the damage her condo sustained. Even if the fire was contained to the condo beside hers, there will be significant water and smoke damage, and to be honest, I'm not sure her place will be saved. If half of the building is destroyed, why not take them both down and start over.

That's what I'd do if I was in Mr. Fitzgerald's shoes.

But we don't have to worry about that now. She has a roof over her head and is safe, and that's the most important thing right now. Everything else will be figured out along the way.

I let her sleep for about another thirty minutes and then decide it's time to get her to the shower and bed. I'll give her the master bedroom and take the smaller one across the hall. The twin bunk beds won't be ideal, but I refuse to let her sleep in there. She and my baby will be comfortable. Period.

"Hallie," I murmur, reaching down and running my hand along the side of her face. "It's getting late."

"Hmm?" she murmurs, her gorgeous blue eyes slowly opening.

"It's getting late, honey. I'm sure you want to shower off the smoke smell."

"Oh. Yeah." She slowly sits up and swings her legs off the couch.

Ignoring the way my body misses her nearness, I'm transfixed on her movements as she raises her arms over her head and stretches. "Let's get you showered and into bed," I repeat, standing up and extending my hand down to her.

She doesn't need help standing, but I seem to enjoy touching her as often as she'll let me. Hallie places her hand in mine and stands up. We walk together toward the short hallway that leads to both bedrooms and the bathroom. I pause outside the small bathroom. "You should have everything you need. There's towels and washcloths in the cabinet and some shampoo and whatnot in the shower stall. We can grab what you need tomorrow at the store, but in the meantime, use anything of mine."

"Thanks," she replies quietly, stepping inside.

"I'll go grab you a pair of joggers and a T-shirt to sleep in and throw them on the sink. Holler if you need anything." I take a step back and give her space.

The corner of her mouth curls up. "I think I can manage showering but thank you for the offer."

She has no clue how badly I want to assist with the task.

I nod and turn toward the master bedroom where I set bags of clothes. I easily find what I'm looking for and slide the rest of the clothing into the closet. When we buy her new clothes tomorrow, she can use the dresser to store them and I'll take my stuff across the hall. Until then, I want to leave as much of it here in case she needs something else.

Grabbing a second pair of joggers and clean boxers, I take those over to the other bedroom and toss them onto the bottom bunk. Is it just me or does that twin bed look even smaller than normal? Oh well. Better I sleep there than Hallie.

When I return to the bathroom, I find the door closed and hear the water in the shower running. I knock softly on the door. "I'm setting some clothes on the sink for you."

"All right," she replies.

As I move inside the small space, I'm assaulted by the shower steam. Even though the fan is running, the room quickly fills up with steam. It's something that can't be avoided. Placing the clean clothes on the sink, I keep my head down and prepare to slip back out. However, I spot her dirty clothing sitting in a pile and want to get those in the washer so she can wear them again tomorrow.

Bending down, I scoop up the pile, but the moment I stand up and prepare to leave, I catch movement out of the corner of my eye. I try not to look, but my eyes betray me and swing toward the shower stall. Thanks to the glass door, I catch sight of Hallie standing beneath the water, rinsing her hair. The door is foggy but still gives me the view I shouldn't be taking. Water cascades down her naked body, reminding me of the shower we enjoyed together all those weeks ago.

Before my cock can respond, I slip out of the room, chastising myself every step of the way. She's not here for me to gawk at or fuck. She's here because she's in trouble and I have the means to help.

I'd do well to remember that.

I take her clothes to the washer and drop a pod into the basin. I can throw my own clothes in the next load, even though this won't be close to full. I'd rather get hers going now. I have something else to wear tomorrow. She doesn't.

Keeping myself busy in the kitchen, I clean up the mess from our quick dinner and start making a list of the things I need to either bring from my place or go to the store to buy. When my list is about complete, I hear the door to the bathroom open and look to the right just as she's stepping through the kitchen entryway.

"That felt amazing, but I still smell smoke."

"You may for a while," I concede. "That burning plastic scent has a way of sticking with you."

She nods.

"I grabbed your dirty clothes too and threw them in the washer. They'll be ready to go for you in the morning."

"Thanks," she replies, her wet hair hanging limply around her face.

"I don't have a brush, but there's a comb in my bag in the closet. Use whatever you need." I feel like I'm just repeating myself, but I want her to understand what's mine is now hers for as long as she needs it.

"Okay." She shifts her weight from side to side, and my cock can't help but notice how delectable she looks in my clothes.

"I'll run through the shower while you get comfortable. Take the master bedroom. There's a TV in there. I don't have satellite or cable here, but there's plenty of DVDs in the closet."

"I can sleep in the smaller room," she insists, but I'm already shaking my head.

"Not going to happen, Cupcake. My baby deserves the big, comfy bed, not the small twin one."

She sighs, and if she's about to argue, she must think better of it. "Fine. There's no use fighting about it."

I flash her a quick smile. "Good."

Hallie turns to walk out but pauses in the entryway. "Thanks again, Logan. You didn't need to do all of this for me, but I appreciate it."

"You're welcome."

Giving me a small grin, she spins around and takes a step toward the hallway.

Shoving my hands in the pockets of my jeans, I confess, "Hal? I stole a peek while you were in the shower."

She flashes me a wide, saucy grin that makes my balls heavy. "I know."

Then she saunters away, adding a little extra swing to her hips, and I'm left standing here with a hard dick and an overactive imagination.

Maybe living with Hallie wasn't my best idea after all.

It's wild how quickly we fall into a comfortable routine. It's been a week since we've been living at the cabin. Today is Hallie's first day back to work since the fire, so I decide to do something nice for her. I take an early lunch from the hardware store and head down the street. I grab a bowl of the tomato bisque soup and grilled cheese sandwich from Frannie's to drop off to her at the preschool. I know she only has a small window between the morning class and the afternoon one, and she didn't take anything with her when she left for work, which means she'll likely have to leave to grab something to eat. This way, she can stay there and relax.

We learned toward the end of last week that the fire was electrical. Something in the attic in the Smithers's unit sparked and caught fire. Even though the fire didn't spread to Hallie's condo, the damage was significant. I was able to go in and grab some of her belongings, but unfortunately, so much of her stuff was ruined from smoke and water. Even after washing her clothes, there's still a heaviness of smoke and fire to them, and she decided just to throw them all away.

Blair and Ellie took her to the store and helped her pick up new things, though she didn't buy nearly as much as I expected. When she got home and explained she'd be needing maternity clothing soon, I understood her reasoning a bit more. But I'm also the type of guy who says if she needs something, she should get it, dammit.

She still wears my joggers and T-shirts to bed every night. Even though they're big on her, she looks adorable as fuck and comfortable in them, so who am I to argue? There's something primal about seeing her in my stuff, so there's no way in hell I'm going to complain. In fact, I just ran to my place over the weekend and picked up more so she had more options. Sharing clothes with Hallie definitely isn't a hardship.

As I'm walking back to the hardware store with her lunch, I pass the small floral and gift shop. Making a quick decision, I slip inside the store and walk to the counter.

"Hi, Logan. How are you?" the older shop owner, Gladys, greets.

"I'm doing well, Mrs. Gibson."

"Well, what brings you in today?"

"I'd like to grab some flowers from the case," I tell her, eyeing the glass refrigerated cooler on the side wall.

"If you don't see what you're looking for, let me know and I can make it up for you quickly," she offers, following me to the case.

I scan the premade arrangements, not really sure what I'm looking for. But when my eyes land on the three red roses with yellow sunflowers, I know I found it. "I'll take that one, please."

"You got it. I'll meet you at the counter."

When I reach the register, I pull my wallet from my pocket and grab some cash.

"Would you like to fill out a card?" she asks, sliding the vased bouquet into a clear bag and tying it closed for easy transport.

"No, that's not necessary." I mean, I'm going to hand them to her. She'll know who they're from.

"Are these for that sweet Hallie? You two are so cute together. Shame about her condo. I heard she's staying with you at the cabin," she says, typing into her old fashion cash register.

"She is, and yes, they are for her."

"Well, I think it's super sweet you two are together. You deserve some happiness in your life. I don't think I've seen you smile much since your daddy died and that horrible woman stuck her claws into your business like that," Gladys says, shaking her head.

I'm not surprised by her comment. Everyone in town knows what happened between Shay and me. Nothing in this town is private for very long.

"And to think, a baby. Your mama is beside herself with joy. She stopped in the other day to grab a gift for your gram and was just gushing," she tells me as I hand over the cash to pay for my purchase.

"She's very excited," I confirm, taking the change.

"She is, but who wouldn't be? There's something so magical and special about the first grandbaby. And great-grandbaby in Bernice's case. I'll be seeing her this week at bingo. I had to miss the last two weeks because my Johnny was down with the shingles. Terribly painful, that is."

"I'm sorry to hear that. Hopefully he's on the mend soon," I tell her, reaching for the vase.

"He better be. Driving me bonkers is what he's doing," she quips, and I can tell by the smile on her face she's teasing. At least a little. "Tell that pretty girl of yours hello."

I don't have the heart to tell her she's not my girl. At least not in the traditional sense. We're not dating, despite having a baby together. "Will do. Have a great day, Mrs. Gibson."

"You too, Logan!" she hollers as I exit the shop and head back to the hardware store.

I don't even go inside, just climb into my truck and start the engine. I technically get an hour lunch, and while most days I don't use all my allotted time, I decide I'm taking it today. Backing out of the spot, I pull onto the road and head for the preschool. Her morning class should be ending now, so if I time it right, I'll get there right when they're done and leaving.

When I pull onto the street with the church and school, I find the small lot beside the building brimming with minivans and moms. I snort as I pull in and park in the back row, far away from running and screaming children. I hop out, grab the bag of food and flowers, and walk toward the door. I can see Hallie there, sending the kids out as parents step forward to claim them. She's talked about the process of keeping the kids as safe as possible. When the child arrives, the parent signs them in and notes who will be picking them up at the end of class. This way, Hallie knows who to watch for and can make sure the kid is taken by the appropriate person.

As the last kid is sent out, she looks up and sees me approaching. A wide grin spreads across her face. I also catch several glances from the moms walking away, but I pay no attention to any of them. My eyes are on one woman and one woman only.

"What are you doing here?" she asks when I reach the door.

"I brought lunch," I tell her, holding out the bag.

"Come on in." She steps back and allows me to enter before pulling the glass door shut and making sure it's secured. "We can go down to the small office area."

Holding the flowers, I follow her past two brightly decorated rooms, filled with small tables and chairs and learning toys. A smile tugs on my lips. I can picture Hallie sitting at those small tables with her students, teaching them colors, shapes, numbers, and letters. She's made this place a fun learning environment, and I'm certain her little students adore her.

Once we're in the small office area, I place the flowers on the desk as she opens the bag. "Is this what I think it is?"

Ever since the night of the fire, Hallie's been talking about Frannie's tomato bisque soup and grilled cheese sandwich. "I had her add pickles to your sandwich."

Her eyes widen. "Seriously?" She digs into the bag, surprised when she pulls out one container of soup and one bag with the sandwich. "You're not eating?"

"Naw, I just grabbed something for you and my baby," I reply with a wink.

She blushes and looks away. Her eyes settle on the flowers. "Those are gorgeous."

I shrug, feeling a little silly by my own sudden bout of shyness. "It was an impulse stop after I left the diner. I thought they might brighten your day."

She unties the clear bag the vase is in and inhales. "They're beautiful. Thank you," she replies, giving me a happy smile.

"You're welcome. Well, I'll let you eat in peace. I gotta get back to the store before Shay decides to fuck up the inventory system again."

She makes a face. "Sorry you have to deal with her."

"Me too." I shove my hands into my pockets and rock back on my heels. "I can see myself out. Go ahead and enjoy your lunch."

"Okay. See you at home later."

I nod, walking out of the office and down the hall, despite the fact I wanted to kiss her goodbye. The entire time I go, I replay her statement. *See you at home later*. She didn't call it your place or the cabin. *Home*. Suddenly, that doesn't sound too damn bad, and it's not because she's having my baby. That's just an added bonus. It's her.

The thought of going home to her feels pretty damn good right now.

With a little extra spring in my step, I leave the preschool and head back to the hardware store. Not even Shay's whining and incessant talking can dampen the mood I'm in. All I have to do is make it through the next six hours of work, and then I get to head home.

To Hallie.

Life has never felt this good.

CHAPTER
Twenty one

Hallie

One thing I've learned over the last few months is life continues to march forward, whether you're ready for it or not.

It's late October, and I'm still living with Logan in his cabin. Why? Because I like it.

And him.

I received word last week that my condo was going to be torn down. The smoke and water damage was extensive, and the landlord will be taking both units down. He's also considering selling the land and letting someone else deal with rebuilding, since he's in his seventies. He and his wife bought the units a decade ago as a way to give them a little extra cash and him something to do by maintaining them, but now that it requires a complete rebuild, he's not interested in taking on that kind of challenge at his age.

Thankfully, I had renter's insurance. Don't tell my mom, but her urging me to take out a policy was the best decision I made. I'm in the process of finalizing my payout with them, but it appears I'll have enough to replace most of my lost belongings. I've been slow to make new purchases, mostly because my priorities have shifted.

After the fire, I grabbed some basic necessities, but the day is coming quickly when I'll be needing maternity clothes, so instead of replacing dozens of items I won't be able to wear for a while, I'll pick up the things as I need them.

Logan and I haven't talked too much more about what will happen when the baby arrives. I'm going to need a place by then, and with winter knocking on the door, I'm not sure when the right time is to move. But we're both going to need to get back to our normal lives soon, preparing for the arrival of our baby at our respective houses.

First though, I need to find my own place, and I'm dreading it more than I ever thought possible.

I assumed living with Logan would be stifling, but it has been anything but. We actually live together quite well. Better than I anticipated. He's incredibly attentive and caring, making sure I have everything I need, from three meals a day to plenty of my favorite snacks. He builds fires and keeps the cabin the perfect temperature. He doesn't seem to care that I keep stealing his clothes either, but they're just better than my own. I sleep more soundly, more comfortably when I'm in his joggers and oversized T-shirts. I may never be able to go back to pajamas.

Do you think he'd miss a few pairs of sweats and some shirts when I move to my own place?

However well it's going here, there's also one big problem. One he's not aware of.

I'm horny as hell.

I blame the pregnancy but him a little too. He walks around in well-worn jeans and a long-sleeved Johnson Hardware T-shirt, sometimes with a hoodie over the top of it, and at night, it's always joggers. When I'm really lucky, he's shirtless—usually after his shower and when he's getting ready for bed. Those are the nights I have to take care of business myself, if you know what I mean. With images of a shirtless Logan, his sweats hanging dangerously low on his hips and the outline of his magnificent cock bulging through the material, I have to double-click my own mouse.

Usually twice.

Even then, I wake in the morning with the same achy feeling washing over me I dealt with the day before. It's a nonstop cycle, one I can't seem to...quench.

It's a chilly Sunday morning; the day before my sixteen-week checkup. The late October sky is cloudy, the winds howling outside the protective walls of the cabin. The small bathroom is filled with steam and the scent of Logan's bodywash. I've been using it ever since we started staying here, because I'm a psycho like that and can't get enough of the smell. It's like a pregnancy craving, except worse, because I can't get close enough to the scent, and considering it's on my own skin, that's saying something. But my oversensitive lady bits know it's not the same as smelling it from his skin as it is my own.

I'm hopeless.

And desperate.

I slip my bra and panties on before reaching for my brush. Just as I start to run it through my hair, I take in my appearance in the mirror.

That's when I see it.

"Holy shit," I mutter, my eyes dropping down to my stomach. There is the slightest bump protruding from my body, one that I swear wasn't there yesterday. It's like it just...popped out. "Oh my God, Logan!" I holler, reaching for the doorknob and taking off out of the bathroom. "Logan!"

He comes flying around the corner from the kitchen, worry and fear written all over his handsome face. "What? What's wrong?" he asks when he reaches me.

"Look," I whisper, placing my hands on the swell of my baby.

"Holy shit," he mutters. A smile instantly spreads across his lips as he gazes down at my stomach. "May I?"

I nod, my throat thick and dry with emotion.

He seems somewhat hesitant, then places both of his warm hands on my skin. He strokes my belly with his fingers as a chuckle slides from his lips. "My baby."

I blink rapidly, trying to keep the tears at bay, but there's something so special about this moment. "Can you believe it? It's like it just popped out overnight."

He glances up at me, but keeps his hands on my belly. "Some of the sites I read said those exact words. It's like it just...pops."

We stand there, both smiling at each other. This is an incredible moment, and I'm so glad he was here to share it. "I still can't believe you read all those online pregnancy sites."

He shrugs, refusing to get embarrassed. "I want to know what's going on with you and the baby every step of the way."

All I can do is grin at his thoughtfulness.

Something dark passes through his eyes as the hum of awareness races through my veins. It's as if we both realize at the same moment I'm standing here, wearing only my bra and panties. My nipples harden as the familiar ache of need crashes into my entire body like a tornado. It's reckless and unrestrained, just like a force of nature hell-bent on destroying everything in its path.

He clears his throat before his eyes slowly drop to my near-naked body. I can feel my panties growing damp, and maybe in another time, it would be enough to embarrass me. But not now. Not today. All it does is cause my desire to rage on.

"Hallie." That one word sounds like a plea.

My body is humming, my brain not fully processing what's about to happen. I step forward, pressing my breasts to his chest as my hand glides around to his back. "Yes?"

"I'm not...this isn't...we shouldn't." The tone of his words doesn't match what he actually says.

"No, I think we should, and do you know why?"

Logan's eyes are dilated as he stands board-straight in front of me. "Why?"

I exhale and lift my chin. "I have a problem, Logan. A big one, and you said you'd always be there to help me if I needed it."

His Adam's apple bobs. "I did say that. What's your problem?"

Deciding not to beat around the bush, I tell him my truth. "I need orgasms. Lots and lots of orgasms. The ones I'm giving myself aren't helping. I need...you."

His groan sounds pained as he closes his eyes and shakes his head. "Hallie," he mumbles, as if not wanting to hear it.

"I'm serious. I need sex, Logan. Desperately. I'm so keyed up, I might actually explode," I insist.

He chuckles and meets my gaze once more. I also notice he moves his right hand and places it at my lower back, holding me against him. His cock is hard, rigid, and ready, and I pray that's a sign of what's to come.

Or who's to come...

"I'm not sure that's a can of worms we should open, Hal." There's regret in his words, and it makes my heart beat a lot faster.

"It would be, like, you performing a service. A very vital, important one." I hope I don't sound too desperate, even though I am. "A dick service, if you will."

He throws his head back and laughs. "I thought those services were illegal in Wisconsin."

I shrug my shoulders and place my hands on his chest. "It's only illegal if money is exchanged. I don't plan to pay you."

"I don't get paid?" He feigns shock.

Leaning forward, I whisper, "You get to come, Logan. A lot." And because I'm leaning against his body, I feel his cock twitch against my stomach.

If there was any fight left in him, it evaporates in this moment. He reaches for my hand and practically drags me to the master bedroom. The moment we cross the threshold, he's spinning me around and pinning me to the wall. His mouth descends in a bruising kiss, one that speaks of good things to come. His fingers thread into my hair as mine reach for the button on his jeans. Reaching into his pants, I cup his erection and give it a gentle squeeze.

"Fuck," he mutters, ripping his mouth from mine and gasping for air.

"Yes, exactly."

He chuckles, taking a step back. "Let me get a look at you."

I whine. Yes, whine. "Looking? I like your first suggestion better."

Smiling widely, he insists, "We'll get to that very quickly, Cupcake. First, I want to do something I've been dying to do since your birthday."

Logan drops to his knees in front of me, reaches up, and grabs the waist of my panties. With little finesse, he pulls them down and helps me step out of them. "My God, you're fucking beautiful," he says, reaching around and grabbing my ass in his hands. "Your ass is a fucking work of art."

A small bubble of laughter slides from my throat. "Sure, now you like it."

He pauses and glances up, confusion written all over his face. "When have I not liked it?"

"Never mind," I reply, hoping to get right back to business.

"No, tell me. What's wrong?"

I huff out a deep breath, hating I even responded the way I did. "It's nothing. Just something you said back in high school."

Now he's super confused. "What'd I say?"

I don't want to tell him. I don't want to kill the mood, and not just because I'm horny as hell. "It doesn't matter," I whisper, suddenly feeling vulnerable.

His eyes are intense as he insists, "Yes, it does. Tell me."

I exhale once more and close my eyes. "You were with your friends, and everyone was talking about girls. You said I was pretty, but my ass needed its own zip code. It's fine, Logan. I've come to terms with the fact I'm not built like other girls, and—"

"Stop." His voice is firm. "It's not okay, Hallie. I'm so sorry. I don't remember saying that, but if you say I did, I believe you." He shakes his head and closes his eyes for a moment, pain lacing those beautiful orbs. "I was a stupid kid. That's the only excuse I have. And stupid is the right word, because if adult Logan could go back and kick teenager Logan's ass, he would. Not just because he was an asshole for saying it—because he was! But simply because your ass is fucking amazing, and I'm not just saying that because of the dick thing I said when I was younger. I'm dead serious." He grips my ass a bit firmer and licks his lips as he gazes at my pussy. "Your body is amazing, Hallie. Don't ever doubt that. I'm sorry I was a dick in high school, but you have to know I think you are the most incredible woman I've ever met. You're beautiful, inside and out."

I swallow over the sudden lump in my throat.

"This body is growing life. *My* baby."

Before I can reply, he leans forward and presses his mouth to the swell of my abdomen. It's soft and gentle and tells me exactly what kind of father he's going to be. The kind every child wishes they had. How lucky is this baby?

When he looks up at me, there's a mixture of awe and lust in his eyes. And the moment he mutters, "Mine," I almost come on the spot.

Instead, I nod in agreement.

Part of me feels like he's talking about more than just the baby...

Then, he pushes my legs apart and leans in, swiping his tongue between my wet folds. A loud moan fills the entire room and my legs threaten to buckle. "Come 'ere," he says, leading me to the bed. "Can't have you falling."

When I'm lying on the crumpled bedding, he slips his body between my legs and positions his face over me. He lowers his mouth and feasts. His tongue flicks over my clit, licks me all over, and slides into my pussy. I can tell this is going to be fast, the buildup of an orgasm growing by the second.

I reach down and slip my fingers into his hair, hanging on tight. My nails dig as my hips rock against his face, chasing the orgasm he's promising. It hits quickly and almost out of nowhere. I didn't even have time to prepare. I come hard, my body convulsing and shaking as waves of euphoria wash over me.

When I'm finally able to open my eyes, the first thing I see is his cocky grin licking juices off his lips. "All good now?"

"Hell no. That barely took the edge off," I tell him, sitting up and reaching for his shirt. When I give it a yank, he falls down on top of me, carefully holding his weight off me.

"So, you need more, huh?"

I nod, pushing his shirt up and over his head. When it's gone, I grapple for the waist of his jeans, trying to shimmy those around his hips.

"Hold on," he says, climbing off me and removing his pants. Since he's not wearing shoes, it doesn't take long to get pants, socks, and boxers off. I'm eternally grateful for his swiftness, but also a little sad the strip show is over.

Just as he starts to climb back on the bed, he pauses. "Shit, I don't have any condoms with me." He runs his hand through his hair.

I blink at him in confusion. "I don't think I can get pregnant again."

He cracks a smile and brushes wet hair off my forehead. "I meant to protect you."

"Yeah, but…" I swallow, zeroing in on his erection, which is jutting straight out from his body.

He snaps in front of my face. "Focus, Cupcake."

"I am. On what I want."

He grins and bends down. "I just thought I should protect us both from…well, everything."

"I haven't been with anyone else. Have you?" I ask, panicking a little at the idea of him sleeping around these last few months. Not that it wouldn't have been within his right—he is single after all—but the idea sits like a lead brick in my stomach, you know? And I'm not diving into the why right now.

"No." His reply is instant. "I haven't been with anyone since you, and it was a while before that, and I always used protection."

I nod. "All right, then I think we're safe. And it's not like we haven't done it without a condom before."

He smiles. "Right." Then, he slides a hand between my back and the bed and flips open the clasp of my bra. "Your tits were amazing before," he says, sliding the straps of my bra off my shoulders, "but now, they're a fucking work of art." Bending down, he sucks one nipple into his mouth, making me gasp. He cups one in his hand and runs his tongue around the nipple of the other. "So full and ripe, like the rest of your body."

I'm practically panting with need. Reaching out, I wrap my hands around his cock and stroke from root to tip. A string of curse words falls from his lips. "You keep doing that and this'll be over before I even slide inside your pussy. Remember how you said you've been taking care of your issue yourself? Well, so have I, darling, and it barely takes the edge off."

My core clenches, and my brain conjures up images of him in the shower, stroking himself to orgasm. "So, we've both been taking care of our own needs, while the other was across the hall doing the same? Isn't that sad?" I question as he guides himself to my entrance.

"A little sad, yes," he states, pressing the head of his cock inside my body.

I shift my hips, taking him a little deeper. "I have a proposition for you."

"Another one?" he asks, stopping to look down at me.

"Yes. For as long as we're here, living together, we can help each other out."

He gives me a slow, sexy smile. "With orgasms."

I nod.

His brown eyes sparkle as he thrusts, filling me completely. I cry out as the pleasure holds, refusing to let go. "Deal."

My body hums to life as he moves in and out. His pace is swift, his strokes fluid, and by the looks of the tension lines around his eyes and forehead, he's close already. Good thing I am too, because if he keeps this up much longer, I'm going to come again in a very short amount of time.

But that's one of the things about Logan. He's been able to draw any number of orgasms out of me with very little trying. Our bodies just work together, as if they were made for each other.

Holding himself up, he reaches down and pinches my nipples, driving me closer to the edge. My body tightens. I can feel every stroke of his cock within me, and I feel him so deeply, I don't know where he ends and I begin. The invisible cord between us starts to tense as his hips pick up speed. He pistons forward, rocking his hips and hitting that magical place deep within me.

I cry out, and my nails bite into his flesh. "Oh God, I'm coming," I tell him as my release sweeps in like waves on the shore. Over and over, they pound, just as Logan does.

Closing my eyes, I ride the waves of bliss until I feel him go still above me. "Christ," he mutters as his own orgasm hits.

The rocking of his hips continues, and before I even realize what's happening, he's drawing a third one from me. I mumble something that might not be actual words as the smaller release slowly ebbs.

When he finally lowers himself, he's careful not to apply the weight of his body to mine. "We're going to do that again soon, right?"

"That's the deal," I murmur, running my fingers across his sweaty back.

"Yep, that's the deal."

And what a deal it is.

Problem is, I may not actually want to look for my own place to live now. I might find every excuse in the book to stay, as long as those orgasms keep coming, and if the ones that follow are anything like these, I'm never going to want to leave.

Who knows, maybe he won't notice I've never left.

We can just stay here, in his cabin, in our own sex-fueled bubble.

That's what dreams are made of.

He turns onto his side, taking me with him, and holds me against his body. The strong beating of his heart echoes through me, and as his fingers dance across my skin, I'm lulled into a deep sleep. The last thing I remember is the feel of our bodies pressed together and the sweet hum of relief sweeping through my veins.

Best. Nap. Ever.

CHAPTER
Twenty Two

LOGAN

The following Sunday, we're all gathered at Blair's dad's house. Today is a combination couple's bridal shower and gender reveal with all their closest family and friends. Even though the couple requested no gifts, Hallie, TD, Ellie, and a few others and I went together and bought the whole house air purifier system Blair has had her eye on the last several months. It wasn't nearly as expensive as it should have been, considering I was able to purchase it at cost through my business. All Blair and Gabe have to do is arrange to have it installed.

"Can I get you something to drink?" Blair's little sister, Aggie, asks, walking around and being the perfect hostess.

"No, I'm good, but thank you," I tell the cute little eight-year-old. Despite having a different mom than Blair, they share the same father. The bond the two of them have built over the last few years has been pretty cool to watch. Blair adores Aggie, and you can tell the feeling is mutual. The little girl moves on, asking everyone else in the large room.

"She is the cutest," Hallie says to me, her eyes bright with happiness as she watches the young girl do a twirl in her black and pink sparkly dress, having to push her glasses back up on her nose after her spin.

"She is," I confirm.

"You two should be finding out what you're having soon, right?" Ellie asks, moving over to the seat beside Hallie.

"Actually, we want to be surprised."

Ellie's eyes go wide. "Really? I'd have to know." She looks at me. "The fact you wanted to be surprised surprises me a little. You're always so organized."

"I was bullied into it," I quip, flashing a smile.

"Shut up," Hallie retorts, elbowing me in the side, causing us both to laugh.

Ellie just stares at us, a knowing grin on her face. "Interesting."

Before either of us can ask more about her statement, Blair's stepmom, Patience, steps into the middle of the room. "May I have your attention, please? Frank and I wanted to welcome you all to our home this afternoon as we celebrate Blair and Gabe. I see no one honored the bride and groom's wishes for no gifts," she says, referring to the pile of gift bags and wrapped boxes over by the windows.

"And I know everyone is anxious to have them open their gifts, but there's a looming question out there I think everyone is even more curious about. Boy or girl?" she asks, practically bouncing up and down with excitement.

Blair's mom walks into the room carrying a large black balloon. On it are the words "Boy or Girl?" It's great to see both of Blair's parents in the same room again. For so many years, there was no communication between them, the anger from a nasty divorce spilling over into the relationship of father and daughter. But over the last year or so, Donna has put aside her anger over her ex-husband's affair with his young nurse nearly twenty years ago and has been able to forge a civil relationship with both Frank and Patience.

Of course, having reconnected with a man she dated years ago might have helped too. This isn't the first time John has come with Donna to Pine Village, and despite the way Donna and Frank's marriage ended all those years ago, everyone seems to have finally found peace and is moving forward.

"When Blair had her ultrasound a few weeks ago, the results were sent to Donna in Merrillville, who cooked up the big reveal for today. Blair, Gabe, will you both come up to the front, please?" Patience states.

When the happy couple moves to the front and center of the room, they're both wearing matching smiles. Gabe has Blair's hand tucked tightly in his and doesn't pass up the opportunity to place his other hand securely on her stomach. Blair's a few weeks farther along than Hallie, so her belly is rounder already. I can also tell she's carrying a bit differently, and according to the internet, that could mean they're having different sexes.

"Take this, Blair." Patience hands over a large safety pin. "On the count of three, pop the balloon."

Aggie starts jumping up and down, the excitement felt through the entire room. "Please be a girl, please be a girl."

Everyone chuckles as Blair glances up at Gabe. When he nods, after a brief silence communication, Blair says, "Come on up here, Aggie. We need your help popping this balloon."

Her little sister moves so quickly she almost stumbles. I find myself moving to the edge of my seat as we wait to find out if they're having a boy or a girl. Aggie takes her position right between Gabe and Blair, and together, the three of them hold the pin.

"Three...Two...One..."

They thrust the pin up into the black balloon and watch as pink confetti rains down on them. "Yay!" Aggie hollers, bouncing up and down and twirling in the confetti. "I knew it!"

Gabe takes the pin in one hand and his fiancée in the other and draws her into his arms. He kisses her with a passion that has me turning my head to avert my eyes. When I do, they land on Hallie, who seems incredibly happy for her best friend and brother. There are tears in her eyes as she looks on.

I want to take her in my arms. I want to kiss her the way Gabe kisses Blair. But I don't know what this is. We're getting along so well, and ever since last Sunday when she made me an offer I couldn't refuse, the sex has been out of this world. We've shared a bed every night since, some nights content to just falling asleep in each other's arms and others spent ravishing our naked bodies. Either way, I've enjoyed the hell out of them, wishing there were an unlimited amount of them on the horizon. But the truth is, I have no idea what our future has in store, so I'll just continue to take it day by day and see how this plays out.

She must feel my eyes on her and turns. The smile on her lips remains as she stares back at me. I reach for her hand, entwining our fingers, and give hers a gentle squeeze in silent support. We sit here, watching the group as all the grandparents celebrate the news of welcoming their first grandchild—a granddaughter—on both sides.

"No one seems to care there's a million pink confetti particles spread all over the floor," Hallie mutters softly.

I shrug, watching as Aggie continues to play with the pink mess. "It's fun."

"Fun until you have to clean it," she mumbles. "But I do see the appeal. If we did that, we'd just do it outside."

"There's still time," I inform her, bumping her shoulder with mine.

"Nope. I've dug my toes in now. No reveal. We will be surprised."

I nod. "I can't wait for the moment we look down and see our son or daughter for the first time. To watch you fight like the warrior you are to bring him or her into the world. That's when we'll find out. The ultimate surprise."

Her ocean blue eyes turn misty. "See? I was right."

I scoff and blow out a breath. "I don't know about that. I think waiting to find out what we're having was my idea."

As expected, her eyes narrow as a look of pure annoyance takes over her face. "What? It was my idea."

"I mean, I don't want to fight about it. Your idea, my idea, it's all the same."

She watches me before nodding. She shifts in her seat and turns her attention to her brother and best friend, who are gearing up to open their shower gifts. "Except it was my idea."

"Whatever you say, idea thief."

That's when I get whacked on the arm. A bubble of laughter slides from my mouth as I look her way. She's grinning too, and it takes everything I have not to pull her into my arms and kiss her. In fact, I'm pretty sure I've never wanted to kiss someone more than I want to kiss her, and the fact I shouldn't—mostly because we haven't outlined our relationship status or lack thereof to anyone—makes me want to do it that much more.

All I know is when we're alone later, I'm definitely laying one on her. I'm going to kiss her with an entire day's worth of pent-up frustration, and even then, it won't be enough.

It may never be enough.

On a Wednesday in mid-November, the bell sounds over the door, but since I'm in the middle of mixing paint, I keep my eyes focused on the task at hand.

"There's my favorite grandson."

I grin. "I'm your only grandson," I tell Gram, glancing up quickly before reaching for the paint can lid and hammering it back into place. Once the gallon is placed in the shaker, I give her my full attention. "To what do I owe this wonderful visit?"

"Well, I was in the neighborhood and wanted to drop this off to you," she says, holding out a small white bag with green tissue paper sticking out of the top.

"I'll be finished here in a few minutes. Wanna go wait in my office?" I suggest, hoping she takes my suggestion and goes to have a seat.

"I'm fine here. I'm not old," she counters, leaning against the shelving unit holding the different varieties of paint.

"No one said you were old," I reply, winking at Victor Houston, who is waiting for the paint.

"That's good. I'd have to set them straight," Gram retorts, making Victor smile.

I finish mixing the paint before pulling it from the machine and popping off the lid once more. Once we confirm it's the correct color, I replace the lid and carry the gallon to the front counter. "Need a stir stick?"

"Nope, still got the last one," Victor replies, pulling his credit card from his wallet.

I ring him up and send him on his way to finish their bathroom project. When the bell chimes again, I lean on the counter and give Gram my full attention. "What's up?"

She places the bag on the counter and smiles. "I know you don't know what you're having yet, but I saw this and had to get it."

"I can wait to open it when I get home," I reply, feeling bad to open a gift without Hallie.

"You will do no such thing. She'll have lots of gifts to open at her shower. This one is for you."

I pull the green cloth from the bag and open it up. I instantly laugh when I read what the onesie says. Across the front says "You got this, Daddy" with arrows pointing to indicate the two arm holes, neck hole, holes for both legs, and one for the snaps. "You have a lot of faith in me."

She grins widely. "I'm teasing, but it was too cute to pass up. And it's green, since you don't know the sex of the baby."

"We're going to wait until the birth," I confirm, slipping the onesie back into the bag.

"Good. It's the best kind of surprise. You know, when I had your father, we didn't have all this fancy technology to help determine the sex of the baby."

"That was back when they used horse-drawn carriages for transportation, right?"

"You shit," she barks out, laughing at my comment. "You better behave."

I chuckle. "Sorry, couldn't resist."

"What are you doing for dinner? I'm making lasagna. You can bring that pretty roommate of yours over after work. There's more than enough."

"I don't think we have plans. We can do that."

"Good. Dinner's at six but come a little early. You're setting the table."

And with that, she turns and shuffles out of the store, off to her next adventure and leaving me to get back to it.

I grab my phone and fire off a quick message.

Me: Dinner at Gram's house at 6.

Hallie: Should we bring something?

Me: Not necessary. If I know Gram, she'll have everything.

Hallie: Okay. See you soon.

Smiling, I put my phone away and get back to work.

"See you tomorrow, Logan," Chip hollers as I carry the register drawer to the safe, deposit bag under my arm.

"Have a good night, Chip," I reply.

He exits out the back door and will make sure the lumberyard is locked up for the evening, with the gates secured and the lighting off. I type in the code for the safe and slip the drawer inside. I set the deposit bag on the shelf with it, deciding to just run it to the bank in the morning. Tonight, I just want to get to Hallie and go visit Gram.

Just before I go to shut the door, something catches my eye. The envelopes on the top shelf are moved and askew. Weird, since I haven't needed to check the legal documentation and the extra cash I keep on hand for emergencies in a few years, I straighten them up and finish closing the door, making sure it's locked.

Finally, I head out, flipping light switches as I go. Once the security system is set, I exit the building, locking the doors and heading for my truck. There's a little extra spring in my step as I walk, anxious to get to the cabin to see Hallie.

Before I reach my truck, lights from a vehicle pull into the parking lot. I turn and spot the red cherries on top of the SUV, letting me know it's TD.

He pulls up beside me and rolls down his window. "Headed home?"

"To the cabin to grab Hallie. We're going to Gram's for dinner."

He stares back at me, the start of a knowing smirk teasing the corner of his mouth. "Interesting."

"What is?"

"The fact you fell in love with her. That's interesting, considering a handful of months ago, you both couldn't be in the same place without biting each other's heads off."

His statement catches me off guard. "I'm not in love with her."

This time, he grins from ear to ear. "You sure about that?"

I open my mouth to argue, but nothing comes out.

"Not that my opinion matters, but I really like you two together. She's a hell of a lot friendlier than your ex-wife, and she actually makes you happy."

My mind races, spins like a top.

Am I in love with Hallie?

I respect the hell out of her. She's smart and beautiful and has a heart of gold. She has this natural ability to make me laugh, even if she's pushing my buttons. She's nurturing, caring, and is going to be an amazing mother to our son or daughter. It's one of the things I'm most excited about. Not only meeting the little life we created but seeing her hold the baby in her arms and nursing our baby on her breasts. These are the images I fantasize about now, the ones that keep me company throughout the day when she's not near.

Is that love?

Hell if I know, but I guess it could be.

I thought I was in love once before, but that felt completely different than this. With Shay, it was wild, and I learned after we separated it was more lust mixed with manipulation. Shay could manipulate me into doing anything she wanted from day one, but it got worse after my dad died. I was lost, desperate to find something to heal the ache in my chest. She didn't really seem too interested in helping with that, and definitely didn't want to entertain my idea of having a baby.

What I feel for Hallie is night and day different than with Shay, and if this is love, I'd be all right with it.

"How's Ellie?" I ask, looking to change the subject.

An instant, natural smile spreads across his lips. "Perfect. Best decision I ever made, and do you know why? Because she makes me happy, and every day is better than the one before. It's not all wine and roses all the time, but we talk and compromise. We make it work because any other way isn't an option. I'd do anything to see her smile, because her happiness means everything to me. She's the other half of my soul."

I absorb his words, focusing on the part about her happiness meaning everything to him. Why? Because I feel the exact same way.

Is that love?

I'm pretty sure it is.

"I gotta go," I tell TD, tapping his door as I push away. "Tell El I said hello."

"Will do," he replies, throwing his SUV into gear. "Have a safe drive."

"You too. Be careful out there," I tell my closest friend as I slide into my truck and turn over the engine.

I press a little harder on the gas, determined to get to Hallie. I don't know what I'm going to do about my revelation, but I know I need to see her. Hold her in my arms. Kiss her. Make love to her. I may not be ready to tell her how I feel, but that doesn't mean I can't show her.

If I had it my way, I'd spend the rest of my life doing just that.

Now, I just have to figure out how to say the words I wasn't sure I'd ever be able to say again.

And pray she doesn't throw them back in my face.

CHAPTER Twenty Three

Hallie

He's different.

All through dinner with Bernice, he seemed...attentive. Even more so than usual, which is a lot by normal standards, but tonight it's incredibly noticeable. Usually, when we're around other people, he keeps his hands somewhat to himself, but not tonight. He keeps touching me, touching my belly. Little caresses that send my blood swooshing and prickles of awareness peppering my entire body.

By the time we're ready to leave, I'm so worked up I'm not sure we'll even make it back to the cabin. Hell, I'm not sure we'll make it out of Bernice's driveway.

"Oh, Logan, will you be a dear and go check the light bulb in my bedroom? It seems dimmer and might need changed," Bernice says before we're able to make it to the front door.

"Of course," Logan replies, releasing his hold on my hand and taking off down the hallway.

Bernice lives in a tiny one-bedroom condo in a small area with other older individuals. She's able to still remain independent, but with the added bonus of not having to worry about mowing a lawn or shoveling snow. Plus, she's close to the community center where she plays bingo often.

"Go ahead and have a seat. He'll be a few minutes," Bernice announces, pointing at the couch.

The moment I take a seat on the floral sofa, she takes the place directly beside me. "Thank you, again, for dinner. It was amazing," I tell her, placing my hand on my stomach.

"You're most welcome, dear. You're always welcome here."

I give her a small smile. "Thanks."

"You two make the most beautiful couple. I'm so happy you're together."

"Oh, we're not...you know, together," I stammer, having a hard time getting the right words out.

She gives me a curious look. "Why?"

I open my mouth but close it just as quickly. "Umm," I start, clearing my throat, "Well, we've never really discussed it." I feel a little embarrassed admitting that.

"Again, why?"

"Gram," Logan says before walking around the corner. He narrows his eyes at the older woman sitting beside me and places his hands on his hips. "The light bulb is gone, Gram. Gone. That's not dim. That's dark. How did the light bulb get removed?"

"Oh," she replies with a chuckle. "I almost forgot to tell you. I decided to check it out so you didn't have to come all the way over here to change a silly light bulb."

Logan exhales. "You got on a stepladder?"

"Well, no. You took my stepladder, remember?"

"Yes, because you kept using it."

"So, I didn't have one."

He closes his eyes for a moment. "How did you take the light bulb out, Gram?"

"I used one of the kitchen chairs."

"Gram!" he argues, throwing his hands in the air. "Those move."

"Which made it very tricky when I was climbing on it to take the light bulb out of the socket," she reasons.

He grumbles a few things I can't understand, and I have to bite my lip to keep from laughing. Clearly, she doesn't need to be climbing on anything, let alone a dining room chair that spins from side to side.

"Could you *not* do that, please? Never again. I'll come change your light bulbs."

"You've just been so busy with Hallie and the baby."

"He's never too busy for you," I step in, hoping to help calm the situation before Logan blows the blood vessel beside his eye. "Just call, and we'll come help. Even though I'm sure you're perfectly capable of climbing a ladder and changing your own light bulb, why not take advantage of your young, muscular grandson?"

Bernice leans in and places her warm, wrinkled hand against my cheek. "You're the sweetest, dear. Thank you."

Logan huffs a long sigh. "I'll go get the new bulb," he mumbles.

When he returns to the bedroom, Bernice turns her attention back to me. "Your relationship with my grandson isn't mine to meddle in, I know, but I've been watching you two for so long. There's something there."

"We're just having a baby," I reply unnecessarily, as if she wasn't aware of that point.

Smiling, she reaches down and squeezes my hand. "And I know you're both very excited about that. We all are. But from the outside looking in, there appears to be more than *just having a baby*," she says, using air quotes for the last four words.

Again, I open my mouth, but nothing comes out.

"I'm not trying to make you uncomfortable, dear. I just wanted to tell you what I see from where I stand, because sometimes, when you're close to it, the picture may not be as clear for you."

"All right, Gram, you're all set," Logan announces as he walks back into the living room. "Your room won't be so dim anymore," he adds with the shake of his head.

"Thank you, Logan," Bernice replies, standing up and walking toward him for a hug. "I appreciate your assistance."

He squeezes her extra hard and long. "You're welcome." Then, he looks over at me. "Ready?"

I nod, standing up and making my way to Bernice. I give her a hug too, reveling in the comfort she offers. "Thank you, again, for your hospitality."

"Please come back soon," she tells me as she holds my gaze and places her hands on my cheeks. Then, she lowers her hands to my belly. "Take care of this little angel."

"I will," I assure her.

Bernice turns back to her grandson and adds, "You take care of both of them."

"I will, Gram."

"All right, well, you two better get going. It's getting late. I want you home before the hooligans decide to run amuck through the streets," she insists.

Logan snorts. "You just want us to leave because *Night Court* is getting ready to start."

Bernice fans her face with her right hand as she whispers, "That John Larroquette is such a looker."

I giggle, resulting in Logan narrowing his eyes at me. "I agree. He's a silver fox."

She leans in and whispers, "Have you seen that Jeffrey Dean Morgan? I've become a huge fan of *The Walking Dead* lately. I'd let zombies chase me just to be saved by that man."

"Gram," Logan grumbles, shaking his head. To me, he points and states, "Stop encouraging her."

"Sorry," I say with a giggle. "We better get going before the hooligans are out for the night."

Logan rolls his eyes. "Ross Moore is almost thirty with three kids. I'm pretty sure he's not sneaking around, terrorizing your rose gardens again."

"That young man is a menace. He cut all my prize roses," Bernice bellows, crossing her frail arms over her chest.

"He was seventeen, and I believe he took them to his mother, who was in the hospital."

"Still. I had to remove my horticulture entry from the county fair. I was a shoo-in."

Smiling, Logan steps forward and kisses his grandma's cheek. "Good thing it's November, and not gardening season."

"Good thing," she replies, shaking her head. "Now, go. John Larroquette is waiting."

As we push through the front door, the cold air slaps me across the face. Winter is knocking on the door, and despite living my entire life in Wisconsin, I'm not ready. The older I get, the more I really dislike the cold months. Of course, the fireplace at the cabin has been pretty amazing these last several weeks.

Perhaps my next home should have a fireplace.

"Night, Gram. Lock up."

"Yeah, yeah, I will," she replies as she waves before closing the door and engaging the lock.

Logan takes my hand and leads me to his truck. As I climb inside the cab, I look his way and that familiar buzz of awareness and desire sparks to life. I shift in my seat, the ache between my legs intensifying once more, just from a look. The moment is drawn out, the air growing heavy around us. It's as if he knows exactly what I'm thinking about, maybe because he feels it too.

He leans in and presses his lips to my own in a chaste kiss. "Buckle up."

With a frustrated sigh, I do as instructed. He closes my door and walks around to the driver's door, climbing inside. I want to scream in irritation. I'm wound tight and ready to burst. I'm certain he knows, yet he didn't do any of the things I had hoped. You know, kiss me like his life depended on it or throw me in the back seat and ravish me from head to toe.

We drive to the cabin in silence, and the moment we stop, I have my seat belt released and the door open. Logan hurries to catch up to me, and even though I have a key, I wait for him to use his. By the time I would have dug in my purse and found the right one, he would have the door open and I'd be inside.

When I cross the threshold, I toe off my shoes and leave them by the door. I move into the kitchen and place my purse on the table. My intention is to go straight to bed—and most likely take care of my little problem between my legs.

"Are you mad at me?"

"Yes," I state, crossing my arms and spinning to face him.

"Why?" he asks, leaning against the doorjamb.

"Because I..." I swallow over the sudden lump in my throat. I have no idea why I'm so emotional all of a sudden. Maybe because of what Bernice had to say while Logan was changing her light bulb. Add in a rush of sexual frustration, and I can't seem to think straight. Clearing my throat, I lift my chin and reply, "I thought you were going to kiss me earlier."

He pushes off the doorjamb and slowly makes his way toward me. "I did kiss you."

My mouth goes dry as his brown eyes turn molten.

"Was that not the kinda kiss you wanted?"

I shake my head.

When he's standing directly in front of me, he whispers, "How did you want me to kiss you?"

"Like you meant it."

Logan slides his fingers into my hair and gently pulls me against his body. He tilts my head to the side and brushes his lips across mine. He does this twice before firmly pressing his mouth to my own. His tongue slips out, sliding along the seam of my mouth and coaxing it open. Once I grant him access, his tongue delves inside, tasting and savoring. He never hurries, despite me grinding myself against him in desperation.

"I want to take you to bed," he whispers, grazing his lips across my cheek and down my neck.

"That's a given."

He pulls back and holds my gaze. I'm not sure what it is, but something passes in the depths of those dark chocolate eyes. Before I can ask about it, he takes my hand and slowly leads me out of the kitchen, flipping off the light as we go.

When we reach the bedroom, he stops me in the middle of the room. Carefully, he starts to undress me. With each item of clothing he removes, he places kisses somewhere on the exposed skin. He spends a little extra time showering my belly with love. There's nothing sexier than a man who worships a baby belly.

Finally naked, he quickly removes his own clothing and guides me to the bed. His mouth claims mine once more as he covers my body with his. My legs instantly wrap around his hips, which opens me up perfectly for him. With a kiss that could make me forget my name, he shifts his lower body and presses inside me. One long, fluid motion, and he's seated fully.

We groan together without breaking the kiss. My hips start to rock to a silent rhythm, as his body does the same. My hands sweep across his back before settling in his hair. My nails bite into his scalp, causing a sigh and moan to slip from his mouth. Logan adjusts his position so he's on his right elbow and slides his hand from my side to my stomach to my breasts.

We're both seeking pleasure in the other but doing everything we can to give it too.

My release comes fast and hard and I'm not prepared for it. I don't want this to end. I want to keep going, to keep pushing toward the release without toppling over the edge. But now that it's within my grasp, I can't stop it. I explode with so much force, I swear my soul leaves my body.

And he's right there with me.

He claims my mouth once more with his and comes, mimicking the movements of his lower half with his tongue. No words are spoken. We just feel. And what I feel is love. For him. For this life we're creating.

The one that wasn't mine to begin with.

A single tear slides from my eye, and he brushes it away. "Don't cry, Hallie," he whispers, brushing his mouth across mine again. It's as if he can't stop kissing me.

Not that I want him to.

When the tremors of release subside, he rolls us both to our sides and curls me against his body. He's warm and comfortable, and exactly where I want to be. In his arms. Surrounded by his strength and goodness.

This is the exact moment I realize I fell in love. I wasn't expecting it—I definitely wasn't looking for it with him—but it happened. When I least expected it, my heart was stolen by the one man who drives me crazy.

Now what? What am I supposed to do?

Confess? Chances are he doesn't feel the same. We both agreed to sex while we were staying together, but that's as far as it went. There were no promises for the future outside of co-parenting our baby, no declarations of happily ever after. We were never going to be a couple.

It's sex, plain and simple.

Despite feeling a hell of a lot like more.

The sooner I come to terms with the truth, the better off I'll be.

So even though my heart feels like it's breaking, I burrow into his chest deeper and hold on tighter, because if this is as far as it goes, I'm going to take it while I can. I'm going to love Logan, probably well after our living arrangement comes to an end and I'm alone once more. Only then, I'll have to continually see him. A lot. It will be both heaven and hell.

All because I fell in love when I wasn't supposed to.

Just like every time before.

I fall for the wrong guy and end up getting hurt.

"Hey," I greet Blair as I join her for lunch the following Wednesday at the local pizza joint.

"I'm so glad you texted. I was wanting to see if you were interested in a shopping trip soon. I want to go to Hudson and hit a few stores for last minute wedding stuff. Did you get your dress?"

"Yes, it arrived in the mail the other day," I tell her. "It fits now, but something tells me it'll be another story in a month."

Blair and Gabe's wedding is just over four weeks away and coming fast. Between Thanksgiving next week, the holiday season, Christmas and a wedding, the days are flying by and the to-do list is growing.

"I can't wait to see it," she replies with an eager grin.

"Anything from TD and Ellie?" I ask, hoping she might have the inside scoop on their push to have a baby.

"No, nothing," she replies, understanding what I was meaning. "I hate that we're both pregnant and she's not."

"Me too. I was hopeful there'd be a honeymoon baby," I reply.

"Me too. It'll happen for them. I feel it."

I hope she's right. Ellie is an amazing mother to Brody, and I know there's nothing she wants more than to have a child with TD.

"How's everything else going?" she asks, sipping her water.

"Okay. Fine. I'm looking for a new place."

She looks at me in confusion. "You are? I thought things were going well with you at Logan's."

I shrug, reaching for a napkin and tearing off the corner. "It was—is. But I can't stay with him forever," I state with a chuckle.

"Why not?"

"Because we're not together. I don't live with him."

She arches a single eyebrow upward. "Does he know that?"

"Of course he does. We've never made promises," I insist, rolling the small scrap of napkin into a long string.

"Yeah, but...things change."

"Not this. It's too complicated, and we don't need things to be more complicated, Blair. We're having a baby, yes, but that's all it will ever be. We barely get along," I reply with a humorous laugh, mostly because I realize I don't even recall when our last argument was.

"Just don't rush into anything—" she starts, but I cut her off.

"This is the perfect time to rush, Blair. It's almost the holidays. I'm starting to show. I'm going to need to start setting up a nursery and getting ready for the baby. It's the perfect time for me to find my own place, so I can get settled. Besides, I'm certain he's ready to get back to his own place. It's closer to work, and with the weather changing and the snow coming, the last thing we need is to be trapped out at the cabin. Being in town, near our jobs and necessities, is the right move."

My oldest friend just stares back at me. Her eyes are mostly curious. I don't see any irritation or shock; it's like she's trying to understand.

"What does Logan say?"

I shrug and look away.

"You haven't asked him what he wants?"

"Of course not. It's not his decision."

"No, but he should have some input, don't you think?"

Again, I don't really have an answer, at least not one she's going to like. "Listen, I need to do this. Logan and I didn't go into this arrangement with any preconceived notions. Yes, we're having a baby, but we're not in love. We'll raise the baby together, living in two separate households. That was the plan from the beginning, right?"

She nods. "I guess."

"Good. It's how it has to be. I know I said it already, but I need to do this. For me. I need to move forward."

Blair gives me a small grin laced with sadness. "Okay, let's look for a place for you to live."

CHAPTER
Twenty four

LOGAN

I finish inputting the last of the hours into the computer, letting the system do its thing. If I had to manually figure payroll deductions and taxes, I'd be in a world of trouble. No way could I do everything by hand the way my grandfather and father did before me. Thankfully, there are software programs to help with this sort of thing.

"I need more."

I take a second to finish my task before glancing up to face my ex-wife. She's wearing painted on jeans, heels, and a sweater that leaves little to the imagination. Basically, she looks like she stepped out of the changing room at a high-end boutique, not working at a small-town hardware store.

Leaning back in my chair, I run my hand through my hair. "Need more what?"

"Money. On my check."

"Not happening. You already make more than you should," I tell her, returning my hands to the keyboard and starting the process of printing the payroll.

"I need it, Logie," she whines, making the hairs on the back of my neck stand up. Before I even know what's happening, she's walking around my desk and practically throwing herself across my body.

"What for?" I ask, trying to push her off without hurting her. "Get off."

"You'll have to help with that," she sings in that overly seductive way I used to find sexy. Now, I want nothing to do with it.

Or her.

"Not happening," I state when she's off my lap. "And neither is a raise."

"But...I own the business."

"You're *part* owner of the business, but that doesn't mean you can just take whatever you want. You're already making way more than necessary, Shay."

"I don't understand you. Just write another check."

Sighing, I rub the spot at my temple that's beginning to throb. "That's not how this works. You get a salary, yes, but that doesn't mean you have access to the business's money whenever you want it. After taxes are done and the year-end complete, you'll get a portion of the profit sharing, like always." The majority of any profit goes back into the business for maintenance or upgrades, but we do contribute a small portion to Shay and me as owners, as well as part of the bonus structure for our employees.

"Well, I need it now."

"No," I tell her pointedly, returning my attention to the computer screen.

"You don't make the rules! I'm your equal," she insists, stomping her high-heeled foot like a pouty child.

"Not true," I say, sitting back in my chair once more. "I do all the clerical work and still work the floor. You show up whenever you feel like it and don't even pretend to work. We are not equal, Shay. And you're not getting more money. This business is small. We don't make millions. If you need more money, go find another job."

As expected, my insistence and use of the J-word has her in a tizzy in point-five seconds flat. The truth is, Shay hasn't worked a real job a day in her life. When she graduated high school, she jetted off to New York for her modeling career. When she slept with the wrong person and was shunned in the modeling world, she came running back to her hometown. She bounced from boyfriend to boyfriend, sucking and bleeding them dry for everything she could.

Then, she turned her sights on me.

I'm still dealing with the consequences of my stupidity all those years ago.

"I can't believe you won't give me money."

"I can't believe you're even asking. I'm not a bank," I tell her, continuing to stand my ground and refusing to let her manipulate me or the situation.

"You're the worst," she pouts, crossing her arms over her chest and tapping her foot on the floor.

"The feeling's mutual," I inform her, returning my attention to my computer so I can get this finished.

"I feel bad for Hallie."

That grabs my attention real quick. "Leave Hallie out of this."

She tightens her arms over her chest, practically forcing her boobs out of her sweater. She's about a quarter of an inch from a nip-slip, and that's the last thing I want for myself or anyone else here. "Does she know what kind of controlling man you are?"

My eyes narrow. Being controlling is the furthest from the truth. I let a lot slide throughout our short marriage, and it wasn't until I started putting my foot down and stopped letting her control the entire relationship, when things really blew up for me. But I was never an equal. It was her way or the highway, and as soon as I started standing up for myself, she was done.

"Get out," I state.

"Fine, but she'll learn how you really are sooner or later, and when she does, I'll be there telling everyone I told you so."

"The fact that you're still this delusional shouldn't be as shocking as it is. Stay away from Hallie. This has nothing to do with her, nor whatever relationship you think we have. Frankly, nothing outside of these walls is any of your business. And speaking of business, aren't you supposed to be out front, working?"

I knew that last part would really piss her off, but I don't care. I'm tired of tiptoeing around my own business because I don't want to deal with her.

"You're an asshole," she counters, narrowing her eyes at me as she flips her long, perfect blond hair over her shoulder.

"What's new?"

"I can't believe I was married to you," she argues.

"The feeling's mutual again, darlin'. Now, I have work to do, so unless you're here to talk to me about my latest offer to purchase your half of the business, I suggest you leave my office and find something to do. Although, it is probably time for a coffee break. Maybe get your nails done again this week? I bet you could use a good massage, since you do so much work around here." The sarcasm is heavy in my tone, but I don't care. I'm done with her.

She flips her hair once more and storms out of my office. Of course, I'm hopeful she actually heard what I said—especially the part about my offer to buy her out—but I know it fell on deaf ears. No way would she give up the cushy lifestyle she's living, complete with free house and business where she doesn't have to put in the work.

My latest offer to buy her out has crossed over the fifty percent mark of the business's value. My lawyer told me I'm crazy, but I have to try. I'd rather be in debt for the rest of my life but free of her than deal with her on an almost-daily basis. I'm hopeful that since she's requesting more money, for whatever reason, she'll actually consider the offer. It's very generous, and while it wouldn't exactly set her up for life, it would help ensure she doesn't have to rush out and find another job right away.

I can't help but wonder what she needs money for. She really does make a good salary for someone who barely puts in any time at the business. But when my father left us the company jointly, he thought he was setting me up for life. He knew I loved the store and would do anything to see it succeed. Little did he know, the marriage was already on the rocks and giving her half the business just made it worse.

My phone vibrates in my pocket, and I pull it out with a smile, already anticipating who is messaging me.

Hallie: Hope your day is going well. I have big news to share. I'll bring Frannie's fried chicken home for dinner, if that works for you.

The smile on my face grows. The last few days, Hallie has been craving fried things. Last night I brought my air fryer out to the cabin and made her mozzarella sticks, fried pickles, and chicken nuggets for dinner. You would have thought I made her a filet mignon meal with all the trimmings.

Me: That's fine. I'll be there after we close.

Hallie: See you then.

I reply with the thumbs-up emoji and place my phone on the desk. The last week or so has been…off. Ever since I made love to her—that's the only way to describe it—she's been a little distant. Her words have been cordial but lack the usual enthusiasm I've come to expect from her.

We also haven't had sex since that evening. I know it's only been eight nights, but it has just felt different. She says she's tired, and while she does fall asleep almost as quickly as her head hits the pillow, she isn't as touchy-feely as she has been. She still lets me hold her, but even then it lacks the depth and warmth we've been experiencing.

I keep telling myself it's the pregnancy and hormones and to quit looking into it, but there's worry niggling in the back of my mind, a fear of her pulling away bubbling to the surface.

Shaking my head, I push all of that aside and return my focus to work. Payroll isn't going to print itself, and I know the employees would appreciate getting paid by the end of the day. So as much as I'd love to spend my afternoon thinking about Hallie, I put my time and energy into work, knowing I'll be going back to the cabin soon enough.

I can't wait.

When I pull up the lane leading to the cabin, a renewed wave of anticipation washes over me. All I want to do is get there, take her into my arms, and kiss her, so that's exactly what I plan to do as soon as I cross the threshold.

I park my truck beside her Jeep and climb out, a little extra spring in my step as I walk. I open the front door, the scent of fried chicken filling the space. I open my mouth, prepared to holler a greeting, when my eyes land on the stack of boxes and bags, it causes me to pause.

"Oh, hey," Hallie says, walking out of the bathroom.

"Hi." My eyes sweep up and down her, taking in the black leggings, oversized crewneck sweatshirt, and warm fuzzy socks. "What's all this?" I ask.

"That's my news," she exclaims. "Come in the kitchen. The chicken will get cold."

I follow behind her, my legs a bit wooden as I walk toward the kitchen. There are two plates and forks set on the table, as well as bowls of pasta salad, mashed potatoes, and gravy, along with a covered platter of Frannie's mouthwatering fried chicken.

"Want something to drink?" I ask, already reaching for the peach lemonade she's been drinking lately.

When she looks over and sees what I have, she just smiles. "Thanks."

We sit down at the table and start dishing out the food. Just as she reaches for her fork, her eyes go wide, and she stills. "What's wrong?" I ask, instantly on alert.

"Come here," she whispers, waving me over.

I'm there in an instant, ready to carry her out to my truck and rush her to the nearest hospital. "Are yo—"

"Shhhhh. Just be quiet," she murmurs, reaching for my hand. "I felt something."

Hallie places my hand on the swell of her belly, directly over the top half of the baby bump. Her right hand is resting over the top of mine, with her left directly alongside my fingers. I'm just about to ask what's going on when I feel it. The faintest little thump against my hand.

"Holy shit!" I proclaim, my eyes wide as I feel the movement of our baby beneath my palm. "That's incredible."

I leave my hand there for several minutes, just feeling the baby move. I know in this moment; I'll never forget what this feels like. I'll never forget this night.

When the baby seems to settle down, I reluctantly get up and return to my seat. I'm on cloud nine, floating from the excitement of what just happened and am so grateful I was here to be part of it.

I grab my fork, suddenly starved from the long day, and ask, "So what's your good news?"

Frankly, I'm not sure it could get any better than this.

Just as I go to take a bite of my potatoes, she drops the bomb. "I found a new place to live."

The fork halts in front of my mouth as I look across the table. She's practically bouncing with eagerness, her smile a mile wide, and while I should be happy for her, my heart breaks into tiny little pieces. "You did? That's great," I force out, setting my fork back down on my plate without taking the bite of food. "I didn't realize you were looking."

She shrugs sheepishly. "Well, I just started, and it sort of happened. I was talking to the pastor at the preschool yesterday, and he mentioned one of the families had a house for rent. He gave me the number for the Gustafsons, who offered to rent it immediately. Isn't that great?"

I nod because it's the expected response, but I don't consider this great at all. "Wow, so you can move in right away?"

She takes a bite of her pasta salad. "Yep. And the best part is they left a lot of furniture in it and told me I can use whatever I need. They have a storage unit available for anything I don't want, but since I'm starting over with a lot of that kind of stuff, I'll probably use what's available. Then I can focus on getting things for the baby and not furnishing an entire house."

My throat is so dry, I'm not sure I'll ever be able to quench my thirst again. "Huh, what are the odds?"

Something flashes in her eyes, a sadness of sort, but it's gone as quickly as it appears, making me think I imagined it.

"Since it's available right away, I figured, why wait? The weather is getting colder by the day, so it's best I get in sooner rather than later. Plus, I'm sure you're ready to go home too. We've been here a lot longer than either of us could have predicted," she adds, and with each word, it's like the knife in my chest slowly turns.

I open my mouth to tell her she can just stay here, but that's not what comes out. "Yeah." My brain finally catches up a little, and I add, "There is no rush, though. You're welcome to stay here as long as you need."

She gives me a small smile. "I appreciate that, but this is what's best. For me."

I nod, even though I don't understand. But I also know I won't argue, not if this is what's best for her. What's best for me—which is her here, by the way—doesn't matter in the grand scheme of things if she's not happy. If moving out and living separately again is what's best, then that's what needs to happen, even if it kills me inside. "Okay."

"When I got home, I decided to start packing up my things, so it's all ready to go. I already had the utilities transferred to my name and move in tomorrow. Gabe said he was available to help. I don't think it's going to take a lot of people. I don't have that much stuff," she says with a chuckle, continuing to eat her chicken as if she's not completely ripping my heart out and stomping it into the ground.

Of course, she doesn't know that. She has no clue how I feel, and how can I tell her now? She's so excited about the move, about returning to her own place. She's always been incredibly independent, and apparently, that's still the case now. It's what's best for her, right?

We eat the majority of our meal in uncomfortable silence. Any conversation is led by Hallie, but it feels forced. Like maybe she doesn't really know what to say, so she's just saying anything to keep words flowing. Even though my stomach is in knots, I force food down my throat.

When most of the food on my plate is gone, I get up quickly and start to clean what little mess was created by the meal. I bag up the chicken, knowing she'll be munching on that later—probably right before bedtime—and place lids on the bowls of sides.

After everything is put away, I turn to face Hallie and find a deep sadness written all over her face. A single tear slides down her cheek, and it's that one little slip of moisture that has me moving in her direction. She's standing and in my arms a second later. I hold her tightly to my chest and listen as she cries. Her sorrow mimics what I feel in my heart, and I'm certain it may never beat right again. When she leaves, she'll be taking it with her, whether she knows it or not.

She pulls away and sniffles. "Sorry, I just got a little emotional," she whispers.

Swiping the wetness from her cheeks with my fingers, I give her a small smile. "It's okay."

She looks up and holds my gaze. "I loved living with you."

My heart skips a beat in my chest. "I loved living with you too, Hal."

"And even though you drive me crazy, I'm going to miss you. You've really become a...friend to me."

A friend.

Not exactly what a guy wants to hear after he's fallen hopelessly in love with a woman.

But I push my own feelings aside. "I will always be here for you. Not just for the baby either. I'll always be here for *you.*"

She nods and swallows hard. "I, uh, I think I'm going to go lie down."

"Let me know if you need anything," I tell her as I release my hold on her.

Hallie turns and walks away, and I instantly realize she's about to do that for the last time. Our time together is almost over. Tomorrow, I'll be moving her into her own place. I'll go there and help her set up a nursery. Then, I'll do the same thing at my own house. Our lives will always be linked, but never in the way it has been this last month and a half.

The cabin feels empty and cold.

It feels like she's already gone.

CHAPTER Twenty five

Hallie

I love my new place. Yet, hate it at the same time.

Why? Because he's not here.

The older ranch-style house sits on a large corner lot. It has three bedrooms and two baths, which is way more room than I need, but I do admit, it'll be nice to have a little space when the baby comes. The problem is, it doesn't feel like home. It feels cavernous and empty, despite coming with many of the furnishings I would need. A lot of the furniture is somewhat dated or not exactly my taste, but the fact I don't have to run out and buy complete sets of furniture all at once is a godsend.

I did purchase a new bedroom set and had it delivered this morning. Since the master bedroom is large with an en suite bathroom, I opted to go with the king-sized bed, despite being the only one sleeping in it. I'll deal with that sad realization later.

Everyone who helped me move my belongings has left for the day. Gabe and Blair were here, as was Logan. He helped make sure everything was where I wanted it, and then Gabe and Logan moved what was left in the larger of the two guest rooms to the storage unit.

I'll be using that room for the baby, so while they were both here, they decided to go ahead and clear out the space. This way, I can paint while the room is empty, and I have a place to put the baby furniture and necessities when I purchase them.

When the work was done, Blair and Gabe left to go home. We're going to Hudson tomorrow to get a few last-minute things for the wedding, which is coming up in just a few weeks, as well as discuss the baby shower I'm throwing her. Logan hung around a bit longer after they left. He made sure all the light bulbs were changed, checked all the outlets to ensure they were in proper working order, and changed the locks on the doors. Not that I minded, especially since he was doing it all for me and the baby. He's being a big help, which is greatly appreciated.

However, now he's gone, having decided he was going to return to his own house for the first time since the fire destroyed the duplex I was living in, and I'm left wondering if I'll ever be able to be alone again.

I miss him. Terribly. There's a hole the size of Alaska in my chest where my heart used to be, and I have no idea how to fix it. I had hoped being in my own space, starting to make a new life here, would be the answer I was looking for, but all I see is emptiness. All I feel is loneliness.

And he didn't sign on for this. He went into this as a friend doing the right thing for the mother of his child. Then said mother fell in love with him. Never once did he tell her there was a happily ever after at the end of our time together. We are partners for the sake of a child, and could be on friendly, cordial terms because of it.

Nothing more.

The baby chooses that exact moment to start kicking, and as my hand covers the thumps, I almost call out to Logan. He'd want to feel the movements, despite having felt them a few times since last night, but he's not here. He won't be here at night to feel the baby move, talk to my stomach, or fall asleep with his hand placed protectively over the top.

I slip into a deeper, darker misery as I lie on the old, yet surprisingly comfortable couch. Sadly, there's no fireplace at this house, so I reach for the throw blanket Blair washed and placed across the back of the couch. It's not as fuzzy as the one I used at the cabin, but it does the trick. I'm cocooned in warmth and coziness, despite feeling so alone in the moment.

I chose this.

I made the decision to leave.

To start my new life without his everyday presence.

It may not be the choice I wanted to make, but I hadn't lied to him when I said it was the right one for me.

It is.

I just lied about the reason why.

But I couldn't tell him I'd fallen in love with him.

That's my secret to bear.

"I'm so glad you came with me. It's been forever since we've been able to spend more than just a quick lunch together," Blair says as she drives toward Hudson to make the few stops she needs for wedding supplies.

"That's because you're a brilliant doctor, changing the world one patient at a time," I insist, so stinking proud of my dearest friend.

"Well, you're an amazing teacher."

I feel the blush creep up my neck at her compliment. "I try. Anyway, what all do we have to get today?"

"Not a lot. Patience and my mom have taken care of so much already, but there's a few things I didn't want their help with," she says, slowing down as we approach the city to maintain the speed limit.

"Like?" I ask, curiously.

She glances my way and blushes a deep shade of red. "I need some lingerie. For our wedding night."

"Oh." I'm beaming with excitement. "Are we going to that cute boutique where Ellie got her stuff for her wedding night and honeymoon?"

Blair nods. "She told me they have a maternity section. I really hope so. I don't want to look like a beached whale trying to fit into something that's not designed for her growing body."

"You'll be breathtaking in anything, as long as I don't picture the man appreciating you to be my brother."

She barks out a laugh as she nears an intersection and turns on her blinker. It only takes a few turns before we're pulling into the boutique parking lot and stopping in the first available spot. "They really should have maternity parking spots," she says, slipping out of her SUV and shutting the door.

I come around the back of the vehicle. "Agreed."

We make our way to the sidewalk and to the glass door with the Honey Rose logo. The pieces displayed in the windows are tasteful, like nightgowns and satin robes, but the moment we step inside, there's pieces for every shape, style, and spice level. "Wow," I mumble as we both pause inside the door, almost a little overwhelmed with where to start.

"Hello and welcome to Honey Rose. I'm Rose, the owner. How may I help you?"

"Umm, I'm getting married in a few weeks and am looking for something for my wedding night," Blair says, looking around at the variety of lingerie.

"Oh, congratulations."

"We also have a baby on the way, which might complicate things a bit," Blair says, placing her hand on her protruding belly.

"Not at all. We have a beautiful maternity line that should suit your needs. Follow me," she replies with a pleasant smile.

We walk to the right, past a section of red and black pieces that leave very little to the imagination. "The line is called Blush, and it's designed to accommodate a woman's growing body," she informs us, pulling a delicate pink bra and panty set from the display. "Their products were designed by expecting women with a lot going into the comfort of each piece. There's just enough stretch in the material without feeling like it's cutting into your skin. There is a wider range of sizes with this line, since no two expecting women's bodies are alike."

"Oh, look at this," Blair says, turning her attention to a stunning white nightgown hanging on a mannequin. It has spaghetti straps that are adjustable and a lace-covered bodice. The satin begins directly below the breasts and hangs perfectly around the mannequin's pregnant belly, the hem hitting mid-thigh.

"This is one of the new pieces in their fall catalogue. Isn't it stunning? The straps cross at the back, and you can pair it with any of the matching white panties in a variety of styles," Rose states, pulling several pairs of panties from the basket beside the mannequin.

She checks out a few of the varieties and settles on a pair of white lace boyshort briefs. "What do you think?"

"My brother is going to lose his mind," I tell her honestly.

Blair grins from ear to ear. "I agree."

"Let me know what size of teddy, and I can take this up to the front counter for you," Rose says, pulling the medium size from the rack when Blair requests that size. "If you'd like to try it on, you're welcome. We just ask you leave your own panties on while trying anything intimate on."

"Of course. I'd like to look around for a few minutes," Blair replies.

Rose nods. "Take your time, and if you have any questions or need help, just holler."

"Thank you."

When the owner of the boutique walks away, I lean toward Blair and whisper, "Is it weird I had no idea they had pregnant mannequins?"

"Me either," she replies with a giggle. "Oh, what do you think of this?"

I glance her way, and the moment I do, I spot a long, light pink nightgown on the far wall. "That's pretty." My feet are already carrying me toward the piece that caught my eye.

It's a shimmery, silky material and goes to the ankle with a long slit up the side. The top has ruching around the breasts in a simple, yet elegant way I find classy. It's a stunning piece, and I bet any man who sees his woman wearing this would fall to his knees and worship the ground she walks on.

"You should get that."

I glance over at my friend with a look of shock. "What? Why?"

She shrugs, finding her size in a few breast-feeding nightgowns. "Logan would love it."

I snort. "Logan? Why would I care what Logan thinks about this?" My heart beats a little faster at the mention of his name.

"Why wouldn't you? You're in love with him, aren't you?"

My eyes widen as I look up at my friend. "I'm not—"

"Oh, stop. You can lie to yourself, but you can't lie to me. I know you, Hallie, just as well as you know me. You fell in love with him and then ran scared."

I replace the nightgown in my hand and cross my arms over my chest. "You're wrong."

The look on her face tells me she doesn't believe me. "About which part? About falling in love with Logan or about running scared, because from where I stand, both are very much true."

All I can do is narrow my eyes at her, wishing what she was saying weren't true. But the fact remains: I both love him and ran from him as a result of it.

"I'll take your silence as the answer to my question, but what I want to know is, why?" She steps forward and places her hand on my arm. "Hal, if you love him, why not stay?"

A lump forms in my throat and I have to fight to keep tears at bay. "Because he didn't sign on for this."

"For what?"

"Me."

"You're having his baby," she reasons unnecessarily.

"Right," I counter. "He's here for the baby, not me."

"Oh, Hal," she replies, chuckling as she shakes her head. "You silly, silly girl. He's in love with you too."

This is the moment my jaw drops to the floor. "Excuse me?"

"A blind person could see it. He's in love with you."

"Uhh," I start, clearing my throat. "How do you know?"

"Because I have eyes. And so does he. He watches you everywhere you go. When you guys were at football games, he would smile and watch you cheer instead of what's happening on the field. Even back at your birthday party in July, I could see it. Hell, even before that, I've always wondered. You two would bicker like an old married couple, and not because you didn't get along. It was foreplay, and now, it's love."

I don't know when I started crying, but a few tears escape my eyes before I even realize what's happening. "I didn't mean to fall in love with him," I whisper, saying those words aloud for the first time.

She gives me a sad smile. "I know. It always happens when you least expect it. It did for me with Gabe. I still fought my feelings and left, so I have a pretty good idea of what you're thinking and how you feel. The problem is all the cards haven't been laid on the table. You've only shown part of the hand, Hal."

My throat is so dry, it's hard to form words. "But...but what if he still says no?"

"Then at least you'd know how he feels. Right now, you're assuming, and you remember what Mrs. Voight used to say in English class, right?"

I can't help but roll my eyes. "Assume just stands for ass out of you and me."

Blair snickers and nods. "Exactly. So stop being an ass, and tell him how you feel."

"You're bossy today," I grumble, even though I know she's right.

I'm just scared.

"How does it feel? You're the one who's usually Miss Bossy Pants," she replies, winking before turning her attention back to a piece of black lingerie. "Do you think your brother would want to rip this off my body on our honeymoon?"

I groan. "Why? I'm gonna need one of those flashy things from *Men in Black* after that question," I argue.

Her full-belly laughter makes me smile. "Just teasing you. Anyway, I hope you really consider telling him how you feel. I think you'd be surprised by his response."

I nod, choking back another wave of emotion. "I try not to compare them," I start, shaking my head.

"Good, because they're not the same. Curtis was a decent guy, but not the one for you. His priority was work, and for some, that's fine. If he would have chosen work over your plans with him every now and again, that was one thing. But he did it all the time. You were constantly disappointed because you were second to him, and you deserve someone who puts you first."

"Thanks," I mutter, fingering the pink nightgown as it hangs on the rack. "I sometimes, you know, wonder if it was me. Am I high maintenance?"

Blair snorts. "Are you kidding me? Shay Johnson is high maintenance. You are far from it." She gives me her complete attention. "Listen, I know I've said this before, but what happened with Curtis wasn't your fault. You wanted different things. Your brother is an example of a man who knows how to commit to his work but can still put me first. Yes, he has to leave at times for patients, but he always makes me feel loved and cherished the moment he's back, and I do the same.

"Now, Logan? From what I can tell, he's a Gabe. When you're around, you're all he sees. Did he make you feel cherished when you were together?"

I don't have to think back over the last few months. I already know the answers. "Yes."

"There you go." She pulls a bra and panty set off a rack.

Looking at our time together, he just felt...different. But, if I'm being honest, he's always been different. Even when we were just friends—or friends who bickered and tried not to kill each other every time we were together. The truth is, a big part of our relationship was built on friendship, and while I'm afraid to lose that, I know Blair is right. If I don't take the risk and tell Logan how I really feel, I'll always wonder what could have been.

And I've never been one to back down, so why start now?

With a smile, I feel a wave of anticipation sweep through me. I don't know when I'm going to talk to him, but it'll be soon. Maybe I can invite him over for dinner soon and tell him then.

When Rose returns to see if we need any more assistance, I pull the nightgown off the rack once more and hand it over. "I'll take this."

She smiles widely and nods. "Excellent choice."

The decision to buy the nightgown was for myself more than it was for Logan. I don't know how things will play out for us, but I know if I don't risk anything, I'll risk losing everything.

And something tells me, what I could have with Logan will be just that.

Everything.

CHAPTER
twenty six

LOGAN

I'm so fucking miserable.

She's been gone a single night, and I'm in agony. My heart just fucking hurts.

That's my fault too. I was too chickenshit to tell her how I feel, but she threw me off when she told me she was leaving and already had her bags packed. I wasn't expecting that to be her surprise. Then she said it was the right decision for her, and there was no way I could tell her then and ask her to stay.

Even if I really wanted to.

Last night, I slept for shit. My bed, while comfortable, was anything but when it came down to sleeping alone. I've gotten used to having Hallie there, in my arms, and my God, do I miss that. So much so the thought of crawling into that bed again tonight brings a sense of dread.

Maybe I'll just crash on the couch.

The sun has long set, the only light on in the house is in the kitchen. Hell, even the TV isn't on. Usually, I can find a basketball or football game for background noise, but tonight, even that doesn't sound appealing. It's as if I'm destined to be surrounded by solitude and silence.

A loud knock hits the back door just as it's pressed open. "Knock, knock," TD hollers as he steps inside.

"Hey." Pulling two beers from my fridge, I ignore the fact the beer is about the only thing left in there and hand one over to him.

"Jesus, what's that smell?" he asks, making a face.

I shrug, opening my beer and taking a long pull. "No clue."

He sniffs again. "Is that moldy cheese?"

"What are you doing here?" I ask, leaning against the counter and taking another drink.

"Saw your light on. Didn't know you were back."

I stand here, drinking my beer a little faster than normal, because I know what's coming next. The questions I'm expected to answer, and frankly, I just don't have them right now.

"Just got back last night," I tell him, hoping that'll be the end of it.

"Where's Hallie?" he asks, setting his beer down on the counter.

"Her new place."

"Ahhh," TD replies.

"But I'm guessing you already knew that." It's a small town, after all, and Hallie's good friends with his wife. The only reason Ellie wasn't there yesterday to help her clean and move some of her belongings to the new place was because she was working.

He lifts a shoulder and continues to just stare at me.

"What?" I finally ask when the silence stretches on longer than it should.

"What happened?"

"What do you mean? We weren't dating. Our living arrangement was only temporary. She found a place and moved out. I'm back here. End of story."

He turns and leans against the counter, clearly getting himself comfortable. "That might be how the story started, but that wasn't the end."

"Stop talking in gibberish and get to your point," I tell him, setting my own bottle down on the counter when it's nearly empty.

"You fell in love with her, and now you're a miserable sack because she left. But what you're not realizing is she only left because you didn't tell her how you feel."

That familiar lump I've felt in my throat since she told me she was leaving returns. "Don't you know everything," I mutter, deflecting.

"It's easy to see from the outside looking in. My question is, what are you going to do about it?"

"Nothing."

"Bullshit," he retorts immediately.

Throwing my hands in the air, I ask, "What am I supposed to do then? Since you're the expert on relationships now, tell me, oh wise one."

"I'm no expert, Logan, but I can speak from experience. I was afraid to ask Ellie out because it could ruin our friendship. Despite being in love with her for as long as I could remember, I kept my distance. Why? Because of fear. That's exactly why you're keeping your distance from Hallie now. You're afraid to tell her."

"She told me this is what she needs."

He just stares back at me, as if waiting for me to catch up.

I shift on my feet and run my hand through my hair. "She'll probably tell me to get fucked."

TD barks out a laugh. "Yeah, she probably will." He sobers a little before adding, "You have to give her all the pieces to the puzzle and let her put it together. If you only give her half of them, the picture isn't going to turn out the way it should."

I roll my eyes. "Jesus, it's like talking to Dr. Phil."

He grins widely. "I am pretty brilliant, aren't I?"

"No," I counter. "But I do see what you're saying."

"Listen, it's your life and your decision. If you decide to tell her and she says no, she just wants to remain friends and co-parents, then at least you know how she really feels. Right now, you have no idea what's going on in her head over there, and she has no clue what's going on in yours. Tell her how you feel and go from there. Either way, you'll know and won't be trapped in limbo. You can move forward."

I exhale, knowing he's right, but refusing to give him the satisfaction.

He smiles, as if reading my mind. "I think you'd be surprised, Logan. I'm pretty sure she loves you too."

My heart starts to gallop in my chest at the prospect of telling her how I feel and having her reciprocate. But just as quickly, it's pushed aside by doubt and uncertainty. I blame years of dealing with Shay for my hesitancy now, but truthfully, I have no one to blame but myself. It's my life, my control to take. Just because I got dumped on in the past doesn't mean I will again moving forward.

Maybe it's time I actually take a risk.

For me.

"Thanks for the stale beer," he says, dumping the rest of his out in the sink and tossing the bottle in the recycling bin.

"That's partially on you, man. I haven't been home in almost two months. What did you expect?" I ask, smiling for the first time in days.

He makes a face and heads for the door. "I'll bring the beer next time."

"Probably a good idea."

He stops before exiting. "Think about what I said. If you decide to tell her how you feel, I think you'll be happy with the outcome."

I nod. "Thanks."

"Oh, I almost forgot. El is wanting to host Friendsgiving next Sunday. She's makin' a turkey and a few sides. Gonna eat at noon, and she wants you there."

"What can I bring?" I ask.

He holds my gaze. "Just your baby." Then, with a wink, he leaves my house, knowing he got the last word in, since there's no way I can bring the baby without Hallie.

Asshole.

But I find myself smiling as I go over and lock the door behind him.

Mostly because I know the guy is right. Deep down I knew this was the right step to take but kept convincing myself otherwise. I guess I just needed to hear someone else say it, and TD has always been the one to talk sense into me when I needed it most.

I'm not going to let the demons of my past keep me from taking a shot at my future. One ex-wife and rough marriage doesn't mean all of them are destined to be like that. And Hallie and Shay are about as night and day different as you can get. I'm happy when I'm with Hallie, and when we're not together, I wish we were. I think about her constantly, and not just because of the baby.

I think about her.

Because I love her.

I know there's a chance she's going to tell me to get lost, but I have to at least tell her how I feel. If I don't, I'll always wonder. So tomorrow, after work, I'll take her dinner. I'll plead my case and see if she reciprocates any feelings for me, the way TD thinks she does. If not, I'll walk away having tried.

But if she does, I'll spend the rest of my life showing her how much she means to me.

My phone goes off, waking me from a heavy sleep.

I glance at the clock on my nightstand, noting it's after two. Worry grips my throat as I reach blindly for my phone. My first thought is Hallie. Is something wrong? Is it the baby? But when I finally have the device in my hand and look at the screen, it's with a mixture of relief and confusion.

It's not Hallie.

It's the security system at the hardware store.

It takes me a few seconds to fully become awake, as I tap my passcode into my phone. I go to the app for my security system and pull it up. The door alarm has been disabled, but the alerts are popping up for movement within the building. I pull up the camera with the alert and press the button for live play. There, on the screen, is a shot of my ex-wife. She's in my office, pressing buttons on the safe built into my wall, and opening the door. My mind reels, especially since I wasn't aware Shay knew the combination to the safe. I'd gone to great lengths to keep it from her. There's only two people who know the combination and the other person isn't her.

All I can do is watch as she fumbles around on the top shelf and pulls envelopes down. She roots through them before pulling the one I keep emergency cash in and opening it up. I watch as she flips through the cash, taking a big chunk of it, and slipping the rest of the envelopes back on the shelf. She closes the safe, slipping the money into her oversized purse, and heads toward my office door. Before she goes, she moves to my desk and sits down. I watch as she digs in my drawers, pulling the ultrasound out. She stares down at it for several seconds before snorting and tossing it on the desk. "I can't believe you slept with that fat cow."

My blood boils as she gets up from the chair and practically struts out of my office, flipping off any lights she turned on as she goes. I switch the camera view to the one behind the counter, which covers both the register and the front door. She keys in her code, messing it up the first time and receiving the warning alert from the unit. Finally, she gets it right and steps outside, using her key to lock the door as she goes.

For shits and giggles, I tap on the camera in the parking lot in time to see her climb into her SUV—a new one, by the way—and take off out of the lot like she didn't just fucking rob me. Because that's what she did. She stole money from me. From our business.

And there's no way in hell I'm letting this slide.

I just have to figure out what to do about it.

I go back to the cameras and download the clips of her actions from the last few minutes to my phone. I'm pretty sure she has no clue how to mess with the camera system, but I'm not taking any chances here. I'll still download it all from the server as soon as I get to the store in the morning. She clearly doesn't realize or remember there's cameras all around the business.

Hell, I barely remember them. They're always recording, but I rarely have to use them. A year or so ago, we realized a young man was stealing tools and reselling them around town. I was able to pull up the cameras as far as thirty days back and watch how it happened. When I took the information to the police, the teenager admitted to what he was doing, and as it turned out, he was selling his hocked items to help pay rent for his mom. After finding out her hours were cut to part time and she was struggling to make ends meet, I didn't press charges against her sixteen-year-old boy. Instead, he spent the summer doing community service, cleaning up our lumberyard and around town. He did a decent job and learned a valuable lesson by the end of his time and turned out to be a good kid.

However, I haven't really had to use the cameras since. They're there to protect the business, employees, and patrons, and right now, I'm damn glad I have them. Right now, I have to figure out what I'm going to do about Shay. She snuck into the business in the middle of the night and took money. One of those envelopes is my personal stash, while the other is what I consider petty cash. I'm not sure which envelope she took from, but neither is good for her.

A smile crosses my lips as I lie back, an idea beginning to form.

Finding my ex-wife stealing from me might turn out to be the best thing to happen.

I didn't sleep a wink after watching what happened at the hardware store, which resulted in me appearing way before my usual 7:00 a.m. arrival. The rest of the crew doesn't get here until seven thirty, with the exception of Shay. She'll arrive anywhere between eight thirty and ten thirty, depending on what extra dose of drama she embarks on. Today, I'm looking forward to her arriving later, which gives me time to put my plan in motion.

First thing I do is make a pot of coffee. I'm definitely going to need it. Once I have a travel mug filled, I get comfortable at my desk. My eyes instantly land on the first ultrasound picture that was tossed onto my desk in a fit early this morning. I swipe my finger over the little bean in the image and press it down to try to smooth out the creases she made when she haphazardly threw it aside. I picture Hallie, her swollen belly growing with our child, and the overwhelming urge to talk to her comes over me. Since it's not even six o'clock, I resort to firing off a text message, hoping it doesn't wake her.

> **Me:** Just wanted you to know I'm thinking of you and baby. Have a good day.

She doesn't reply, which brings me a mixture of sadness and relief. Even though I'm not getting the opportunity to talk to her, at least I didn't wake her.

I pull up the security system and find the videos on the server. I download them to my computer and pull up my email. I compose the document and include the video attachments as planned and hit send. All I can do now is wait, but at least this time, I feel like the end result will be worth it. Either way, I'm holding all the aces in the deck of cards.

My ex-wife isn't going to know what hit her.

Fortunately for me, my attorney is an early bird too and I have an email reply within thirty minutes. He's working on my request now from his home office and will have it back to me within the hour. I'm all smiles as I send a quick reply of appreciation. Needing to keep my hands busy, I go out to the small woodworking shop in the lumberyard. When I was younger, I'd spend all sorts of free time out here, building and creating. This room isn't used nearly as much as it used to be, but it comes in handy when I need to think. I grab a small strip of oak trim and an idea forms.

Over the next thirty minutes, I cut the wood down to four pieces of the size I want and miter the ends. I use a hand sander to make sure the pieces are smooth and router the edges so they're slightly rounded. Then, I grab the wood glue, pegs, and clamps, and before I know it, I have a perfect picture frame. When it's finished drying, I'll be able to touch it up with fine sandpaper and stain it. I can't wait to see the final product, complete with ultrasound photo tucked inside.

When it's time to open the business, I head inside. "Hey, boss. You seem awfully happy," Chip greets, pouring coffee into his mug.

"Gonna be a good day, Chip. Oh, when Shay gets in, will you send her into my office, please?"

"Will do," he replies, flipping on the lights and grabbing the cash register drawer I set out on the counter earlier.

She finally arrives a few minutes before ten, and my heart rate accelerates. I keep myself busy, making sure I have everything documented and ready to go, and wait for her to be sent in here. Even after I overheard Chip telling her I'd like to see her, it takes another fifteen minutes before she finally shows her face.

"I need to leave early today," she says as she flounces through my doorway.

"Why?" I ask, even though I don't really care.

She shrugs and flips her hair. "Wouldn't you like to know," she replies with a devious grin on her face.

I lean back in my chair, my thumb tapping on my desk. "Get a new car?" I ask, recalling the brand-new sporty BMW SUV I saw in the video.

She bats her black eyelashes at me. "I did. Rick said it suits me better than the older model I was driving," she informs me. Her previous one was only two years old and came with every lap of luxury a person could imagine. It also cost more than my house did, which isn't surprising for someone like Shay. She picks at her fresh manicure and asks, "So what did you need?"

"Yes," I start, sitting up in my chair and pulling up the video on my computer. "We had an incident very early this morning."

She pays me no attention. "Oh?"

"Someone broke in."

That catches her attention.

When she doesn't say a word, just looks up at the video I'm now playing for her, I continue. "Apparently, someone thought it was a good idea to enter the business around two this morning and open my safe. They took money that doesn't belong to them."

She snorts and rolls her eyes. "Whatever. That money is mine too. I own this business," she replies smugly.

"Actually, the money you stole *wasn't* all business money. Part of it was my personal stash I keep in my safe. You not only took some of the petty cash, which is a felony, by the way, but you also took cash from me. Also illegal."

For the first time since she arrived, I see her appear a little nervous. "So? What are you going to do? Have me arrested?" she asks, laughing with a bit too much force.

"Actually, yes."

Her eyes widen and the smile falls from her painted lips. "Excuse me? You can't do that."

"I most certainly can. It's no different than if any other employee or customer steals. You're not above the law."

She narrows her eyes at me and sits up straight in her chair. "This is a joke, right?"

"I would never joke about this," I tell her, relaxing even more as she starts to really squirm. "You're fired, and TD is on his way."

He's not—yet.

"You can't do this!" she bellows, jumping up and starting to really panic. "I *own* this business. It's not stealing when it's your own money, Logan."

"I beg to differ, Shay. You're part owner, but that doesn't give you the right to take money." Deciding to lay all my cards on the table, I add, "Unless..."

Her blue eyes brighten as she poses in front of me. "Unless what?"

"Unless you sign these." I pull the updated contract out of my top drawer and slide it toward her.

"What's this?"

"A contract to sell me your half of the business."

"What? No!" she demands, pushing the papers back toward me.

"Fine," I reply, gathering up the contract and making a big deal out of restacking them together. "I understand you'd rather take your chances with the court system, but I assure you, I'm in no mood to suggest community service. Hey, wasn't orange one of the colors you said washes out your complexion?"

She huffs and crosses her arms, stomping her feet. "This is an outrage."

"What's an outrage is you stealing from the business and from me. You took money that doesn't belong to you, Shay, and for what? A new vehicle?"

"Because Rick says I deserve the best of everything!" she bellows, her eyes wide and frantic.

"Well, I hope Rick comes to visit you in prison."

She flops down into the chair and bursts into tears. Big, fake ones. Ones that used to wield power over me, but since, mean nothing. "You can't do this," she wails, her perfect makeup remaining in place as she cries.

"I can, and I will. The only way out of this is to sign the papers."

"That's extortion."

"No, it's good business. I'll pay you for your half of the business, and in return won't release the security videos to TD." Fighting a smile, I add, "I wonder how easy it would be to leak them on the internet?"

She gasps and cries harder.

I sit up straight, lean forward, and fold my hands together. "Listen, Shay, you don't want the business. You want the status that comes with it and to make sure I'm not happy. Well, you've had me by the balls for years, sweetheart. No more. I'll pay you for your half of the business right now. My attorney has the contract ready to go, and the bank is prepared to cut the check. You could have it by mid-afternoon. All you have to do is sign your name and walk away."

She sniffles again and reaches for the papers. She scans them over. "Wait, this is less than the last offer!"

"That was a one-time deal, Shay. You declined. Then, you stole from me. I'll pay you exactly fifty percent of what this business is valued at today and not a cent more. It's either that or you take your chances with TD. And you know how he's always felt about you," I add, letting myself smile for the first time.

As if realizing she's truly fucked, she groans and wipes frantically at her eyes. "He's always hated me."

"With good reason, but that's a conversation for another time. Make your choice, Shay. You can walk out of here right now with a bunch of money. You keep the house and anything else you were awarded during the divorce. The only clause is you can't come after me for any sort of support in the future."

She seems resigned to realize her game is over. I hold my breath as she reaches for an ink pen and signs her name across the line.

I've done it.

I officially own my entire family business.

"You'll be sorry," she mumbles.

"No, you will. You had a pretty sweet gig here," I start, reaching for the papers and signing my own name across the other line. "You barely worked and have been compensated too well for it. Now, you get to take your money and move on."

She huffs, as if realizing she's about to be fairly wealthy from the sale. "I've already moved on. With Rick."

I shrug, not caring in the least.

"He's a lawyer. Wealthy. Comes from a great family. Not some small-town hardware store guy like you," she states, assuming she's going to hurt me with her words. Unfortunately, they're meaningless.

"Great. Go have a nice life with Rick. I hope his wife doesn't mind you hanging around her husband." I don't know Rick or if he's married, but I do know Shay, and when something that looks like realization flashes in her eyes, I know I've hit the nail on the head.

"When I walk out the door, that's it for us," she says, and I almost laugh in her face.

Instead, I look her straight in the eye and say, "Don't let the door hit your ass on your way out."

With a huff and a cloud of expensive perfume, Shay storms out of my office and out of my life.

Hopefully, forever.

I lean back in my chair and smile. I'm a free man. I'll be in debt for the rest of my life, but I don't give a shit. I've done it. I'm rid of my terrible ex-wife and officially the sole owner of my family's business.

There's just one more thing I have to take care of...

CHAPTER
twenty seven

Hallie

It's been a long day.

The kids seemed extra wound up from the weekend and struggled to fall back into our classroom routine. Add in the fact I haven't been sleeping well since I moved out of the cabin and into my own place, which contributed to my own battle to remain focused and calm when needed.

Of course, a big part of my distraction was thinking about Logan and the early morning text he sent me. I thought about replying a million times, but each reply I came up with felt wrong. Not heartfelt enough, not aloof enough, and everything in between. So instead of firing off a reply, I kept staring down at his message, wishing things were different.

I need to talk to him, but telling someone you love them isn't something you send in a message. It should be done face-to-face so he can see everything in my eyes and hear everything written in my heart. But he's still working, preparing to close his business down for the evening, and I'm left fighting with myself on when the right time to have this conversation is.

Now, I'm home and staring at the fridge, trying to decide what I want to eat for dinner. Honestly, I wish I would have ordered a pizza on my way, but I convinced myself I should just eat some of the food I purchased to stock the fridge. However, now that I'm here, looking at the ham lunch meat, salad fixings, and carton of eggs, none of it sounds good.

There's a knock at the front door, resulting in me closing the fridge. It's probably Blair, and I'm certain she's not delivering pizza. When I glance through the peephole, my heart skips a beat.

What's Logan doing here?

I release the lock and turn the knob, coming face-to-face with the man I love for the first time in two excruciatingly long days. "Hi."

"Hey," he replies, a gentle smile on his scruffy face. He looks...good, despite looking a bit tired. His jaw is covered with dark stubble, and my thighs clench at the thought of it rubbing against the sensitive skin.

I glance down, noticing the pizza he's holding in his hands for the first time. "What's that?" I ask, my mouth watering as the aroma hits my nostrils.

"Dinner. I took a chance you haven't eaten yet," he tells me, holding up the box.

"Did you get breadsticks?" I ask, ignoring the way my stomach growls hungrily.

He grins a goofy smile and holds up the white bag. "Of course."

I step back, granting him entrance and closing the door behind him. He hands over the pizza and breadsticks before bending down to remove his work boots. I'm struck with a wave of sadness as I realize how much I've missed seeing those boots by the door, even in just a couple short days.

When he takes off his coat and sets it on the back of the couch, we walk to the kitchen together. "What can I get you to drink? I have water, green tea, or juice," I tell him.

"Tea sounds good."

I pull the jug out of the fridge and pour two glasses, while Logan grabs two paper plates. When I join him at the table, he has a slice of ham and mushroom pizza on my plate and two slices on his. He doesn't say a word as he pulls the soft breadsticks apart and sets two in front of me and hands over the cup of cheddar cheese sauce. Like the weirdo he is, he doesn't dip his breadsticks into any sauce, choosing to eat them dry like a psychopath.

We're silent as we dive into the food. I have both of my breadsticks consumed and am reaching for my slice of pizza before he finally speaks. "I had an interesting day."

"Yeah?" I ask before taking my bite. "Mine was a little chaotic."

"Tell me about yours first," he states, wiping the corners of his mouth before he takes another bite of pizza.

"It wasn't bad, just the kids were wound up today. It took almost the entire class time before they were able to settle down and concentrate on learning," I tell him with a shrug, leaving out the part about my own mind being distracted.

"I'm sure some days are like that," he says. "Especially after the weekend."

I nod. "You're right. Mondays can be the hardest." After taking another bite of my pizza, I ask, "So tell me about your day."

Logan sets his half-eaten slice of pizza down on his plate and smiles. "I bought the remaining half of the business today."

My mouth falls open as I absorb his words. "What? Seriously? She sold it to you?"

His grin sets my heart off with a wild pitter-patter beat, but I ignore it, trying to remain focused. He tells me about waking up at two this morning by the notification of movement within the building and watching her steal money. He goes on to detail the confrontation and about how she didn't want to sign the papers but opted to do that and take the money. The other option of possible jail time didn't sit well with her, as I expected it wouldn't.

"Holy shit, I can't believe she did that," I say when he's done telling me all about it.

"Honestly, me either. She has always been self-absorbed and high maintenance, but I didn't peg her for a thief." The look in his eyes is a little sad, and I'm sure he feels her betrayal deeply.

"I'm sorry."

He shrugs his broad shoulders and holds my gaze. The room is suddenly a little warmer than it was before as he stares across the table at me.

My throat is thick and dry, but I somehow manage to say, "I'm happy for you. Looks like you finally got everything you wanted."

Logan stands up and is moving almost as soon as I have the words out. My eyes widen as he drops to his knees beside me and takes my hands in his. "Wrong. There's something big and important I'm missing."

Air stalls in my lungs, and I find it hard to breathe. "There is?" I whisper, a bubble of hope erupting in my chest.

"Yeah. You," he tells me, reaching up and cupping my cheek with his warm hand. "My life is missing you, Hallie. You and our baby. You're giving me so much by having my baby, but I realized when you left it's not enough. I want more. I want you."

He blurs, thanks to the tears filling my eyes. "You do?" I croak out.

Sliding the pads of his thumbs across my cheek, he brushes away the tears that start to fall. "I do, because I love you."

His words are like an arrow straight to my heart but in a good way. Elation and joy fill my entire being as I reach for him, wrapping my arms around his shoulders and pulling him as close to me as possible. "I love you too," I insist quickly, afraid he'll take the words back if I don't get mine out as rapidly.

He chuckles and hugs me back. Then, he suddenly stands, takes my hands, and helps me stand before him. With the softest touch of his lips, he brushes his mouth across mine. "Say it again."

Smiling, I murmur, "I love you too."

"Yeah, you do," he retorts, making me laugh.

"Never mind. I take it back."

"Nope, no takebacks, Cupcake. You love me." He slips his hand between us and rests it on my baby bump.

Smiling up at him, I shake my head. "Fine, I don't take it back, but only because you love me too."

"Damn right I do."

Then, he finally kisses me the way I've imagined he would after a declaration of love. His lips are insistent, yet gentle, as he coaxes my mouth open so his tongue can sweep inside. My body fires to life in that familiar way only he can cause, and my need for him becomes urgent. His hands are everywhere, gripping at my clothing and moving it out of the way to get to bare skin.

"I need you, Logan," I whisper with a pant.

He stops what he's doing and meets my gaze. His eyes are gentle and the softest smile spreads across his lips. "I need you too, Hallie. Always. I'm sorry I let you go before. It wasn't what I wanted, but I thought that's what you needed."

I reach up and run my palm down his scruffy cheek. "I only needed that because I thought you didn't feel the same. I was protecting myself."

"Never again. You never have to protect yourself from me, especially your heart. Whatever you want, it's yours."

I grind myself against his erection. "There is one thing I really, really want."

He closes his eyes as I reach down and grip his cock, slowly stroking him through his jeans. "And you can always have that, Cupcake. Always."

"Good." As I dive for his belt buckle, something else hits me. "Oh, there's one more thing I want."

"Name it," he insists, his own movements paused.

"I don't want to sleep without you again."

"Done," he replies quickly, grabbing my sweater and gently pulling it up and over my head.

"That's it?" I ask, the cool air causing my nipples to pebble even harder.

"Yep. You want me in your bed, I'm there. No place I'd rather be, actually."

"We have to decide where we're going to stay," I start, fumbling to remove his belt.

"Makes no difference to me. I'm not attached to my house."

I pull back and look at him. "You're not?"

He gives me a cocky, easy grin. "Nope. I'm attached to this pussy, though, so wherever it is, that's where I'll be."

I roll my eyes. "Classy."

He slides his hand into my maternity pants and strokes my swollen clit through my panties. "You like the caveman side of me. That side is the one you invited back to your bed on your birthday," he says, shifting his fingers behind my panties and meeting wet flesh. "You couldn't get enough of me."

He pushes two fingers inside my body, and even though he's one-hundred-percent correct, I refuse to let him hear me say it. "Whatever you say."

Logan adds a third finger, causing my body to tighten around his digits. "Say it, Cupcake. Tell me you couldn't get enough of me." He slides his other hand up my stomach and pushes aside the material of my bra. He pinches my nipple, sending shock waves of pleasure rippling through my body. "Tell me, Hallie."

Glancing up, I look him straight in the eye and state, "I couldn't get enough of you. Now take me to bed and show me how much you love me."

Grinning from ear to ear, he pulls his fingers from my body, lifts me into his arms, and takes off at a rapid pace toward my bedroom. The moment he places me on top of the soft mattress, he cups my jaw and whispers, "I'll always show you how much I love you."

After our clothes are stripped away and he's entering me, he adds, "You're my world, Hallie. Don't ever doubt it."

The most euphoric feeling washes over me. It's from the way he makes my heart feel, as well as how he makes my body feel. The two combined are better than anything I've ever experienced in my life. Sex has always been good, but add in the factor of being in love, and it takes it to a whole new level.

When we're both boneless and sweaty, our limbs entwined together, I sigh in contentment. "Just so you know, that part about me not being able to get enough of you doesn't count."

He barks out a laugh. "What?"

"It doesn't count when you have your fingers buried inside me. That short-circuits my brain."

He chuckles, gliding his mouth across my neck. "Well, then I'm going to have to ensure I keep my fingers inside your sweet pussy at all times then."

I snort a laugh. "That'll make going in public interesting."

"Ehh, who says we ever need to go out in public?"

I glide my fingers across his chest, reveling in the feel of his hard muscles beneath my fingertips. "We both have jobs."

He sighs. "I would quit tomorrow if it meant I could stay home and make love to you all day long."

Closing my eyes, I rest my cheek against his arm. "That'd be nice," I murmur, sudden exhaustion taking over.

His chuckle echoes through my ears as his hand rests on my stomach. I feel the baby kick beneath his touch, as if our son or daughter knows whose hand it is and is happy to have him back.

Me too, baby.

"I love you, Hallie. Thank you for making me the luckiest son of a bitch on the planet."

With a smile on my lips, I murmur a soft, "Love you too, Logan."

And I fall asleep happier than I ever thought possible.

In his arms.

The only place I ever want to be.

EPILOGUE
epilogue

LOGAN

I'd never wish the night away, especially tonight, but all I can think about is getting Hallie back to our place and stripping that dress off her body.

Some might say we've moved fast, but there's nowhere else I want to be. Once we both confessed our love last month, we've been together ever since. Every night. In fact, over the last few weeks, I've moved all my personal belongings from my house to hers. I know she's just renting, but she has more space. Plus, we've inquired about buying the house from her landlord, who is very interested in talking after the first of the year. We're still trying to decide what to do with my house, but we're in no hurry. It can sit empty until spring for all I care, just as long as I get to keep waking up with Hallie in my arms.

Today was the big day. Blair and Gabe's wedding.

It was a beautiful event at the church, and now the reception is in full swing. Half the town is here, despite the fact they wanted a smaller, more intimate affair. But when both the bride and groom grow up in a small, close-knit town, it's hard to draw the line for invitations. My first wedding was a grand affair, complete with the world's longest list of invites. That was Shay's idea. I'd been fine with fifty or sixty of our closest family and friends.

"Promise me something," Hallie says as she steps up behind me, her arms wrapping around my waist.

"Anything," I reply, turning and kissing her forehead over my shoulder.

"If we ever do this, we're eloping. Like to Aruba or the Virgin Islands."

"Deal," I reply with a chuckle, turning around so she's in my arms. "And for the record, we'll be doing this someday."

"Yeah?" she asks, a happy grin spreading across her beautiful face.

"Definitely. I know a good thing when I see it, and you are the best thing to happen to me," I tell her, loving the way her belly presses into me.

"I am, aren't I?"

A bark of laughter slips from my lips before I press them to hers in a chaste kiss. "You are," I confirm. My hands immediately go to her stomach, where I'm rewarded with a hard kick from our son or daughter. "Best feeling ever."

She rests her head against my shoulder. "It is. Until she kicks me in the bladder."

"He," I correct, just trying to get a rise out of her. Even though I'd be perfectly content either way, I have a strong feeling it's going to be a boy. My gram confessed to me earlier this week she feels the same way, and she's always had a sixth sense when it comes to these things.

"We'll find out in April," she sings, practically vibrating with excitement.

"Yes, we will. That's when you'll have to look at me, with love and adoration in your eyes, and say, 'You were right, Logan. You're always right.'"

She snorts and shakes her head. "I will never say *those* words," she sasses, causing my black slacks to suddenly get a little tight in the crotch.

I can't help but laugh. Leaning forward, I place a small kiss on the tip of her nose. "Come on, Cupcake. I wanna dance with my baby and baby mama."

If you would have told me six months ago I'd love being wrapped in Logan Johnson's arms, I would have called you a liar. No way would I have thought I'd be anywhere close to where my life is sitting at the moment. Having a baby, living with the man I love, and hoping to spend the rest of my life beside him. It most definitely isn't what I pictured, but I wouldn't want it any other way.

"What time do you think we can slip out?" Logan asks, his body pressed tightly against mine as we move on the dance floor.

"Soon," I murmur, thinking about the lingerie I have waiting back at the house. I've successfully hidden the nightgown I purchased that weekend I went shopping with Blair, with the goal of wearing it tonight after the wedding reception.

"What's that look for?" he asks, pausing his movements.

"What look?" I ask coyly.

The start of a wicked grin starts to spread across his face. "The look that says you want me to strip you naked right here in the middle of the dance floor and do naughty things to your body."

My heart rate jumps significantly. "Well, maybe not here, considering my entire family is in attendance," I quip, glancing over to see both my brother and his new bride, as well as my parents, dancing.

"Hmm," he hums, pulling me snuggly against his body. There's no missing the erection pressed against the side of my stomach. "But it definitely has something to do with me stripping you naked."

"It does," I confirm. "I might have purchased something special for later this evening."

His already dark eyes turn molten. "Yeah? Tell me more," he mutters.

"Well, it's a very light shade of pink and hugs my girls..." I shift my leg to brush against his cock. "...perfectly."

A gravelly groan hits my ear as his hands press firmly against my lower back. "Vixen."

"Mmm," I sing, leaning forward so my mouth brushes against his earlobe. "It's silky and long and has a slit from my ankle all the way up to my..." I pause for dramatic effect. "...hip."

Suddenly, I'm moving. He takes my hand in his and practically drags me off the dance floor, heading straight for the exit.

"Wait, my stuff," I blurt out, noticing a few wedding guests turning our way.

Logan stops and exhales. "Be quick," he insists, making me laugh at his clear discomfort.

Leaning forward, I kiss his cheek before glancing down at his crotch. "That looks painful. I'll be speedy fast," I say before moving toward our table to retrieve my wrap and clutch.

It's cold outside and the wrap isn't super warm, but it's at least a layer of material against my bare arms and neck. "We're taking off," I tell Marcus, TD, and Ellie.

"See you two later," Ellie replies, a knowing grin on her face.

Marcus's eyes are on his phone. "Shit, I gotta go."

"What's wrong?" TD asks.

"Ava broke down," he announces, standing up and slipping his phone back into his pocket.

"Oh no. Where?" I ask, wondering if we need to swing by and pick her up.

"Eldridge Road. She wasn't able to make it completely onto the side of the road, so I need to get over there and pick it up before there's an accident," he states.

"Do you want us to meet you there? We can give her a ride home so you don't have to worry about it," I offer, even though Eldridge Road is in the opposite direction of where Logan and I live.

"Naw," he replies, pushing in his chair. "She said someone just picked her up and is taking her home."

He's gone before I can ask who, but as long as she has a ride, that's the most important thing.

"You two behave tonight," I tease, throwing a wave to TD and Ellie.

"We won't," she quips back, a grin on her lips that tells me they'll take full advantage of the empty house when they get home.

I head to where Logan is still standing. "Everything all right?"

"Yeah. Ava broke down, so Marcus had to take off to tow her car."

"That's too bad," he says, extending his hand for me to take.

"It is, but she has a ride home, so I'll send her a message tomorrow to check on her."

He nods, guiding me to the exit. We hurry to his truck, which he gratefully started to get both the engine and the cab warm, and climb inside.

As soon as he's in the driver's seat, he reaches for my hand, bringing it to his lips and placing a kiss on my knuckles. The familiar butterflies take flight in my stomach, something that still happens whenever he's near. I hope that burst of anticipation and excitement never stops. I know my love for him won't. The man I once thought a pain in my ass quickly turned into the one I can't see my life without.

"Now, tell me more about that pink nightie waiting for us at home."

another EPILOGUE

Ava

I fire off a quick thank you to Marcus, feeling awful he's having to leave Gabe and Blair's wedding reception to come bail me out of trouble, but that's what happens when you're the only repair shop and tow service in our area. As my rear end isn't completely off the road, I don't want to leave it until morning, since it could cause an accident for a passing vehicle, despite having the emergency hazards on.

I wrap my arms around myself, hating the fact I'm not wearing a winter coat. It just didn't go with the dress I wore to the wedding, but I'm desperately regretting that decision now. This sweater is warm but not providing nearly enough comfort in a disabled car in the dead of winter. I make a mental note to stock up on emergency supplies for my trunk very soon.

A pair of headlights fill my rearview mirror and stop directly behind my car. My heart starts to beat hard as I reach over and press the lock button. Twice. I clutch my phone in my hand, ready to dial 911 when the person who stopped behind me opens their driver's door. I can't tell who it is or what kind of vehicle, thanks to the blinding lights in my mirrors. My heart pounds even harder as I feel the person approach my door and knock on the window. I lift my phone, ready to call for help.

That's when I catch a glimpse of a familiar face.

"Hey," he hollers, lifting his hand and giving me a friendly, nonconfrontational wave.

"Mr. Pierson?" I holler through the closed window, surprised to find the father of one of my students standing beside my disabled vehicle this late at night.

He flashes me a warm, disarming smile that makes my heart flip in my chest. "Just Gavin, Miss Rutledge. To you, I'm just Gavin."

Want more Logan and Hallie?

Will they have a boy or a girl?

Find out in their delivery bonus scene by visiting my website, under

Pretty Drunk in the Pine Village tab, to download a digital copy.

Don't miss a single reveal, release, or sale! Sign up for my newsletter.
http://www.laceyblackbooks.com/newsletter

BOOKS ALSO BY lacey black

Rivers Edge series
Trust Me, Rivers Edge book 1 (Maddox and Avery) – FREE at all retailers
Fight Me, Rivers Edge book 2 (Jake and Erin)
Expect Me, Rivers Edge book 3 (Travis and Josselyn)
Promise Me: A Novella, Rivers Edge book 3.5 (Jase and Holly)
Protect Me, Rivers Edge book 4 (Nate and Lia)
Boss Me, Rivers Edge book 5 (Will and Carmen)
Trust Us: A Rivers Edge Christmas Novella (Maddox and Avery)
    ~ This novella was originally part of the Christmas Miracles Anthology
BOX SET – contains all 5 novels, 2 novellas, and a BONUS short story
With Me, A Rivers Edge Christmas Novella (Brooklyn and Becker)

Bound Together series
Submerged, Bound Together book 1 (Blake and Carly)
Profited, Bound Together book 2 (Reid and Dani)
Entwined, Bound Together book 3 (Luke and Sidney)

Summer Sisters series
My Kinda Kisses, Summer Sisters book 1 (Jaime and Ryan)
My Kinda Night, Summer Sisters book 2 (Payton and Dean)

My Kinda Song, Summer Sisters book 3 (Abby and Levi)
My Kinda Mess, Summer Sisters book 4 (Lexi and Linkin)
My Kinda Player, Summer Sisters book 5 (AJ and Sawyer)
My Kinda Player, Summer Sisters book 6 (Meghan and Nick)
My Kinda Wedding, A Summer Sisters Novella book 7 (Meghan and Nick)

Rockland Falls series
Love and Pancakes, Rockland Falls book 1
Love and Lingerie, Rockland Falls book 2
Love and Landscape, Rockland Falls book 3
Love and Neckties, Rockland Falls book 4

Standalone
Music Notes, a sexy contemporary romance standalone
A Place To Call Home, a Memorial Day novella
Exes and Ho Ho Ho's, a sexy contemporary romance standalone novella
Pants on Fire
Double Dog Dare You
Grip
Bachelor Swap, A Bachelor Tower Series Novel
Perfect Kiss, Mason Creek Series book 9
Waiting For Love, The Love Vixen Series book 11
Quarterback Keeper, a surprise baby novella
Kissing A Stranger, book 4 in the multi-author The Kissing Games series

Burgers and Brew Crüe Series
Kickstart My Heart, book 1
Don't Go Away Mad, book 2
Same Ol' Situation, book 3
Wild Side, book 4
What's It Gonna Take, book 5

Home Sweet Home, book 6
Too Young to Fall in Love, book 7
Without You, book 8
Time For Change, book 9
You're All I Need, book 10

Pine Village Series
Pretty Remarkable, a free prequel short story
Pretty Incredible, book 1
Pretty Dependable, book 2
Pretty Drunk, book 3
Pretty Relentless, book 4
Pretty Wild, book 5
Pretty Desperate, book 6

Snowflake Falls Series
Merry Little Mix-Up, book 1
Merry Little Sugar Rush, book 2

Co-Written with *NYT Bestselling* Author, Kaylee Ryan
It's Not Over, Fair Lakes book 1
Just Getting Started, Fair Lakes book 2
Can't Get Enough, Fair Lakes book 3
Fair Lakes Box Set
Boy Trouble
Home To You, a second chance novella
Beneath the Fallen Stars
Tell Me A Story
Royal – Writing as Rebel Shaw
Crying Shame – Writing as Rebel Shaw
Watch and Learn – Writing as Rebel Shaw

ABOUT
lacey black

USA Today Bestselling Author Lacey Black is a Midwestern girl with a passion for reading, writing, and shopping. She carries her e-reader with her everywhere she goes so she never misses an opportunity to read a few pages. Always looking for a happily ever after, Lacey is passionate about contemporary romance novels and enjoys it further when you mix in a little suspense. She resides in a small town in Illinois with her husband, two children, adorable black lab puppy, crazy cat, and three rowdy chickens.

Website: www.laceyblackbooks.com
Email: laceyblackwrites@gmail.com
Facebook: https://www.facebook.com/authorlaceyblack
Instagram: https://www.instagram.com/laceyblackwrites/
Bookbub: https://www.bookbub.com/authors/lacey-black
Amazon: https://www.amazon.com/Lacey-Black/e/B00MW2UGZI
Twitter: https://twitter.com/AuthLaceyBlack
Goodreads:
https://www.goodreads.com/author/show/8414783.Lacey_Black

Sign up for my newsletter so you don't miss a single sale, reveal, or release!
http://www.laceyblackbooks.com/newsletter